A CREATIVE KIND OF KILLER

A CREATIVE KIND OF KILLER

BY JACK EARLY

Carroll & Graf Publishers, Inc.
New York

In memory of my uncle,
Robert K. Krausse,
who wrote for the detective pulps
and was proud of it.

A CREATIVE KIND OF KILLER

1

I must have passed the corpse half a dozen times without noticing it. That's what comes of taking your surroundings for granted. I've lived in the same neighborhood in Manhattan for almost all of my forty-two years and even though both of us, the neighborhood and I, have gone through a lot of changes, I don't always see everything. Things are just there, like lines on a map. On the other hand, when I need to be, I'm very observant. Walking past The Sweatshop Boutique I needed to be observant but I wasn't. Nobody was until, early on Sunday night, a kid, sixteen years old, and her boyfriend, seventeen, stopped to take a long look at the window display.

The Sweatshop Boutique is one of those new shops in SoHo where all the clothes look like a joke and the mannequins are posed in tortured positions. Maybe it's the weight of the price tags that makes them look that way. Anyhow, The Sweatshop had three mannequins in its window, all wearing the latest designer rags: big, puffy-sleeved blouses under overlarge vests with long skirts or baggy pants. The hair was pink, blue and purple in various lengths and each of the dummies was adorned with jewelry made out of what looked like parts of a chain-link fence hanging from the wrists. Around the necks were things like angle hinges and wire cutters. And the one sitting in the chair, the one with the pink hair and a padlock around her waist, was bleeding from the head.

The two kids, newly in love, holding hands, spied the stain, which went down the right side of her forehead, over the eye, down the cheek, and correctly identified it as dried blood. The girl's knees started to buckle and the boy began to hyperventilate. They had seen a lot more gory stuff at the movies but instinctively they knew this was no movie; this was real. Smart kids. But I only learned all this later.

The Sweatshop Boutique is right across the street from my apartment on Thompson Street and when I heard the sirens I looked out the window. Neither of my kids was home and even though it was only six-thirty the sound of police sirens on my block always gives me a twinge. There were four blue-and-whites pulled up in front of the boutique, two at right angles, two blocking off the street. The cops were jumping out, guns drawn. From my POV I couldn't see who they were after so I thought I'd better get a closer look.

When I got downstairs a few of my neighbors were already huddled in the doorway. Mrs. Castelli, a piece of light blue netting over her newly permed and bleached hair, gave me one of her best smiles, a swatch of crimson lipstick on her front tooth.

"So what is it, Fortune?" she asked me.

"I don't know yet. I heard the sirens and came down. You've been here longer than I have."

"Me, I was lighting a candle over at St. Anthony's. Thirty years ago today Mama passed away." She crossed herself. "I got here just when the police cars come screeching down the street."

Doug Fanner, the super of my building, was to my right, one booted foot propped on a cement ledge as if he were at a bar. He was a man in his mid-thirties with a wide face and a neatly clipped mustache. His brown eyes had the look of a schemer, and I'd never had much use for him.

"You know what it's about, Doug?" I asked.

"Who, me?" he said, pulling back as if I were accusing him of something.

"I thought you might have heard," I said.

Still defensive, he answered, "I just finished putting away my cleaning stuff when I saw the cops pull up."

I didn't bother asking what he was doing cleaning on a Sunday evening; I was just grateful he cleaned at all. Usually he forgot. I turned to my left and said, "How about you, Nick? You know what's up?"

Dominick Scola, short, with shoulders like a guard for the Jets, his black hair growing low over his forehead and bushy brows, shrugged. "I heard the girl screamin', that's all."

"What girl?"

He looked around, up and down the street, his brown eyes watery and red around the rims from one too many the night before. "There she is, yeah, over there wit that cop. See?"

I looked in the direction his shaky finger was pointing. The girl was really a girl, not a woman, no more than sixteen. A cop stood on one side of her, a young boy on the other.

"What was she screaming about?" I asked Nick.

"Who knows?" The shrug again. "I was comin' out to go to the store and all of a sudden like I hear this screamin'. You didn't hear it, Fortune?"

"I must have been in the bathroom." I'd taken a shower ten minutes before the squad cars arrived.

"Yeah, you musta been, 'cause there ain't no way nobody coulda missed that screamin' unless you was dead. Or inna terlit."

I pictured myself swimming around in my toilet, fighting to get out. "So what happened?"

"The broad is screamin' and the guy is tryin' to pull her away and—"

"Away from what?"

"They was lookin' in the window of that friggin' store. Oh, sorry, Mrs. Castelli."

"You watch the mouth, Nicky."

"Yeah, sorry. Anyways, they was starin' at the window, and the broad was screamin' and the guy's tryin' to get her away, that's all."

"What did you do?" I asked.

"Huh?"

"You help the girl, call the police?"

"I didn't wanna get involved, Fortune. You know how it is."

Unfortunately, I did know how it was for him. Nick Scola was a penny-ante crook and wino who still lived with his mother at age thirty-one. "So who called the cops?" I asked.

"I did."

I turned to see Father Paul standing next to me. He was six feet four, two inches taller than I was, and as blond as I was dark. We'd known each other all our lives. "Tell me," I said.

"I was coming down Thompson as they were running up. I saw that something was wrong and I stopped them. They said a mannequin was bleeding in the store window."

"Bleedin'?" Nicky said.

Father Paul ignored him and went on. "I said we should call the police and I escorted them up to Angie's and we made the call. That's all I know, Fortune."

"It's these artists with their galleries and their lofts and all their money that's causing all the trouble, isn't it, Father?" Mrs. Castelli asked, her cheeks flushing to match the color of her lipstick.

"Now, Alberta, don't get yourself in an uproar." He patted her shoulder with his big hand and it was as if he was Christ himself the way she calmed down in an instant. The neighborhood people loved Father Paul; most of them had known him when he was a kid. "We don't know what this is all about, do we?" he asked.

"It just seems like all the trouble's come in the last ten years with...*them*."

She meant the people who had created SoHo, the area below Houston Street that went south to Canal, east to Lafayette and west to West Broadway. There were a lot of artists, writers, actors and musicians. Meryl Streep lived down here and so did the guy who wrote *Eye of the Needle*, Ken Follett. I liked what had happened to the neighborhood, thought it was pretty interesting, but a lot of the people, old and young alike, resented it. Anything new scared them.

Just then I saw two cops lifting one of the mannequins out of the window. The way they were carrying her I knew it wasn't a dresser's dummy. Off in the distance I heard the sound of an ambulance siren. It always made me think of World War Two movies. When had we adopted that sound?

A bunch of the cops came out of The Sweatshop, their guns put away. Then the ambulance siren came closer and one of the cops moved his car, which was blocking off the street. The ambulance turned the corner from Prince into Thompson and screeched up in front of the boutique. Two guys jumped out from the front and one of them went around to the back, opened the double doors, pulled out a litter and, escorted by two cops, went inside the store.

"How could a dummy be bleedin'?" Nick asked, realizing by the arrival of the ambulance boys that something bad must have really happened.

Mrs. Castelli crossed herself.

"Maybe," I said, "it wasn't a dummy, dummy."

"Hey, who you callin' a dummy, Fortune?" He jutted out his lower lip, making him look like the big baby he was. A big, hairy baby.

"No offense, Nick. Just kidding."

"You think you're better than the rest of us, dontcha?"

What I thought was that I was more sober than Nick Scola but then, most people were. "C'mon," I said, "where's your sense of humor?"

"I ain't got none," he said sourly.

This came as no shock to me. I gave him a pat on the back and directed his attention to what was going on across the street. The ambulance guys were coming out the door carrying the litter. A sheet covered the body.

"Holy shit," Nick said.

"Nicky, please," begged Mrs. Castelli.

"Sorry."

Father Paul said, "I think I'd better go over."

I followed him.

He walked up to the ambulance and blocked the guys carrying the litter. One of the cops stepped up to him.

"Excuse me, Father, we got to get this body to the morgue."

"If you don't mind," he said in his voice like maple cream, "I'd like to see if it's one of my parishioners."

"Oh, yeah, sure." The cop nodded to the ambulance guy at the head and he rested the litter against his thighs as he pulled back the sheet.

I looked past Father Paul's shoulder. Death hadn't aged her; it had only made her look dead. She couldn't have been more than seventeen and I could see that she'd been pretty. The pink wig had fallen off and lay on the litter like a discarded Muppet. Her own hair was blond and she had fair skin and a small, full mouth. I figured her for blue eyes. Something had happened to the top of her head. The hair was soaked with blood but from my angle I couldn't tell if it was from a blow or a gunshot. Most likely a blow since people hardly ever shoot anyone in the top of the head. Still, you never knew these days. There was a line of dried blood down the right side of her face that disappeared under her chin where the sheet met her neck. I thought of Karen, my daughter, and my heart seemed to slide down to my belly and stay there. Karen was just about the same age as this kid. Where the hell was she, anyway?

"I don't recognize her," Father Paul said. "Do you, Fortune?"

"No," I answered, my voice coming out hoarse. I'd seen a lot of dead bodies in my time but I never got used to seeing dead kids. I turned away and walked back toward my building.

"Anybody we know, God forbid?" Mrs. Castelli asked.

I shook my head and started up the street toward the girl and boy who'd discovered her. I don't know what I thought I was doing. It wasn't like I was on the case. I guess it was instinct or habit, or maybe it was just that I didn't like kids getting bumped off. A few years before, in the category of who asked, I'd worked my butt off trying to locate Etan Patz, a six-year-old who'd been snatched in the block between Wooster and West Broadway. But I hadn't had any more luck than the guys who were officially on the case. Still, it made me feel better to help.

As I approached the Eurogallery I noticed the owner, George Mayer, standing in the doorway. He was wearing one of his usual cowboy outfits, and a large, tan Stetson sat on his head looking ridiculous. In the winter he wore a coyote coat, and the license plate on his red Ferrari said VROOM. George thought he was a swinger and the locals thought he was an *asino*.

"What's going down, pal?" he asked.

"A girl was killed," I answered.

He stuck a thumb under his belt and adjusted his hat. I wondered what they thought of him in Queens when he went home to visit.

"You mean murdered?" he said.

"Looks that way."

"Bad for business," he said morosely, "very bad."

My mouth hanging open I watched him go back into his gallery. I don't know why I was surprised. People like George Mayer were interested only in money. The life or death of an anonymous girl wouldn't mean anything to him.

I continued up the block and when I got closer to the two kids I saw that the girl's face was red from crying and that some of her brown hair had come loose from her ponytail. The striped ribbon that held it back had come undone and the two tails hung over her shoulders rumpled and creased. She was wearing a red windbreaker, a man-tailored pink shirt, maybe from L. L. Bean, jeans, no designer name on them, and a pair of blue and white Adidas. The boy had short brown hair, wore glasses and was dressed almost identically to the girl except his windbreaker was blue and so was his shirt. Pink and blue: these kids took their roles seriously. They seemed to be in a time warp and I wondered what they were doing here.

"Hi," I said. "You kids okay?"

[7]

The cop who was standing with them was one I knew. "We don't need your help, Fanelli."

We were great friends. "Take it easy, Dunne. I'm just being neighborly."

He laughed derisively. "Ya think these kids are gonna hire ya or somethin'?"

"Never crossed my mind." I turned and looked into the frightened blue eyes of the girl. "That must have been a very scary experience for you," I said.

She nodded and the boy moved closer to her as if his body would shield her from my question.

Dunne said, "Look, Fortune, we're gonna take these two with us now so go move some cars around your parking lots or something."

Six years since I quit the force and some of these guys still couldn't stand it that I'd inherited a little money from an aunt, made a lucky investment and didn't need to be a cop for the city anymore. They were hanging on for their pensions and hating every minute of it but treated me as if I'd betrayed them. I decided to ignore Dunne and I asked the girl another question.

"Did you know the girl in the window?"

"No," she said, "no. I never saw her before." Her face crumpled and she brought her hands up to cover it as she started to cry.

"You crazy or something?" the boy said to me.

"Get the hell out of here, will ya? See what ya done, ya asshole?" Dunne said. "Beat it before I run ya in."

"You'd love that, wouldn't you?" I said.

"Keep it up, Fanelli, just keep it up." He took a step toward me that was supposed to be menacing but it only looked as if he might lose his balance.

"Save it," I said and turned away from them.

Walking back down the street I found that I was absolutely certain the girl had been lying. As unlikely as it seemed, there was no doubt in my mind that she knew who the dead girl was.

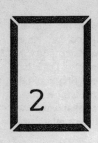

2

"Where the hell have you two been, dammit?" I yelled.

"Hey, Dad, it's only seven-twenty," Karen said. "The movie got out at seven. It takes twenty minutes to walk home from the Greenwich."

"We told you we'd be home by seven-thirty," Sam said. "We're early."

I felt embarrassed. These were good kids and they hadn't done anything bad. I was twitchy because of the homicide across the street. I hate admitting when I'm wrong but I do it anyway.

"I'm sorry," I said. "I'm a little jumpy tonight."

"You talk to Mom or something?" Sam asked.

"Very funny," I said.

"I wasn't trying to be funny."

Karen said, "Maybe you don't know it but sometimes you're a real drag after you talk to Mom."

"I am?" I hadn't realized that Elaine still got to me.

"A real grouch," Sam said.

"No kidding?"

"Would we put you on?" Karen said. "You're a pain in the butt when you've either talked to Mom or seen her and that's the total truth. What's for dinner? I'm starving."

"Me, too," said Sam.

I wondered, as I watched them walk past me into the kitchen, why they had never mentioned this before. Karen stood at the stove lifting the cover from the sauce pot. She was a pretty kid; no Elizabeth Taylor, but pretty. Dark hair and eyes, straight nose, dimple in one cheek. She was tall, like me. And her figure was neat, trim. For sixteen, I realized, she was pretty mature looking. Or were they all that way now? I thought of the scared kid with the ponytail. Not all.

"What kind of sauce, Dad?"

"Truffles and peas," I said.

"Oh, gross me out," said Sam, holding his belly. "What's truffles?"

Karen said, "It's something pigs dig up, isn't it, Dad?"

Sam bent double, made a sound like he was vomiting and fell over onto the kitchen floor, eyes closed in a mock faint.

I looked down at my son the comedian. He was fourteen and painfully thin. But worse than that, for him, was that he was only five feet three and had been that height for the past two years. Karen towered over him but she never used it against him. He was a good-looking boy with reddish brown hair he wore just below his ears. He looked a lot like Elaine.

"Truffles are a delicacy," I said.

"So why can't we have food instead of delicacies?" Sam said from the floor, his green eyes open now. "Why can't you cook normal like other mothers?"

"Maybe because I'm a father," I said. "Get up, brat. This is a great dish." I kissed the tips of my fingers with a smacking sound.

Karen was setting our round oak table. "You can't have burgers and fries for every meal, Sam."

"Why not?" he said getting to his feet.

"Because we have to learn about good food."

"Why?"

"Oh, don't be such a baby," she said, exasperated. "Want me to wash the arugula, Dad?"

"It's done, but you can get it out and put it in the bowl with the endive."

"You see," Sam whined, "that's just what I'm talking about. Arugula and endive! Other people have lettuce and tomato salads, other *normal* people."

"So we're not normal," I said. "Have us committed."

Sam slumped into a chair at the table. "I don't get no respect," he said imitating Rodney Dangerfield.

When the vermicelli was done, I drained it thoroughly, put it on a platter and added the pea-truffle sauce. Karen tossed the salad with a lemon-oil dressing I'd made earlier. Sam got the seltzer bottle from the fridge.

I watched them roll up their pasta (no spoons for them) and waited for a response. Sam grabbed his throat and pretended he was being poisoned, his fork dropping back into his bowl. Karen ignored him, chewing very slowly, savoring her food, deliberating.

"Well?" I said.

She held up a hand for me to wait until she had swallowed. Then she took a sip of seltzer and turned toward me, her long dark lashes slightly shading her almond-shaped eyes. *"Buono,"* she said, *"molto buono."*

I smiled.

"Cut the Italian," Sam said. "Can't we be normal?"

"Normal what?" I asked.

"Normal Americans."

"Oh, Sam, we *are* normal Americans; that's the trouble," Karen said sighing.

"Eat," I said. I wasn't sure I'd ever understand these kids. One wanted to be normal and the other didn't.

"It's really fine, Dad," she said.

"Oh, gimme a break. *Fine*, for godssake," Sam said.

"Thanks, honey," I said. I was always pleased when they liked my cooking. Sam hardly ever did, or at least he pretended he didn't, but Karen was very appreciative. Cooking was something I took pride in. I'd taught myself after Elaine walked out.

"How come you kids never told me before that I'm a pain when I talk to your mother?"

They looked at each other, a quick, furtive glance, but I caught it. I'm not a private eye for nothing! "Give," I said.

Karen said, "I don't know why I never told you. I just didn't, but it's getting more and more obvious. *Were* you talking to her today?"

She tried to sound offhand about it, but I knew better. Karen had suffered most from Elaine's defection, feeling it had something to do with her because they didn't get along. Sam felt it, too, but it was different for him. His hurt came out in his quest for normality. He was, after all, the only kid on the block with a father for a mother, although certainly not the only kid from a so-called broken home.

"No, I haven't talked to Elaine in a week." I didn't add that I'd tried to reach her but she was too busy to return my calls. The world of a soap-opera producer was pretty important stuff, all right.

"So why were you so uptight about us coming in at seven-twenty, Dad?" Sam asked.

I noticed his plate was half empty. "I might as well tell you," I said. "You're going to hear it on the street anyway." I told them about the murder at The Sweatshop and how the girl was so young. Karen reached out and covered my hand with hers. She was a real sensitive kid. She knew I'd been thinking about her. "I want you kids to be extra careful around here until we know what's up, okay?"

They agreed.

Sam asked, "You gonna be on this case, Dad?"

"Not unless somebody asks, and I can't see why anybody would."

As if on cue the phone rang. We all laughed.

Sam got up to answer it. "Should I say you're available or not?"

"Just tell whoever it is I charge one fifty a day plus expenses."

"Right."

The phone was on the wall near the door to the living room so I could step into the next room if I wanted privacy.

"It's for you, Dad," Sam said, holding out the phone.

"Who is it?"

"I dunno, some dude."

"Thanks, sport." I'd tried to teach him always to ask who was calling, but he never did. Karen, on the other hand, never failed to ask; she was at the age where it was important to screen all calls. I took the phone from Sam and stepped into the living room: my office.

"Mr. Fanelli?" a man's voice asked.

"That's right. Who's this?"

"You don't know me; my name's Horton. I'd like to see you."

"What about?" I noticed the guy had a slight wheeze in his voice, like the sound of a slow-closing door.

"I'd rather not say over the phone."

"That doesn't give me much incentive, Mr. Horton."

There was silence for a few seconds and then he said, "You were recommended."

"Yeah, by who?"

"Father Paul."

"Why didn't you say so right away? Okay, when do you want to meet?"

"What about tonight? Now?"

"I'm in the middle of my dinner." I looked at my watch. "How about in half an hour? You know this neighborhood?"

"I can find my way around."

Good for him. "There's a bar on Sullivan between Prince and Spring. It's called Barney's."

"Is it one of those wine bars?" he asked.

I laughed. "No. Why?"

"I don't like those places."

"Neither do I." This guy sounded okay. "How will I know you?"

"I'll know *you*," he said. "Half an hour." He hung up. Believe it or not I didn't look into the receiver like they do in the movies. Instinctively, I knew I wasn't going to see anything there. I walked back into the kitchen and hung it up.

"Hot case, Dad?" Sam asked. His plate was clean.

"Yeah, big time." I resumed eating. "I see you really hated this meal."

"A person has to have sustenance," he said.

"I'm going out for a while," I said. "You two have homework?"

"Done mine," Karen said.

"Me, too."

"You sure, Sam?" He wasn't getting the best grades this year. I knew he was brooding over his size.

He said, "Would I lie?"

"Yes."

"You're right. But tonight I'm telling the truth. I did it earlier because tonight there's a movie I want to see."

"What movie?" I asked.

"Slime Pit."

"Oh, no wonder you got your homework out of the way. You wouldn't want to miss *Slime Pit*. Maybe I should cancel my appointment and stay home to watch it with you."

"Not a bad idea," Sam said.

"You going to watch *Slime Pit*, too, honey?" I asked Karen.

"Oh, Dad," she said as if I'd asked her if she wanted to watch open heart surgery. "I'm watching 'Masterpiece Theatre.'"

"Yuck," Sam said elegantly.

Karen was a kid after culture. It was okay with me. "It's a good thing your mother gave you that little set for Christmas," I said. I liked to give Elaine points when I could. She didn't earn them too often.

"Yeah, it's a good thing," Karen said sadly.

Now I was sorry I'd reminded her of her mother. But she probably thought about her without my help. I'd have to try Elaine again the next day. If she didn't return my call I'd go up to her office.

"Well," I said, getting up from the table, "I'm going to change my clothes."

"You have a date?" Sam asked.

"Not the kind you mean, buster. When you get a little older you'll find out women aren't the only species you change your clothes for. It's your turn for the dishes."

"Yeah, I know. I'm nothing but a slave in my own house."

"We did our share," Karen said.

"Spare me."

I walked down the hall to my room. It was the same room I'd shared with Elaine for ten years. She'd been gone for seven. This had been our second apartment. The first was a studio. We thought it was a palace. Then when Elaine got pregnant with Karen we moved here. It was a great apartment. Six rooms. I could afford to move into a co-op or a loft now but I thought it was best for the kids to stay put; they needed the continuity. When the kids were grown, I figured I'd co-op the building I owned on Mercer Street and move there. Or maybe I wouldn't. I liked it here. Change wasn't my strong suit. That had been one of Elaine's biggest complaints about me. The hell with Elaine.

I changed into tan slacks, a dark brown shirt and my brown tweed sports jacket, no tie. I traded my Nikes for a pair of Frye loafers. I looked in the mirror. Not bad for an old man. I ran a brush through my black hair and tried not to notice the white, like spills of cappuccino foam. I noticed anyway. I suppose it was distinguished-looking since it was at my temples, but it gave me a twinge. Getting older was change and like I said I didn't take to change. But the skin was still good; only a few lines near my eyes and one on either side of my nose.

My mother said we Fanellis had olive oil in our blood, which made us look younger than we were. I ran a finger down the bridge of my nose and felt the bump that had always been there. It was the same one my father had had. I looked just like him except by my age he looked beat. Poor soak.

I put my wallet in my back pocket and put on my hip holster with my .38. I suspected I wouldn't need it with this guy Horton but it was better to be safe than sorry. Sorry could mean dead.

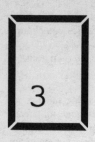

3

It had gotten cooler since I'd been out earlier, but it was still one of those gorgeous April nights when even the city smells good. The sky was clear and I could see the twin towers looming over lower Manhattan like two solemn sentinels.

I crossed the street and took a fast look in the window of The Sweatshop Boutique. Two mannequins remained. They were facing toward the center where the dead girl had been and the expressions on their plaster faces looked surprised. Why not? There was a yellow sign on the door that read: CRIME SCENE. I continued down the street and crossed Prince, then walked over to Sullivan. On the corner the market was doing a brisk business as usual. Rumor had it that it, and a few others in the area, were owned by Moonies, but I had my doubts. Vegetable and fruit markets seemed to have been taken over by Asians in the last few years, but I couldn't believe they were all Moonies. Whoever they were they worked hard and the produce was beautiful. It should have been, considering what they charged. I called them the Robbers. The only scale in the place was the one *they* used and they did everything so fast it was like Houdini at work. More than once I'd asked them to get a scale for the people to weigh their own vegetables and fruits but they'd just said no and that was that. Their produce was good but the atmosphere was far from homey.

Still, I never knew when I might see Meryl Streep again. I'd seen her in there once on a cold day in December right after her new movie opened. She had a scarf wrapped around the lower part of her face but I knew her by the nose. You can't miss that nose. Then the scarf fell and she looked into my eyes, smiled and said, "Excuse me." I was blocking her from the potatoes. It made my day. My week. My year, maybe.

I turned down Sullivan toward Spring. There were bunches of new shops on either side of the street. They opened and closed so fast you needed a scorecard to keep track. SoHo, in the last six years, had become the chic in-place, offering fashion, food and art. Galleries were everywhere, along with overpriced restaurants. But Barney's was far from chic. It was your typical neighborhood bar: some stained-glass windows, a heavy wooden door and the inexorable smell of stale beer.

The bar itself was mahogany and curved at one end. The stools were wooden with red vinyl seats patched with electrical tape. Four booths lined the wall opposite the bar and in the back room there were tables and chairs. Every night but Monday Barney himself tended bar.

The place was filled with regulars, mostly neighborhood people, some from the Village and Little Italy. There were no gallery or boutique owners here. A few writers and painters drifted in from time to time but none of the successful ones. They drank at another bar on Mercer Street called The Warehouse. It was just as well; they wouldn't fit in at Barney's.

I looked around carefully, said hello to a few guys, and took a place at the bar. My man was not here. Three minutes late. I didn't like lateness, saw no excuse for it, especially if you were the one who arranged the meeting.

"Hiya, Fortune," Barney said. "The usual?"

"Yeah, thanks."

Barney was in his early sixties. He was completely bald, but even so his face belied his age. His skin was smooth and unlined and guys were always kidding him about having had a face-lift. They said the scars were hidden underneath his toothbrush mustache.

"Here ya go, Fortune," Barney said putting my Coke down in front of me. "What's new? Ya hear about the broad what got wasted?"

Some broad. "Poor kid," I said.

"Hey, Barney, a boilermaker down here," a voice yelled from the end of the bar.

"Yeah, poor kid." He went off shaking his head.

I took a large swallow of my Coke. God, I love that stuff. I guess you could say I'm addicted. Well, it's better than being addicted to the other coke. This one may rot your teeth but the other rots your brain.

"Hello, Fanelli."

It was Wayne Morrison. He worked for George Mayer in the Eurogallery. Wayne was about thirty with a baby face and smooth, tanned skin. His auburn hair, which he wore in a modified crewcut, was full and spikey, like a marigold. He wore Levi's, a work shirt and yellow work boots. I'd never seen him in anything else. A bunch of keys hung from his belt on his right hip. The man projected a kind of innocence that could fool you unless you looked carefully into his eyes. They had seen things I didn't care to think about.

I saluted him with three fingers.

"Some kind of trouble today," he said, lifting his beer.

I nodded, wondering if he was worried about business, too. But probably not; he was only an employee. "I didn't see you around today. George tell you?"

He glanced away toward the big color television over the bar, a muscle in his cheek throbbing. "Yeah, he told me."

I wondered if it was the mention of his boss that set him on edge or something else. I asked. "Something bothering you, Wayne?"

"No, nothing." He plunked his empty glass on the bar and turned away. "See you," he said.

I watched him, shoulders hunched forward, as he left the place. I kept my eye on the door for a few seconds. Was Horton going to be a no-show? I swung back to the bar and looked up at the set. Jimmy Connors was giving John McEnroe a hard time. The clientele at Barney's were not particularly tennis fans, but any sport was preferable to no sport. I felt a tap on my shoulder just as McEnroe missed a beautiful passing shot by Connors. I wanted to see McEnroe's reaction, so I didn't turn around. McEnroe sliced the air with his racket and called himself stupid. The tap came again and this time I turned. "Yeah?" I said.

"Mr. Fanelli?"

"Right."

"I'm Charles Horton." He offered me a well-manicured hand, the fingers long and slim.

I felt the pressure of a large diamond pinky ring but it didn't hurt; Horton had a temperate handshake. He was a man in his early fifties, medium height and build with wavy hair that had the gray-yellow look blonds get when it starts to go. He was wearing a dark blue suit, white shirt, blue tie with a thin red stripe and a wider yellow stripe; a white handkerchief peeked out from his breast pocket. His eyes were blue and I could see at once that one of them was glass.

"I'm sorry I'm late. . . . I saw this place but I didn't think it could be the right one." His nostrils twitched as if he were smelling something bad.

"I thought this would be up your alley. You said you didn't like wine bars."

"I don't. I don't like wine. But this . . ." his voice trailed off as he shook his head.

"We can go somewhere else if you want but there's lots of privacy in the back room."

"That will be fine."

"What are you drinking?" My intuition told me it wouldn't be beer.

"Haig and Haig Pinch on the rocks," he said.

I could hardly wait to order it. I called Barney over. "The gentleman wants a Haig and Haig Pinch on the rocks and I'll have another Coke." The odd couple.

Barney gave Horton the once-over, shook his head in disgust and went to look for the Haig and Haig.

"Do you suppose he doesn't have any?" Horton asked, amazed.

"It's possible," I said.

Barney came back after a few minutes with a dusty bottle that was three-quarters full. "I got it," he said as if he'd won the treasure hunt.

Horton smiled thinly and nodded in appreciation. There was a moment or two when Barney didn't know what to charge for the Scotch but finally decided, since he could see that Horton was paying, to make it two bucks. We carried our drinks to the back room.

Only one other table was occupied: two neighborhood women having a Sunday night beer. I took the table farthest away from them. The room was shabby: the paint was peeling from the walls and the linoleum on the floor was cracked and deeply yellowed. A calendar hung lopsided on the wall near our table. It was from Edgar Fuel and the month it showed was February; the year was 1968. Sam wasn't even born then.

"Lovely place," Horton said facetiously.

"I like the ambience," I said. This guy was beginning to get on my nerves.

"Do you have an upset stomach?" he asked.

My sentiments must have been showing. "No. Why?"

He pointed to my Coke.

I said, "I don't drink alcohol."

"I see."

I was pretty sure what was coming next.

"I've always thought it difficult to trust a man who doesn't drink."

I couldn't help smiling. No matter what the background, the class, the situation, they always said the same thing or a variation on it. So I always said the same thing, too: "It's funny, but my experience has been the opposite. Drinkers are a lot less trustworthy than nondrinkers."

Naturally that made him defensive. "You're not a Born-Again or something, are you?"

"Nope. I just don't drink. It's simple."

"May I ask why?"

"I like to be in control. Besides, it killed my father and it's going to do the same to my sister. Look, do you want to tell me what this is all about or should we continue discussing the alcoholism problem in the Fanelli family?"

He took another sip of his drink, a larger one than the last, his one good eye on me, probably wondering if I disapproved or not. I could've put him at ease and told him I didn't care what anyone else did as long as it didn't affect my life, but I decided to keep the advantage. From his inside breast pocket he took a gold cigarette case, snapped it open with his thumb and offered me one of his brown Nat Sherman's. Now I knew why the wheeze in his voice.

"No, thanks."

"A saint in his own time," he said.

I let it pass.

He lit the cigarette with a gold Dunhill lighter, put all the paraphernalia on the table, blew out a stream of smoke, fixed his eye on me and said, "I'm Jennifer Baker's uncle."

The temptation to do a Sam and fall over in a faint was great but I resisted. "Who?" I asked.

He frowned, bringing his sparse gray brows together. "Jennifer Baker."

"I'm sorry, I don't know who that is."

"The girl who was murdered today. The one they found in the dress store."

"Oh. That girl. I'm sorry, Mr. Horton, I didn't know her name. You have my sympathy."

"Thank you. She was a lovely girl. Beautiful. Sweet. Kind. Innocent. That's probably why it happened. The meek don't inherit the earth, do they?" He looked past me for a moment as if he were trying to remember something. Then his eye focused on me again. "He killed her."

"Who did?"

"The same person who killed or kidnapped Patrick."

"Wait a minute, Mr. Horton, you're losing me. Who's Patrick?"

"My nephew. Jennie's brother."

"Why don't you start from the beginning."

"Yes. I should start from the beginning," he said, sounding like his batteries were running low. He swallowed the rest of his drink, glanced at me mournfully, then back into his empty glass.

"Let me get you another Scotch before you begin," I said.

"That would be good of you," he said and his eyes filled. I knew it wasn't because of the free drink. I was beginning to feel sorry for the guy.

When I came back with his drink he was composed once again. His mouth was clamped in a hard, straight line as if to keep out any bad taste, and a fresh cigarette burned between his fingers. I liked him better vulnerable but I was pretty sure that what I'd seen a few minutes before was an unnatural state for him.

"You were going to start from the beginning," I cued.

"Yes. My sister Rebecca married a man named Carter Baker, a lawyer, nineteen years ago. Their two children are...were...Jennifer and Patrick. Everything seemed perfectly normal...well, *looked* normal to outsiders...but it wasn't really. Not that there was any funny business going on, no child abuse or anything like that."

I'd never thought of child abuse as funny business. "So what wasn't normal?"

He shook his head, lips pursed, as if he'd sucked a lemon. "I shouldn't use the word *normal*; it's erroneous. It's just that it wasn't a happy household, Mr. Fanelli. To an outsider it might have looked like one: they had plenty of money, dressed well, had a fine house, but there was no joy. Carter Baker is a strict disciplinarian."

"And Mrs. Baker?"

He blew out a plume of smoke and shrugged. "Oh, you know, it's the usual thing. She's under his thumb."

"You mean he disciplines her as well?"

"I suppose you could say that. He certainly makes all the rules."

"So what happened?"

"The children were very unhappy. Patrick never talked to

me about it but Jennifer did. They weren't allowed to do any of the things other children their ages were allowed to do."

"How old is Patrick?" I sipped my Coke.

"Fifteen."

"So what happened?"

"Patrick left home two months ago."

"Did he disappear or run away?"

"He ran away...I suppose. Still, there's been no trace of him for two weeks."

"You mean you knew where he was until two weeks ago?"

"No, of course not." He lifted his glass to his mouth and the ice rattled as his hand shook; then he put the drink back on the table and went on. "I think Patrick was in some kind of trouble. You see, after he ran away, they heard nothing from him for six weeks and then..."

"The police had no leads?"

"The police were never called in."

I'd been leaning forward and this piece of information pushed me back in my chair as if I'd been punched in the chest. "Wait a minute, Mr. Horton. Are you trying to tell me that a fifteen-year-old kid runs away from home and his parents don't even tell the police?"

"That's *exactly* what I'm telling you."

"Why not?"

"Carter Baker runs his own ship, as he put it. He said if Patrick couldn't abide by his rules and didn't want to live with them, he had no intention of dragging him back by the ear."

"But he's a fifteen-year-old kid!"

"Precisely."

I was astonished. Parents often abandoned their children, but this was something else...something crazy.

"Go on," I said.

"Three weeks ago Patrick sent a postcard to Jennifer. Naturally he didn't send it to the house but rather to a friend of Jennie's, Alison Gordon. It was postmarked New York....Well, I have it with me." He reached into his inside pocket and brought out the postcard.

The front was a painting of a small boy in shorts and a shirt sitting next to a table with a clock on it. Above the boy was a framed painting of a man leaning on one elbow. Next to them both was a shadow of another man. It seemed a funny choice for a fifteen-year-old kid. I'd seen it before at the card shop on Prince. I turned it over. The address side of the card just said: "Alison, this is for Jen." I looked at Horton. "There's no address."

"He sent it in an envelope," he wheezed.

The writing was small and cramped. I read the message:

Dear Jen,
I just wanted you to know that I'm in NYC and doing OK. I can't tell you where cause it's better this way. I have a job and live with a friend. I'm sure now about what I always knew and my friend says I have the talent. I hope I live that long!!! People are weird here. Maybe I'll see you someday.

It was signed, "Your bruth, Pat." I put the card on the table, picture side down. "What talent was he referring to?"

"He wanted to be an artist."

"Did he paint?" That might explain the choice of card but something still nagged.

"He didn't get much chance. Carter discouraged it, of course. He has no time for the arts."

"Baker sounds more appealing every minute."

"Doesn't he? My sister was a wonderful pianist when she married him but he never even let her have a piano. He's a bastard. As far as I'm concerned *he* killed the children."

"You don't know for sure that Patrick is dead. You said he was in trouble. What did you mean?"

Horton gestured toward the postcard. "It's right there. He said, 'I hope I live that long!'"

"But that's just an expression."

"Maybe. A week ago Jennifer appeared at my door. She'd run away, too. I'd always been close with the girl and I said she could stay with me. I had a moral dilemma because I knew Rebecca would be terribly worried even if Carter wasn't. But I was afraid if I told her Jennie was with me Carter would get it out of her and try to bring Jennie back."

"You mean he had a different set of rules for her?"

"Oh, indeed. Double standard." He rubbed his good eye, and the other one, open and glassy, made me think of a Cyclops.

"So you didn't let anyone know."

"Correct. Jennie said she was sure Pat was around the Village somewhere or maybe SoHo, because he'd always wanted to go there. Yesterday she told me she'd met a man who knew him, but Pat hadn't been seen for two weeks." He brought his cigarette to his mouth and the diamond in his ring caught the light from a naked ceiling bulb. "I begged her to tell me who the man was and tried to convince her we should go to the police but she refused. She said I shouldn't worry: the man was going to take her to Pat that night. She also said that soon she'd have a lot of money."

"What did that mean?"

"I don't know. I didn't pay much attention to that part. You know how young girls are, always dreaming and fantasizing, but now . . ." His voice trailed off and his body slumped as though somebody had let out the air.

Yeah, I knew how young girls fantasized and I knew how young boys dreamed dreams of glory, too. My kids would go on dreaming and maybe even achieving but the Baker kids' dreams had turned to nightmares and now to dust.

"When she didn't come home last night I called the police. They said a girl her age would have to be missing twenty-four hours before they could do anything." His mouth curled into a sneer. "I hope the bastards are satisfied now."

"So what do you want me to do, Mr. Horton?" I asked gently.

"I want you to find Patrick if he's alive, and if he's not I want you to find his killer and Jennie's. I'm sure it's all connected. It would be too much of a coincidence otherwise."

"I agree with that. But what about the police? They're going to be looking for Jennie's killer, you know."

His face flushed in anger. "I just told you how interested the police are."

I said, "But now that she's been found..."

"Dead! Found dead. They don't care. Oh, God." He put his head in his hands.

I waited for a bit and then I said, "All right, we'll forget about the police for now. But there's something I want to know. How did you find me? I know Father Paul recommended me but how did you get to him?" It was always important to know all the connections.

"A good friend of mine, Robert Sheedy, the painter...."

He waited to see if I recognized the name. I didn't. I couldn't keep up with everything.

"Well, he lives here on Greene Street. He told me about Father Paul. Bob said the man has his finger on the pulse of the neighborhood, so to speak. I thought he might know something. I wasn't even thinking of a private detective; it was the father's idea."

I nodded. Paul often sent people my way. He said we both helped their souls. Sometimes he even helped me on a case. "This all happened pretty fast, didn't it? Jennifer's body was discovered around six-thirty and you called me two hours later. You didn't waste any time."

"I never do. Time is short, as we've just seen. You never know when yours might run out. The police called me at seven-thirty, I identified... I identified Jennifer at about ten of eight, called Bob at eight and saw Father Paul at eight-fifteen." He finished off his Scotch. "Will you take the case or not?"

I didn't like this guy much; there was something false about him, something unreal. I felt there were things he wasn't telling me, but I felt sorry for him and I kept thinking about the dead girl and about Patrick, who might still be alive. Who was I kidding? It was Sam and Karen I was thinking about.

"Yeah, I'll take it." I told him my fee and asked if he had a picture of Patrick. He said Jennifer had taken them all, but they weren't in her handbag when they found her. That cinched it for me: whoever killed Jennifer had also known Patrick. Horton gave me his card and I saw that he was an antique dealer with a shop in the East Sixties. I got the addresses of Alison Gordon and the Bakers. "I'll wait until the funeral is over before I go there," I said.

"You needn't bother. There isn't going to be any funeral. Carter asked me to have her cremated and to do what I wanted to with the ashes."

"Jesus Christ," I said.

He picked up his cigarette case and lighter, put them back in his pocket and stood up. "It won't be easy to get anything out of Carter, you know. You may even have trouble getting in the door."

"Let me worry about that," I said.

I waved good night to Barney as we walked through the bar. Outside we ambled up to Prince Street together. I looked down at the card he'd given me. "You can always be reached here?"

"I have the same phone number in my shop as I do at home. You'd be surprised at how many collectors call me in the middle of the night. Sometimes I operate as a therapist of sorts." He laughed, a strange sort of hacking sound as if he might suddenly break into sobs. "I'll walk up to Sixth Avenue and get a cab."

I looked east on Prince. "Here comes one," I said. It was easy to get cabs in SoHo.

"Splendid."

The cab pulled up and I opened the door for him. "I'll be in touch. By the way, this has nothing to do with the case but I'm curious, how'd you get the glass eye?"

His good eye blinked and for a moment he hesitated; then he smiled. "I wish I could say in Korea or something like that but the truth is I stuck a pencil in my eye."

"When you were a kid?"

"Four years ago. Good night." He closed the door and the cab drove off.

My estimation of him went up a hundred percent. I always respect an honest man.

4

After I got the kids off to school I decided to call Elaine. Supposedly she was always in her office by eight. It was something she never failed to mention, because she thought my life was sloppy, my hours irregular. They are; I like them that way.

The person who answered the phone said, "Good morning, 'Another Woman's Heart.'"

As always, I was tempted to say, "This is another man's nose calling," or something equally snappy, but I resisted. Instead I said, "Elaine McQuade, please." She'd taken back her maiden name; it fit her new life better, she said.

"Who's calling, please?" the receptionist asked.

"Mr. Fanelli."

"One moment, please."

There was a click and then some music came on the line. It was a soppy instrumental, a lot of violins. I think it was "My Favorite Things."

"Mr. Fanelli," came the voice, "Ms. McQuade is in a meeting right now. Can I take a message?"

I found it hard to believe that there could be much of a meeting going on at eight-fifteen in the morning but what did I know about television land and taking a meeting?

"Tell her to call me tonight."

"Does she have your number?"

"She has mine and I have hers," I said.

"I beg your pardon?"

"Skip it. Just tell her to call me." I hung up. There wasn't much chance that Elaine would call back. She knew I wanted to arrange a time with her to see the kids and she just wasn't interested. I'd definitely have to confront her. Soon.

In the bedroom I reached into the back of my closet where I had hung my old ties. I hardly ever wore one but sometimes they were useful. I was going to see the Bakers today and I felt I'd get further with them if I was wearing a suit and tie. Instinct.

I picked out a red silk with small blue fleurs-de-lys; it would go nicely with my gray pinstripe. I put a clip in my .32 and shoved it in my shoulder holster. Ready.

I walked down Thompson to Prince, across Prince to Sullivan where I turned uptown. It was a nice day but I prayed nobody I met would tell me to have one. None of the stores except the Robbers and the butcher store on Sullivan were open. I knew this because my mother was the butcher. It was only eight-thirty but already she had three customers. I knew them all.

"Here's your big boy, Concettina." Mrs. Albetta said.

"Hello, ladies."

"So handsome," Mrs. Fabrizio said.

"You going to a funeral, Fortune?" Mrs. Rauschenberg asked, flipping my tie. "Or a wedding?"

"Neither," I answered. My mother was behind the counter trimming some veal chops. At her feet was Bruno, her yellow mutt. When he saw me he growled, showing the few teeth he had left. Bruno had always hated me. I ignored him and leaned down and kissed my mother on the back of the neck. "Morning, Mama."

"Morning, Fortunato," she said without turning around. "Where you go all dressed up?"

"Business," I said.

She hacked off a piece of fat with her cleaver. "Ah, business!" She dropped the chops onto a piece of waxed paper, rolled them up and put the package on the scale. "Eight twenty-five, Sophia."

Mrs. Albetta paid and the women all left together for their morning coffee at Angie's. I waited alone in the store while my mother went into the refrigerator for a side of beef. I didn't offer to help; it only made her mad. She'd been running the store alone for more than ten years, since the old man died. But even before that she'd done the lion's share of the work. He was either too tanked up or too hung over to be of much use.

She came back with the beef over her shoulder, the weight of it pushing down her thin frame. She flopped it onto the butcher block and sighed. Mama was on the tall side for a woman of her background and generation, about five feet six. Even though she was slight, over the years she'd developed a good set of muscles. But she was slowing down, getting older, a little weaker. So who wasn't?

"You on a case, Fortunato?"

I nodded. "Don't worry, Mama. I'll be careful."

"You always say you be careful but you get a punch in the nose anyway. Come over here, I gotta make steaks."

I moved over next to the butcher block and Bruno gave me what sounded like a grunt. I looked at my mother's profile. She was still beautiful: aquiline nose, full mouth, delicate chin. Even with the short, oyster white hair and the fine network of lines around her eyes, you could still see the beautiful young woman she'd been.

"It's the girl in the store window?" she asked.

"How'd you know?"

She shrugged. "One and one makes two. Logic, right?"

"Right."

"The children okay?"

"Fine."

"The girl was young, huh? Like Karen?" She stopped hacking away at the beef and looked up at me, her brown eyes singed with sorrow and maybe a little fear.

"Don't worry, Mama. Karen'll be all right."

"I dunno, Fortunato, everything's changed. Used to be so safe in this neighborhood...we never even lock the doors, remember?"

"Yeah, I do."

"Now they take drugs and steal and kill, I dunno. When just the neighborhood people and the factories were here we were better. Do I make this up, Fortunato?"

"Neighborhoods change, Mama. Most of the new people who live in the lofts are nice people."

"It's true, it's true."

"The girl who was killed wasn't even from this neighborhood and for all we know whoever killed her isn't either."

The door opened and Mr. Torterello, bent and leaning on a cane, came in. "Morning, Connie," he said. "Hello there, boy."

I said hello. "I have to go, Mama. I'll see you Thursday for dinner."

"You bring a friend?" she asked, her eyes glistening with hope.

"Just me and the kids, I think. Anything changes I'll let you know."

"Always room for one more," she said.

"Thanks, Mama." I kissed her on each cheek, and she kissed me.

"You got your gat?" she whispered, a smile playing around her mouth.

My back to Mr. Torterello, I patted the left side of my chest. As much as my mother was nervous about what I did for part of my living, she was also realistic. She also knew her references to my "gat" were funny. We said good-bye again and I left.

Walking to my parking lot on Wooster Street, I thought over what my mother had said about the neighborhood. Everything *had* changed. Up until about 1968 the area that was now known as SoHo, which meant South of Houston, had been mostly industrial. Thompson, Sullivan, MacDougal, some of

Prince, and some of Spring housed a large number of Italians, a few Jews, and some Irish in the tenements. Mostly we were poor people. Not desperate. Everybody always had enough to eat but luxuries came hard. Then, in the late sixties, people started buying up the loft buildings that had been factories and turning them into living spaces. And then the galleries moved in and SoHo was suddenly rivaling Fifty-seventh Street as the center of the art world. Tourists came in droves and everybody who had a shop started to get rich. There was a lot of money floating around SoHo and a lot of money brought corruption. It never failed.

Around 1970 my brother-in-law, Roy Sklar, made me a business proposition to buy some empty parcels of land on Wooster and Mercer streets and turn them into parking lots. Everybody thought Roy was crazy but he could see what was coming. I could too and I had a little money my Aunt Gloria had left me so I bought. Elaine had also thought I was nuts and we had had one of our worst fights over it. Roy and I also bought four buildings and in 1980 we sold two of them for a hundred percent profit. Each of us still owned one. The truth was if I got rid of the lots and I never worked again it wouldn't matter. But I liked working. And I liked my neighborhood.

Julio, the guy who worked for me in the Wooster Street lot, was peeling rubber when I walked up.

"Hey, Julio, cool it." I didn't like him driving like a cowboy. It wasn't good for the cars.

Julio got out of the Cadillac he'd been jockeying and in his slow, deliberate way, walked over to me. He was wearing an imitation leather jacket and a checkered porkpie hat. No matter what the weather he'd wear that outfit until May thirty-first and put it back on again September first.

"Here," he said. He handed me some checks from a couple of monthlies who were late. "Finally." Julio was a man of few words.

I stuffed the checks into my pocket. "Where's my car?" I'd called him at seven to tell him to leave it out.

He slammed an open palm against his forehead. "Oh, mon,

I forget." His round cheeks stained red like two cherry tomatoes. "I get it now."

I cooled my heels and turned off my eyes and ears for five minutes while Julio tore around the lot moving cars to get to my Volks. At last he pulled the yellow wagon to a screeching halt at my side.

"Here you go, boss."

"Thanks," I said. When I was in I leaned out the window. "Julio?"

"Yeah, boss?"

"Take it easy putting those cars back, okay?"

"Sure thing, boss."

Right, Julio, right. As an example I slowly eased my way out onto Wooster Street. When I got to the corner of Wooster and Spring I could hear the revving of an engine and the peeling of rubber. So much for being a role model.

The ride from the Holland Tunnel to Maplewood, New Jersey, was about forty-five minutes. After the usual run-down area you go through when you enter a town I could see that it was a pretty affluent place. The address I had was one-twenty-one Holcomb Drive. I stopped in a gas station for directions and five minutes later I was there.

It was one of those streets where the houses have manicured lawns on every side and the trees are so green they look like they've been spray painted. Almost all the homes had azalea bushes in front but it was too early for them to be in bloom. Still, I could imagine the bursts of color that would be on display in another month or so.

One-twenty-one Holcomb was on a corner. It was a big white house with black shutters. A glassed-in room, like a large porch, was on the right and a wooden portico on the left. The driveway was empty and the garage doors were shut. I parked the car, got out and walked up the cement path, which was bordered by low bushes. The big front door had a brass knocker in the shape of a lion's head. I used it. Nothing happened. I decided to try the bell at the right of the door.

Still nothing. I pushed it again and this time I realized there'd been a humming coming from within, because now it stopped. A vacuum cleaner. The door opened.

A large woman in an apron, her hair in pink rollers under a scarf, stood blinking at me. I knew this wasn't Mrs. Baker.

"Hello," I said. "The Bakers in?"

"Nobody's home. I'm the cleaning girl."

She hadn't been a girl for at least forty years and it made me feel bad that she referred to herself that way. I wondered if Mrs. Baker was the kind of woman who said, "My girl comes in to clean every Monday."

"When will they be back?"

"Who are you?" she asked suspiciously.

"A friend of the family." Maybe the Bakers were with their minister for consolation. "I know about the tragedy," I said.

She clucked her tongue. "Could ya believe it? Two of them, just like that." She snapped her fingers and the sound seemed to surprise her.

"A terrible thing," I agreed.

"Well, you wouldn't know it by the likes of them," she said, bending toward me conspiratorially.

"What do you mean?" I asked.

She pulled back as if suddenly she remembered an old lesson in protocol. "Why should I tell you?"

"I'm a concerned party. A friend. Do you think I could come in a minute?"

Her eyes narrowed. They were like two pieces of burnt coal with just as much life. "In? Why should I let ya in?"

I took a ten dollar bill from my wallet and folded it in my hand where she could see it. "What's your name?"

Her eyes were on the ten in my hand. "Joan."

I smiled to myself. I didn't expect that. I thought it would be Gertie or Hazel or one of those. "Okay, Joan, my name's Fortune and I'd like to talk to you. It's important." I wiggled the bill.

Joan stuck her head past the door, looked up and down the street, saw that no one was around, then motioned me in.

Was she afraid her reputation would be tarnished if she let a man into the house when she was there alone?

A white staircase with a walnut banister swung into the main hall I stepped into. To my right I could see part of the living room. I got an impression of colorlessness as if the entire room had been bleached. A corner of a fireplace, painted white, was visible, and long white drapes covered the one window I could see.

"So whatcha want?" Joan asked. "I got work to do, ya know."

"You look like the kind of woman I can be straight with, so I'm going to tell you the truth."

She bobbed her head as if to say that it was only fitting.

"I'm a private investigator looking into the murder of Jennifer Baker."

"What kind of name is Fortune?" she asked. It was almost a non sequitur but not quite, just a delayed reaction.

"It's really Fortunato, which in Italian means fortunate or lucky."

"I know an Italian. His name's Tony Cardella. You know him?"

"I'm not from New Jersey," I said as if that were the only reason I didn't know Tony. "I was wondering, Joan, if you'd tell me something about the Bakers."

She sniffed. "Like for instance what?"

"Oh, anything you want. Were they a happy family?"

"A private investigator?"

She did it again. Maybe she was out of sync. "Yes."

"How do I know?"

I gave her my card and she read it for an interminably long time, considering it only had my name, phone number and the words "Private Investigation." Finally she looked up at me, her beaky nose twitching over her thin lips. "How do I know this card is yours?"

It wasn't a bad point. "You don't," I said. "You'll just have to take my word for it." To help my word along I reached over, took her hand and pressed the ten into it. She slipped it into the pocket of her flowered apron.

Then she said, "Was they happy? They gone to work today, them two. Now you tell me, was they happy?" The look of disapproval that settled on her face seemed natural.

I felt some disapproval myself along with shock. "You mean they went to their jobs?"

"That's what I said. It ain't normal, if ya ask me. How could ya work when your girl's been killed? Well, they never was normal anyways."

"How weren't they normal?"

"It's hard to put it. I mean, they look all right, to the outside, if ya know what I mean. But it wasn't right. They come and they go, they talk and eat just like anybody but something weren't there. I dunno."

"You mean something was missing?" I helped.

"That's it," she said brightly. "Something was missing."

"What was it?"

She thought for a long time, rubbing her lower lip as if it were a crystal ball. Conceptions did not come easily to Joan, life had ground thought down to mush. You could see it on her finished face. Finally she looked at me, a dim light behind her ashen eyes.

"Love," she said. "Love was missing."

I nodded. "They never hurt the children, did they?"

"Oh, no. Nothing like that. And Mrs. B wanted to be different, I think, but she was too scared."

"Of what?"

"Of *him*. Mr. B. He's cold as a witch's tit. Like this morning. I could tell she didn't want to go to work, her eyes all red like they was, but he insisted, told her there was nothing to stay home for and he needed her in the office."

"She works for him?"

"She's his secretary."

"Did Jennifer ever say anything to you about her brother's disappearance?"

"He run away. No, she didn't talk to me. She was a wild one."

"Really? I heard the Bakers wouldn't let the kids do anything."

"That's right, but Jennie done it anyways."

"How?"

"They all had to be in bed by nine but she snuck out. Through her winder, onto the solarium roof and down that tree next to it. Back in the same way at two, three in the morning."

"How do you know this?" I asked.

She stuck her chin out, defying me not to believe her. "My grandson tole me."

"What's his name?"

"Oh, no, ya don't. You ain't gonna go creeping around him."

"No, I'm not," I said, almost laughing at the image. "I just want to ask him a few questions."

"What for?"

"To find out more about Jennie. Look, Joan, you don't want to see her killer get away with it, do you?"

"It wasn't nobody from New Jersey," she assured me.

"I'm sure it wasn't," I said. "But the more I know about her the easier it will be for me to find the person who killed her. I'd like to know what Jennie did when she sneaked out at night. Did she have a boyfriend?"

"Mebbe yes, mebbe no."

I hated to do this but I had to. "You could be arrested for obstructing justice, you know," I lied.

She took a fearful step backwards and her hands worried the hem of her apron. "Whatcha want to know?"

"Did she have a boyfriend? If you tell me his name I won't have to bother with your grandson."

"According to . . . someone she was seen in the company of a boy name of Leo. I can't think of his other name but he was some football boy or something. Any kid at school could tell you."

Alison would know. "I'd like to see their rooms," I said.

She recoiled as if I were asking the unthinkable. "What for?"

"To get a feeling of them. To see if there's anything that might help me."

"There ain't."

I was annoyed. How would she know what would or wouldn't be helpful? "There just might be," I insisted.

"There ain't." She nodded once for emphasis.

"Why don't you let me judge that?"

She thought about it, then said, "I could get in trouble."

I understood, got out another ten and slipped it into her pocket. She motioned with her head for me to follow. We went up the stairs, past some framed prints of sailboats and at the top, turned right. First she opened a door on one side of the hall and then on the other.

"That was his," she said pointing, "and that one hers."

I stepped into Jennifer's room first. Stunned, I turned around to face Joan.

"I told ya there was nothing to see," she said righteously.

The room contained a single bed with a tan plaid spread, the kind you find in motels, a maple chest of drawers, and one maple armchair. There were no posters, no photographs, no knickknacks, nothing personal. I walked over to the closet and opened it. Empty. I pulled out a dresser drawer and found it empty, too. The desk was the same.

I left the room and crossed the hall to Patrick's room. It was identical. I didn't bother examining the closet or drawers; I knew what I'd find. Back in the hall I stared at Joan.

She shrugged. "They threw everything away when each of them left."

"Threw it away?" I asked incredulously.

"He made her and me pack up all their stuff, clothes and all, and take it down to the Goodwill people. The papers and junk he made us burn. It ain't normal, is it?"

"No, it's not."

Back downstairs I said, "One more thing. Could you give me the address where the Bakers work?"

"It's not in Maplewood."

"That's okay. I've got a car."

"You won't tell him where you got it?"

"I'm sure he's listed in the phone book. I just thought you'd save me the trouble."

"All right. He's got his office in South Orange, in the new complex right where Academy Street meets South Orange Avenue. It's called the Professional Building." She gave the derisive laugh of a woman who instinctively distrusts lawyers and doctors.

I thanked her and she gave me a lopsided smile. The best she could do. I stepped outside. Joan kept the door open just a crack as she watched me go down the walk. At the end of the path I turned and saw that she was still watching. I waved to her and she slammed the door shut. A friendly gesture.

I started the car and put it in drive. Where, I wondered, did a seventeen-year-old girl go every night until two or three in the morning and what was so important that she'd risk the wrath of her father? I had a funny feeling Jennifer Baker might not be exactly the girl her uncle thought she was. That made me think of Karen. Did I really know her? Did any parent *really* know his kids? Later for that one. Now I was going to see these Bakers. I felt like I was on my way to interview a couple of monsters. Maybe I was.

5

Joan had been right. You couldn't miss the Professional Building. It was one of those low, sprawling jobs built out of a yellow bricklike material that made you feel the whole place was anemic. The windows were the kind you couldn't see into, giving it a dark, closed-down appearance. I was glad I wasn't coming here for my annual checkup; the atmosphere would have given me heartburn at the very least.

I parked in the back and entered from there. A roster of names was near the door. The Bakers were on the top floor. I found the elevators and rode up to four. His name was on the door. There was no one in the outer office but I heard a distant buzzer when I opened the door so I was sure there would be soon. It wasn't a fancy place but there was nothing shabby about it either. There was a white Formica desk and blue wall-to-wall carpeting; two brown leather chairs and a small tweed couch filled out the room.

She came out of another office, to the right of her desk, but before she closed the door I caught a glimpse of a man sitting behind a walnut desk.

"May I help you?" she asked timidly.

Joan had been right again. Her eyes were red-rimmed and puffy. Mrs. Baker was a small woman and gave the impression she was frail, brittle. I guessed she was around my age but she looked to be in her fifties. I suspected it wasn't only recent events that had caused this. Her hair was a dull brown and worn short in no particular style. She was wearing a blue polyester suit, a white blouse with a jabot and low-heeled brown shoes. She wore no makeup except a very light lipstick.

"I'd like to see Mr. Baker," I said.

"Do you have an appointment?"

"No." I didn't want to tell her what it was about; I felt if I said it she'd dissolve. But of course she'd have to know. "Are you Mrs. Baker?"

"Yes." She looked surprised, like a woman who was rarely asked to confirm her identity: no one cared.

"I'd like to see you as well, Mrs. Baker. I'm investigating your daughter's death."

She drew in her breath in a great gulping sound and caught the edge of the desk for support. I hadn't been far off.

"Are you all right?"

She nodded, and sounds like strangled sobs filled the room. The inner door opened and a man stood there. Carter Baker, I presumed.

"What is it? What's going on?" He glanced at his wife, then took a step toward me, his fists clenched at his sides.

"I'm investigating the death of your daughter, Mr. Baker," I said quickly.

Again Mrs. Baker made two choked-back cries.

"Rebecca! Please! Control yourself."

She gulped down her despair like unwanted food.

"Who are you?" Baker asked me.

I gave him my card. While he studied it I studied him. He was on the short side, maybe five nine or ten. He wouldn't have been a bad-looking guy if his face hadn't been so tight with anger. His features were regular and he wore steel-rimmed glasses in front of faded brown eyes. His hair was brown, no gray. I wondered how he did it. He was wearing a charcoal gray suit, white shirt and a narrow gray tie with a thin green stripe. His jacket was open and I could see a gold chain looping over his hip. From it hung a Phi Beta Kappa key.

"You're not with the police," he said.

"I didn't say I was."

"You're nothing but a private detective," he said disdainfully.

I didn't think this was the time to tell him I was many other things. "I'm a private detective; that's right."

He held out my card to me. "We don't have to deal with you."

"No, you don't." I didn't take the card.

He let it float to the floor. "Who hired you?"

Instinctively Rebecca Baker bent down and picked up the card. A woman used to cleaning up after her man. Carter ignored her.

"I can't tell you who hired me, Mr. Baker. That's confidential."

"We were with the police all last night. We have nothing to say to you," he stated.

"I assume you'd like your daughter's murder solved?"

"In the interest of justice, of course. As for us it won't help either way."

Only a direct approach was going to help me here. "Did you know Jennifer's boyfriend?"

"She didn't have a boyfriend. She was much too young. I think you'd better leave, Mr. . . . ah . . ."

"Fanelli," Mrs. Baker said looking at my card.

Baker glanced her way. He might as well have been looking at a bug. Then he looked back at me. "Listen, Fanelli, I know your type. Down and out, you'll do anything for a buck."

I wasn't about to tell him the balance in my Dreyfus account, so I ignored the remark. "Your daughter climbed out her window every night after you two went to bed and she stayed out until three in the morning. Her boyfriend's name is Leo."

"Leo Schultz?" Mrs. Baker said, then put a trembling hand to her lips.

Baker whirled on her. "You knew about this, Rebecca?" His face was bordering on crimson.

"No, no," she said quickly. "I only know the name. He's a football player or something. I've seen it in the paper."

"I don't believe what you're saying, Fanelli. My daughter would never defy the rules of my house."

"But she left home, Mr. Baker. Surely that was defiance. Look, I don't want to upset you people. I'm not your enemy. I want to find out who killed Jennifer and where Patrick is."

Baker stiffened at the mention of his son. "As far as I'm concerned, when Patrick left my house he died. Both of the children are dead."

"You're a hard marker, Mr. Baker."

He leveled an icy gaze at me. "You don't know what a hard marker is."

"Tell me about it," I said.

"My father raised me as if I were in the Marines." His eyes clouded over in memory. There was no smile. "Every day of my life I got up at four-thirty in the morning, chopped wood, fixed breakfast and did the dishes before I walked five miles to school."

For a minute I thought this guy was trying for an Abe Lincoln award but when I looked at Mrs. Baker, who was tearing little pieces from my card, I knew he was sincere.

"Still and all I learned valuable lessons," Baker said. "I had a set of values that have stood me in good stead all of my life." The cloud lifted from his eyes and he was back in the present. "I wanted to pass that on to the children. In return they both ran away. Ungrateful," he muttered.

It was as if he hadn't truly realized that his daughter was dead.

"There are things you have to do that you might not like to do to teach children about life, but you do them anyway because it's your duty."

"Like what?" I asked.

He removed his glasses and wiped them with a handkerchief he took from his back pocket. I waited for an answer but none came. Horton had said Baker never abused the kids but now I wondered. "What kinds of things did you have to do that you didn't like, Mr. Baker?"

He put his glasses back on and stared at me. "I never beat

them if that's what you're thinking. But none of this is your business. You couldn't possibly understand. I think you'd better go, as I've already said."

I could see the interview was over. "I don't suppose you have any pictures of your kids you'd like to give me?"

"The only thing I'd like to give you, Mr. Fanelli, is a punch in the nose."

That surprised me. Even though Baker's fists were clenched I didn't think he'd speak that way, much less act on it.

"You know, Mr. Baker, whatever your daughter was into it's all going to come out. You'd do a lot better with me than with the police."

Baker's mouth rolled in on itself and disappeared. "Get out," he said.

"I'm going." I took another card from my pocket and laid it on the desk. Mrs. Baker had completely shredded the other one. "Just in case you change your mind," I said.

I sat in my car in the parking lot for a few minutes trying to figure Baker out. Nobody could really be that heartless, I thought. There was a tap on my window and I looked up. It was Rebecca Baker, looking wild-eyed and disheveled. I rolled down the window.

"I must talk to you," she said.

"Get in."

She ran around to the other side of the car and jumped in. "Please, let's get out of here."

I started the car. "Where to?"

"The mountain," she said. "I'll show you."

We drove up South Orange Avenue and pulled off the main drag onto a winding road through the mountain. The trees were starting to come to life but there wasn't enough foliage yet to keep the sun off the road and out of my eyes. Rebecca Baker was silent and smoked a cigarette. At the end of the road there was a clearing and I parked. It was a great view. I could see New York and I wished I was back there. So far New Jersey wasn't my idea of heaven. I turned to look at the woman next to me.

She was trembling slightly and was lighting her second butt. When she got it dragging she turned to me.

"Carter would kill me if he knew I smoked," she said.

"Would he?"

"Well, not literally, of course." She giggled nervously.

I noticed that the jabot at her neck was open and torn away from the collar. "What happened after I left, Mrs. Baker?"

She shook her head and shoulders as if she had a chill. "We argued. I got away from him. I knew he'd never chase me through the building. He's much too concerned with appearances for that. You mustn't hate Carter," she implored.

"I don't hate him, Mrs. Baker. I just think he's a cold fish. Anyway, what do you care what I think of him?"

"I don't know. It's just that he makes such an awful impression on people."

"Quite a liability for a lawyer."

"Oh, he's different with clients. He can turn on the charm, believe it or not."

It was hard to believe. "You argued with your husband because you wanted to tell me something. Is that right?"

"Yes." She opened her bag and pulled out a powder blue wallet. It was in two sections and had a band with a snap to close it at the end, the kind my sister carried back in the fifties. She opened the wallet exposing a plastic picture folder. From one of the sections she pulled a picture and handed it to me. "That's Patrick," she said softly.

It was a school picture. The boy was beautiful. He had blond hair to his collar and clear blue eyes. His features were delicate, almost feminine. Horton had told me the boy was fifteen but this was the picture of an eleven- or twelve-year-old.

"He's a wonderful-looking boy," I said, "but don't you have something a little more recent?" I knew from watching my own kids how quickly they changed.

"This was taken right before he . . . he ran away. I know, he looks very young. That's part of what was so frightening. How could a boy who looks like that make it on his own? Wouldn't you think someone would have turned him in or whatever you do with stray children?"

I thought of the postcard and that Patrick said he had a job. Who would give this kid a job? Maybe he was lying.

She went on. "He looks like my brother did as a boy. I think that disturbed Carter more than anything. He hates my brother. It's Charles who hired you, isn't it?"

I didn't answer.

She waved a hand in my direction. "Oh, it doesn't matter. I know it must have been."

"Do you have a picture of Jennifer?" I asked.

She flipped the picture folder and pulled out a black and white photo of a group of girls. She pointed to one in the upper right-hand corner. "That's Jen." She started to cry then, great wracking sobs that seemed too large for her small frame.

I didn't want to comfort her at the moment for fear it would cut off the tears she obviously needed to shed. I took the picture from her hand and studied it while she cried. It was taken in warm weather; they were all wearing shorts. There were eight of them. They looked like nice, clean-cut girls and one of them even looked familiar. She was sitting next to Jennifer, smiling. Her hair was loose and hung to her shoulders. She looked like Betsy, a friend of Karen's, I thought. Maybe.

Mrs. Baker seemed to be slowing down and I reached under the dashboard where I kept the Kleenex. I slipped some into her hand, then patted her shoulder.

"I'm sorry," I said. "I really am. I can't think of anything worse."

She nodded and blew her nose. "I'm all right now. Thanks."

"Where was the picture taken?"

"At camp last summer. The children always went to camp. Jennifer hated it but Charles insisted."

"Who's this girl?" I asked pointing to the one who looked like Betsy.

"That's Price Allen. She's a lovely girl. She lives in New York."

It clicked then. Price Allen was the girl who'd discovered Jennifer's body in The Sweatshop window. Why had she lied about knowing her?

"Why'd you ask about Price?"

"Nothing. She looks like a friend of my daughter's, that's all."

She nodded. "They all look so much alike at that age."

I didn't agree. Price Allen looked a lot different from Jennifer Baker, for instance. From the little I could see in the picture Jennifer stood out from the rest. For one thing she wasn't smiling. Her expression was sullen and bored, and I could tell she was wearing makeup. The others weren't.

"Is this the only picture you have of Jennifer?" I asked.

"She was absent from school when they took class pictures this year and the year before. . . . Well, I can't remember. But I don't have any recent pictures. Mr. Fanelli, do you think you can find my son?"

"I don't know. I'd like to try." I didn't tell her there was a chance the boy was dead.

"How can I help?"

"You can tell me anything you think I should know about him."

She touched her temple with the tips of her fingers as if to activate her memory. A look of desperate sadness swept over her face. "I probably don't know much. The children never told me anything. They were afraid I'd tell Carter. I didn't encourage them to talk to me because they were right. I wouldn't have ever volunteered anything, but if he'd asked me, well . . ." She shrugged helplessly.

"Does Mr. Baker hit you?"

"Oh, no. He's adamant about not using physical violence. You see, that's what it's all about. He said he wanted to punch you but he never would. Carter fights that in himself all the time and he always wins. He was an abused child, Mr. Fanelli." She shut her eyes as if to shut out an ugly image. "His father beat him mercilessly. Somehow he can't completely deny his father and so he carries on the traditions and discipline that went with the beatings. He says that that part made him a man. I wish you could see the scars on his back. They'd turn your stomach."

I felt a modicum of compassion for Baker but what he'd

done with his own children obliterated it. "He's a sick man, Mrs. Baker."

"Yes, I know. That's why I don't leave him. I don't know what would become of him."

"I see." Another woman who subjugated herself to her husband. There seemed to be a lot of them around...too many. I wanted to get off the topic of Carter Baker. "Now what can you tell me about Patrick and Jennie?"

"Is it true what you said about Jennie climbing out of the window?"

"I don't know. Someone told me that."

"It wouldn't surprise me. Carter thought she was perfect because she played it that way with him. But I knew she was miserable in our house. What could she have done all night?" She blushed then, realizing the possibilities. "She was so young."

"Unfortunately, they're never too young these days." Was Karen a virgin? I wondered. It wasn't the first time I'd thought about it, but the idea still shocked me.

"Carter never even let her date."

That'll do it every time, I thought. "Did she have any special interests?"

"Music. Disco music. She liked to dance and play that awful stuff. Of course she couldn't do it when Carter was home, but she did when he was out. I can't think of anything else. But Patrick was an artist. Or wanted to be. Carter thought it was sissy stuff. It reminded him too much of Charles. I guess he was afraid Patrick would turn out like Charles."

Even though Charles Horton wasn't one of my favorites I could think of worse people Patrick might turn out to be like. Namely his father. "What's wrong with Charles?"

Her face flushed again. "Well, Charles is a homosexual."

I hadn't spotted it. I was so used to the gay men downtown who wore short leather jackets and had mustaches and muscles that it had never entered my mind about Horton. When they were macho I could tell they were gay; otherwise I didn't think about it. And I certainly didn't care. I'll take a Charles Horton over a Carter Baker any day.

"Do you think Patrick is homosexual, Mrs. Baker?"

Her head snapped back; she was affronted. "I certainly don't. Not that he's anything at his age."

Mrs. Baker lived in a tiny world. Now that I thought about it I realized how the kid could easily have made his way. He said he was living with a friend. Was it a lover?

"Did Patrick have any friends in New York?"

"Not that I know about. I don't see how he could have."

I looked down at his picture again. With a face like that he could have had two hundred friends in an hour. I decided I wasn't going to get anything more from Mrs. Baker. I'd never met a mother who knew less about her children.

I tucked the pictures in my inside pocket and started the car. We drove back in silence. At the parking lot of the Professional Building I asked her if she'd be all right.

"You mean will Carter do anything?"

I nodded and pointed to her torn jabot.

"That was an accident. He's never touched me in anger, Mr. Fanelli. And he won't now. He'll just ground me for a month or so, that's all."

That's all! A grown woman, and her husband was going to ground her like a kid. I wanted to tell her to get the hell out of his clutches but I knew it wouldn't do any good. She was in for life, like prison.

"I'll keep in touch," I said.

"You'd better not. If you find Patrick . . . well, then that'll be different."

"Will your husband take him back?"

She shrugged.

I wanted to ask if she'd leave Baker then to be with her son, but I didn't. I was afraid I knew the answer. We said our good-byes and I watched her walk to the door of the building. She stopped, reached into her bag, took something out. Then she opened her mouth and held her hand up to it. She was spraying her breath so Baker wouldn't smell the cigarettes. She dropped the spray back into her bag and went inside. I wondered what it must be like to feel like a frightened child all your life. I'd never know.

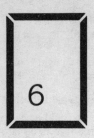

6

My interviews with the Bakers left me with a bad taste in my mouth so I stopped at Sip 'n Sup, a broken-down luncheonette on Valley Street, to chase it away with a cheeseburger and two Cokes. There was no doubt in my mind that Jennifer Baker had been leading a double life and had probably gotten into something way over her young head. What I couldn't figure out was how her murder connected to her brother's vanishing act. I hoped that was all it was and that I'd find him.

The next stop was the high school. It was a big red brick structure. I could see that, at some point, a section had been added to the building, which probably accounted for the lack of grounds around it. I'd asked the counterman at Sip 'n Sup a little bit about the place and he'd told me that although it was in Maplewood it served the students of the neighboring town of South Orange as well. He also said that when he'd gone there in the early fifties it had been a great school with terrific kids. But now it was full of druggies and punks. It's funny how we all feel that way about our alma maters.

The lot behind the school was filled, so I had to park a block away. Inside the front entrance a boy with shaggy black bangs sat behind a small table.

"Can I help you, sir?"

Clearly this was no punk. "I'd like to see the principal."

"Do you have an appointment?"

"No." I gave him my card.

His thick black eyebrows arched. "Well, I don't know."

"I do. It'll be all right."

"I'm not supposed to let anyone in unless they have an appointment." He bit at the flesh around his thumb.

"Don't worry about it. If there's any objections I'll tell them I held a gun on you."

He giggled nervously and moved his chair back an inch or so. I started past him.

"Which way?" I asked.

"At the end of this hall you turn right and the main office will be on your right."

"Thanks. Oh, yeah, what's the principal's name?"

"Mrs. Gordon."

I stopped. Well, Gordon wasn't an uncommon name. Still, I thought I'd check it out. "She Alison's mother?"

His eyes widened. "Yeah, she's her mother. Is Alison in trouble?"

"No, she's not. Thanks for the info." I followed the kid's directions and dammit if I didn't find the main office just like that!

It was your usual school office with a high counter and six workers behind it clacking away at typewriters and answering phones. Two boys in jeans and tight T-shirts stood in front of the counter. A woman behind the counter, with hair the color of a copper pot, told them to sit on the bench and wait until they were called. I was next. We went through the appointment routine when I told her I wanted to see Mrs. Gordon and then I said I was there to see her about the dead student. She blanched.

"I beg your pardon?"

I realized then that the school hadn't been informed of Jennifer's death. "One of your students has been murdered," I said, handing her my card.

"Oh, Lord." She stood rooted to the spot. I could see that she wanted to ask who it was but couldn't.

"Mrs. Gordon, please," I prompted.

"Yes. Just a minute."

A little dazed she walked to a door on my right, knocked and went in. A few minutes passed and the copper-headed woman came out and motioned me over. When I went past her she sucked in her body as if the taint of death might mark her if we touched.

Alison Gordon's mother was a knockout. She was standing behind her desk when I came in and I could see that she was tall, maybe five ten or eleven. Her black hair was pulled back into a chignon but the sides looped and gave her a soft look. Gold hoop earrings hung from her ears. Her eyes were large and gray and she wore a discreet amount of liner and eye shadow. She had a straight nose and a wide mouth. She was wearing a tan linen suit, expensively tailored, and a brown silk blouse; small ruffles poked out from her sleeves. Her body was that of a twenty-year-old but she must have been at least forty. I wanted to ask her if she'd been using the *Jane Fonda Workout Book* but I didn't think it would be a good start. She held my card in one hand and offered me her other.

"How do you do, Mr. Fanelli. I'm Vanessa Gordon."

I took her hand. The skin was soft. "Nice of you to see me. I'm here about Jennifer Baker."

She withdrew her hand from mine and it went to her lips. "But Beth said you were here about . . . Oh, no. You mean it's Jennifer who's been murdered?"

"I'm afraid so." It probably seemed cruel to her that I'd told her so bluntly, but there really was no other way.

She sat down and gestured for me to do the same. As if she were on automatic she opened a drawer, took out an ashtray and a pack of Benson & Hedges. There was a moment when I thought she might be waiting for me to light it for her but then she pulled out a Ronson and lit it herself.

"I shouldn't be smoking in here," she said. "I only do it under stress." She laughed, showing white, even teeth. "I guess that's a lot." The laughter died quickly. "Do you smoke?" She held the package out to me.

"No." I'd seen this kind of behavior before. She didn't want to talk about Jennifer and was using a delaying tactic.

She probably didn't even know it. I hated to remind her but I had to. "Mrs. Gordon, did you know Jennifer well?"

"Yes, I did. She was a close friend of my daughter who's a student here. But I was glad when Jennifer transferred to a private school last week. She'd changed in the last year and I didn't like her influence on Alison. That's my daughter."

"She transferred to a private school?"

"Yes. Her father called and asked to have her transcripts sent to, ah, I can't remember the name of the school right now but I can look it up for you if it's important. At any rate, it was a different school from the one Patrick transferred to. The Bakers must have become disenchanted with our school. We do our best," she said defensively, and blew a wreath of smoke above her head.

I wasn't going to bother with the private school names because I knew they were phonies. Not the schools themselves probably, but the fact that the Baker kids had gone to them. Obviously this was the way Carter Baker got around reporting his kids missing.

"You said Jennifer had changed in the last year. Can you tell me how?"

"I will, but I want to know what happened to her first."

I told her, trying to play down the details as much as possible. It was hard. When a girl is killed and propped up in a store window like a mannequin it's not easy to make the story palatable. She took it fairly well; her eyes filled but the tears didn't spill over. I waited a moment then asked her again to tell me about Jennifer's change.

"She'd always been a nice girl, well spoken, and when she came to the house for dinner she was bright and entertaining but polite. She didn't dominate the conversation or anything. And she always looked neat and clean. But in the last year her behavior as well as her appearance changed. She'd begun to use a lot of heavy makeup, rouge and great sweeps of purple eye shadow. And her lipstick was dark red and thick. I don't mind a little lipstick on a girl... Alison wears a light shade now and then... but this was ridiculous. I suppose the style is what they call punk."

I didn't tell her that punk was already out. Actually, maybe Jennifer didn't know that either. "What about her behavior, Mrs. Gordon?"

She leaned forward and rested her hands on the desk. "She was irritable and jumpy. Often she'd just rattle on at the dinner table about nonsense. She couldn't be stopped. I'd never known her to talk so much. And she never ate a thing. She just pushed her food around on the plate. As if I wouldn't notice. She'd gotten very thin over the last year and it occurred to me that she might be anorectic. As a principal I have to be up on all these things." She toyed with an earring.

I said, "I'm sure you do." She might be up on anorexia but she hadn't a clue about drugs. The description she'd given of Jennifer Baker sounded like the kid was on something. It could have been diet pills but I suspected worse.

"I tried several times," she went on, "to get Mrs. Baker to come in and talk with me about Jennifer but she always canceled at the last minute. And then last week they transferred her. I suppose they saw the change themselves, I mean they couldn't miss it, and thought a new school would help. But this is a wonderful school. We don't have alcohol and drug problems like some places. Public schools always get the blame." She laughed ironically and shook her head. Then the realization that Jennifer was dead came back to her. "Poor Jennie. Did she run away from the new school?"

"There wasn't a new school." I explained. When I was finished her eyes were wide with astonishment.

"But where *is* Patrick?"

"We don't know. But I want to find out. Tell me something about him, Mrs. Gordon."

She leaned back in her chair, an almost dreamy look coming over her face as though she were thinking about an old boyfriend. "A lovely boy. Thoughtful, kind, hardworking. Decent. He's sort of old-fashioned in a way. Nothing macho about him, if you know what I mean." She glanced at me to see if I was offended.

"Do you think he's a homosexual?"

"I certainly don't," she said as though I'd asked her if he was an ax murderer.

"Did he have a girl friend?"

"I don't know. But that doesn't mean..."

"I know," I said. "I was just curious. Did he have a group of friends?"

"I suppose so. He wasn't a loner if that's what you mean. I often saw him in the halls with other...boys."

"That doesn't mean anything either. I'm often seen with the boys. Aren't you seen with the girls?"

She wasn't amused. "I just don't want to give the wrong impression about Patrick."

"You haven't. I'd like to speak with your daughter."

"Why?"

"Because she was Jennifer's friend."

"There's nothing she can tell you that I haven't."

I almost laughed out loud. For a principal Vanessa Gordon seemed to have some strange little lapses when it came to understanding kids. "Come on; you know better than that. Or are you going to tell me that your daughter tells you everything?"

She stood up, her eyes sparking with resentment. "You might find that surprising but there are some girls who do."

I knew, of course, that Alison wasn't one of them. She hadn't told her mother that Patrick was in New York and not at some bogus private school. And I assumed she'd known the truth about Jennifer's whereabouts as well. But I didn't want to give Alison away to her mother. "Well," I said, "I'd like to talk with her anyway. Please."

She pressed her lips together while she thought it over. "All right, but you mustn't keep her out of class too long." She picked up the phone.

I said, "I want to talk to Leo Schultz, too."

"What for? What does Leo have to do with it?"

"He was Jennifer's boyfriend."

She depressed the button on the phone and held it down. "You're way off base, Mr. Fanelli. Leo is practically engaged to a girl named... Well, her name doesn't matter. The point is he couldn't have had anything to do with Jennifer."

"I'd like to talk with him anyway." I could see she was about to argue. "Mrs. Gordon, the police don't know about the existence of Alison and Leo but they will if I tell them." I knew she was just trying to protect her child, her students, her school, but her mother-bear attitude was getting to me. "Okay?" I asked.

She deliberated for a moment then let go of the button; its snap cracked in the room like a tiny shot. "Mrs. Davenport, please have Alison Gordon and Leo Schultz come to my office at once. Thank you." She hung up. "I won't have you harassing them. They're only children."

"Do I look like a guy who would harass kids?"

She didn't answer.

"I have two kids myself," I said.

She said nothing but sat back in her chair and drummed her fingers on her desk.

I said, "Mrs. Gordon, I'll be wanting to speak with Alison and Leo alone."

"Why?" she asked, alarmed.

"Because they might not want to say certain things in front of you."

"You're very blunt, aren't you?"

"I don't play games," I said. "Look, we're on the same side. I'm sure you want Patrick found and Jennifer's murderer caught and so do I."

"And talking to my daughter *alone* is going to do that?"

I shrugged.

She stared at me a moment and then everything, her eyes, face, posture seemed to relax, or maybe they just gave up.

"Oh, I know you're right, Mr. Fanelli. I don't know why I'm behaving like this. No, that's not true. I *do* know. Ever since Mr. Gordon and I separated, Alison has withdrawn from me. It's very painful."

"I'm sure it is." The modern cure-all: divorce. Thanks, folks.

"We used to be close, like girl friends. But I think she blames me for Dick's walking out. She doesn't understand that it takes two."

"How long has it been?" I asked.

"A few months."

I nodded in sympathy.

She emptied her ashtray and put it and her cigarettes away and then came out from behind the desk. I stood up. She was tall all right.

"I have some things to attend to. Mrs. Davenport will send Allison in when she gets here. I hope you'll break the news to her gently, Mr. Fanelli; she's very sensitive."

"I'll do my best." I held out my hand and she took it. I wanted to tell her that being separated would get easier, like everything does with time; that it was a process she had to go through and she and her daughter would work things out eventually. I wanted to give her assurance and hope but I couldn't find the words. Instead I said, "Thanks a lot for your help."

She nodded and left me standing there, feeling sad and hopelessly inadequate.

7

Alison Gordon cried openly when I told her about Jennifer. She was tall like her mother and just as good-looking in a youthful way. There was nothing punk or new wave about this kid; she was as preppy as you could get.

She was wearing a red cotton crew-neck sweater with a pink polo shirt underneath. The collar was up and casual-looking. Her pants were chinos and on her feet she wore tasseled loafers with no socks. She wore no makeup and her black hair was straight and held back at the sides by tortoiseshell barrettes. Ten minutes passed before she was able to talk. I waited. Finally she looked up at me, her gray eyes appearing damaged. If she'd had any innocence left, it was gone for good now.

"I knew something awful would happen," she said.

"Why?"

She shook her head as if to say she didn't want to talk about it.

"I need your help, Alison."

"She was just . . . into things she shouldn't have been into, you know?"

"Like drugs?"

She shrugged. "I don't know. What good is this now? She's dead."

"She was murdered. Don't you want to help put the person who did it behind bars?"

"For how long?" she asked with a cynicism that surprised me.

"Forever," I said.

"Oh, Mr. Fanelli, you know better than that."

It was true, I did. "Well, for a long time, then."

"Maybe."

"I need your help," I said again.

She sighed and picked at her sweater. "Okay. What do you want to know?"

I decided to change the subject for a minute and showed her the postcard from Patrick. "Have you ever seen this before?"

"Where'd you get this?" she asked. "Did Jennifer have it on..." She couldn't finish the sentence.

"Her uncle gave it to me."

"Charles?"

"Yes. Do you know him?" He hadn't mentioned meeting Alison.

"I met him a few times when Jennie and I went into the city."

"You recognize the postcard?"

She nodded.

"It's Patrick's handwriting?"

"Oh, sure."

"And you gave the card to Jennifer."

"It was for her."

"Did she say anything to you about the card?"

"This one?"

I took in the two words like small shocks. "Was there another one?"

"Uh-huh. About a week later he sent another card. The same way, in an envelope to me. That was the one that got Jennie worried."

"Do you remember what it said?" My palms felt sweaty.

"It frightened Jennie. Or at least it was what made her

decide to go to New York. I remember the exact words because we studied it carefully. It said, 'Everything changed. No place to live, no friend.' Ah, let's see . . . oh, yes, then it said, 'Why isn't anything or anybody what they're supposed to be? I wish I didn't know so much. Knowledge kills. Pat.' Isn't that weird?"

"Weird," I said. I felt chilled. "Do you know where that card is, Alison?"

"Jennie took it." Her lip trembled when she mentioned her friend's name.

"Do you remember what the front of the postcard looked like?"

"The front?"

"The picture. Was it this kind of card?"

"Oh. No, nothing like that. I mean it wasn't a painting. It was a photograph of a gallery."

"Which one?"

She cocked her head and stared at the ceiling as if the answer might appear there. "I can't remember. It was in SoHo, I remember that much but I didn't pay attention to the name."

I switched topics again. "Your mother's a very nice woman," I said.

Alison rolled her eyes.

I smiled. "Maybe she's a little bit behind the times."

"A little bit?"

"She thinks Jennifer was anorectic, for instance."

"I know. Can you believe it?"

"No," I said, "I can't. I think it was something else."

She shifted her gaze away from me and stared at her loafers. It was clear that Alison knew something and didn't want to tell me. I couldn't blame her. She wanted to stay out of trouble and didn't want to implicate anyone who was still living. I decided to give the kid a break.

"Look, Alison, let's get some things straight. First of all, anything you say will be in strictest confidence, okay? I'm not going to spill the beans to your mother about anything you tell me. For instance, I didn't let on to her that you knew all along that the Baker kids hadn't transferred to other schools."

She looked at me with new interest. "No kidding?"

"No kidding. Now let me tell you what I think, and you tell me if I'm close. I think Jennifer was using drugs. Maybe some kind of amphetamines but more likely cocaine. How am I doing so far?"

"You're doing good." She slid down in her chair in a dispirited droop.

"I think she climbed out of her window every night and met Leo Schultz and they went somewhere to disco and take drugs."

"How do you know that?" she said and clapped a small hand over her mouth.

"Don't worry, Alison; I promise not to rat on you. Where'd they go to disco?"

"It doesn't matter," she said.

"It might."

"It went out of business."

"When?"

"About three weeks ago."

"Before Jennifer went to New York."

"Oh, sure."

"Did she and Leo stop meeting then?"

"No. Jennie was in love with him."

"And was he in love with Jennie?"

She looked more uncomfortable than she had, if that was possible. "I don't know. . . . I don't think so. He's practically engaged to Beverly Ogden. Her father's the mayor. You want to know the truth?"

"Always."

"I think he just used Jennie."

"For what?"

Two points of color appeared in her cheeks.

"Sex?" I asked gently.

She nodded and the blush spread. "And for drugs. Not that Jennie got them; Leo did. But he liked taking them with her. Beverly wouldn't ever do anything like that. Besides, Leo's this big wheel here: captain of the football team and senior class president, and he couldn't do any of that stuff out in the open, you know?"

I nodded. "But Jennie kept it quiet."

"She was nuts about him. I told her she was crazy and that as soon as we all graduated he was going to dump her, but she wouldn't listen. She never got any sleep and she looked lousy. I don't know why her parents didn't see what was happening."

"People see what they want to see."

"That's the truth. Anyway, all she lived for was Leo and the drugs. Until that second postcard came from Pat. Then she said she had to go to New York and find him. I don't know what she thought she was going to do if she did."

"Did she tell Leo what she was going to do?"

"She told Leo everything."

"Was she in touch with you from New York?"

"No and it freaked me out, too. I was worried, you know? But she called Leo and he told me she was on Pat's trail."

I said, "Then presumably Leo can tell me more about it."

"Oh, God."

"What?"

"He's going to freak. I mean, Leo's parents are these real uptight types. They're just going to go bananas if this all comes out. Does it have to?"

"I don't know. Maybe not." I had a feeling Leo's involvement with Jennifer had nothing to do with her death.

"I hope not, because Leo's parents will kill him. They're these pillars of the community and all that."

"I'll do my best to keep his name out of it. Yours, too, of course. Now, Alison, I want to ask you something else about Patrick. Did he have a girl friend?"

"I think there was this girl he wrote to. He met her over the summer at camp. But there wasn't anyone here."

"Did you ever hear any rumors about Pat?"

"Like what?"

I was pretty sure the question would make her blush again. "Did you ever hear anything about Pat being a homosexual?"

Right again. She laughed. "Pat? God, no. He hated gays. That was a big sore point between him and Jennifer. See, their uncle, the man who gave you the postcard, is one. Well, Jennie couldn't care less, but Patrick hated him for it. They used to have big arguments about it. Pat said their father told them that homosexuals were the scum of the earth and Jennie pointed out that it was crazy for Pat to believe that, when he didn't believe anything else their father said. She never got anywhere with him, though. Personally I think it was because Pat was always being hit on, you know?"

"By men?"

"Well, yeah and other boys. I mean, have you ever seen Pat?"

"A picture."

"Gorgeous, isn't he?" she asked. "I mean, not macho or anything but really beautiful. It pissed him off that just because he looked a certain way people thought he was gay. Do you think Pat's dead?" she asked haltingly.

"I don't know. He's been missing for two weeks and his body hasn't turned up. That's a good sign." I made a mental note to tell Charles Horton to check the morgue. Then I took the camp picture from my inside pocket. "Have you ever seen this?"

She took it from me and her face lit up for the first time. "That's our choral group at Camp Cutchogueapee. See?" she said pointing at a girl in the back row. "That's me."

So it was. She'd lost her baby fat in the last year. "Do you know Price Allen?" I asked.

"Sure. That's her," she said, pointing to the girl in the picture. Then sadly, "And that's Jennie."

"Tell me about Price."

She let out a long sigh. "A real nerd. Very out of it, if you know what I mean. She lives in New York and—can you believe this?—she's never been to the Village or SoHo or anyplace below the theater district. I mean, really. She lives in the Sixties and her parents think the Village is an outpost or something. God! Jennie and I were always teasing her about it and threatening to yank her out of her plastic bubble and drag her down to Sodom and Gomorrah . . . SoHo and the Village." Her eyes changed from a teasing memory to sudden reality. "Now we never will."

I didn't tell her that somehow Jennie had pulled it off alone. I reached over and took the picture from her. "Are any of the other girls in the picture from New York?"

"No, it was just the three of us. The others..."

The door flew open and Vanessa Gordon, her face the color of a peeled stick, burst into the room.

"Mr. Fanelli, please, help!"

I jumped up. "What is it?"

"It's Leo. Please, come." She turned and headed out of the room. I followed.

We ran down the hall, our heels echoing in the emptiness. At the end of the hall a man with white hair and a crooked nose stood in front of a door marked BOYS.

"In here," he whispered as if he might disturb someone.

I saw the upper half of the boy's body right away. He'd fallen out of a booth and lay on the floor, his eyes still open. I knew he was dead before I took another step. The needle was still in his arm right below the elbow. For the sake of the others I touched the pulse in his neck. Nothing. He was gray and his lips were literally blue. I supposed he'd been a handsome boy but the terrified expression on his face had distorted his features. It was hard to look at him. I moved into the stall. To the right of his legs was his belt. He'd obviously used it as a tie for his arm. On the lid of the toilet tank were a spoon, a lighter and a square of tinfoil. I picked up the spoon with my handkerchief. It had a white film on the inside and on the outside it was charred. I put it back. The tinfoil was clean but I knew it had held the cocaine. Floating in the toilet was the blue wrapper for the syringe and needle and the water was pink with his blood. There was more blood splattered on the toilet seat. By that I could figure what had happened. It was the same story with all heads. He'd shot up, then thought it wasn't enough. Emptied the syringe, splattering the blood, and shot up again. Too much. Why were they such greedy pigs? Well, I thought, there's one good thing: Leo Schultz's parents weren't going to kill him.

I came out of the stall and looked at Vanessa Gordon and

the man with the crooked nose. They were flattened against the far wall as if they were about to be shot.

"Did you call the police?" I asked.

She shook her head.

"Somebody'd better."

"I thought you . . ." she said.

I shook my head. "You have to report this. Who found him?"

"I did," the man said.

I looked back at Mrs. Gordon. "Had he already been gotten from class to meet me?"

"Yes," she said. "He was waiting in the outer office and then, after Beth told him about Jennifer and that you were waiting to see him, he asked to go to the bathroom. Beth wanted to help him, prepare him. She didn't realize."

"It probably would've happened sooner or later," I said. "Leo must have thought a nice coke high would help him through the interview. And through feeling anything about Jennifer Baker's death."

We walked out into the hall. Mrs. Gordon looked at her watch. "Oh, God, classes are going to change any minute. I'll go call the police and you guard this bathroom, John," she said to the man. "What about you, Mr. Fanelli?"

"What about me?"

"Will you be staying to talk to the police?"

"I think you can handle it, Mrs. Gordon. You don't need me for this."

We started down the hall together.

"I can't believe that Leo Schultz was a drug addict," she said. "He was a model student. A wonderful boy. I feel sick."

We got to the main office. "Can I give you a piece of advice, Mrs. Gordon?" I didn't wait for her answer. "I have a funny feeling Leo wasn't the only one using drugs. I think you'd better look into this a little deeper."

"I think you're right. I wanted to think my school was different, so I didn't see what I should have seen. I've failed; maybe I should resign."

"What good would that do?"

"Someone else might do a better job." Some of her hair had come undone and a long black strand trailed across her shoulder.

"I think you'll do just fine," I said.

"It's too bad a child had to die to make me see the truth."

"Two children," I reminded her.

"Yes. It was drugs with her, too, wasn't it?"

"Yes, it was. But that's not what she died of, although it might have had something to do with it. You'd better call the police now."

"What about Alison? Does she take drugs, too?"

"No," I said. I wouldn't swear that she hadn't tried them but I didn't see any point in saying that. Alison was not a user; that was clear.

"Thank you," she said. I watched her go into the office, her shoulders slumped as if she'd been beaten. I supposed she had but she wasn't defeated.

At the front door a new kid was stationed behind the table. A girl this time. Was she a user? I wondered. Had she ever tried pot, coke, 'ludes? I smiled at her and she smiled back with her innocent baby face.

I walked to my car and started it. What about my own kids and drugs? We'd spent hours talking about them and both kids had said they would never try them. But what did that really mean? I'd never noticed any signs in either one. Still, an occasional stick of pot or a hit of coke wouldn't show up. There wasn't much I could do about it except to go on talking with them. I would tell them about Leo Schultz. But what would I tell myself?

I couldn't help feeling that if I hadn't come to the school Leo might still be alive. Did his fear of talking to me make him get greedy or would he have shot up twice whenever he heard about Jennifer's death? I'd had to interview Alison and there was no way I could ignore Leo's existence. I was doing my job. Still, a kind of culpability nagged at me. Well, I would have to live with it, like so many other things.

The Holland Tunnel wasn't crowded yet and I was able to go through at a pretty good clip. When I hit the sign in the tunnel that said New Jersey / New York I breathed a sigh of relief. I was always glad to get back to my own turf, and New Jersey never had done it for me. I wondered if it did it for anybody? I couldn't believe anybody lived there by choice, but probably some people did.

I came out of the tunnel and started up Hudson Street. I'd be home in a few minutes. It had been a crummy day. Not one good thing had come of it. Maybe the night would be better.

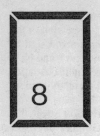

8

Julio was sitting in a Caddie with a friend when I pulled in. I knew he was matching bills but he didn't know I knew. If I hadn't, the sick grin that spread over his face when he saw me would have tipped me off. He got out of the car and then sauntered over to me. Julio never hurried.

"Hey, boss," he said, his hands stuffed into his jacket pockets. "Nick Scola lookin' for you."

"Yeah?"

"He come 'round right after you leave. I tell him you be back later. He come again 'bout half-hour 'go and I tell him you not back yet, right?"

"Right. I wasn't. Did he say what he wanted?"

"To me?" He pointed at his chest with a stubby thumb and giggled.

"Right. Anything else happen today?"

"Nope. Everythin' copacetic."

Julio was always using words he thought were cool; they were usually from another era but I didn't see any reason to burst his word balloon. "Good," I said and made a circle with my thumb and forefinger. "See you tomorrow."

"So long, boss."

At the corner of Prince and Wooster I turned left toward home. The bakery building was still empty and ugly-looking as ever. The price was up in the millions and it had been vacant for almost two years now. There'd been a rumor for a while that Bloomingdale's was going to buy the place, but nothing ever came of it. I didn't like empty buildings and wished a sale would go through. I crossed West Broadway and looked into the fish store. They had great-looking stuff but it was expensive. My kids hated fish and it wasn't exactly a favorite of mine but I did have a passion for fresh tuna. This wasn't the season. I went on and stopped in at Vesuvio's, the bread store. I shot the breeze for a few minutes then went on to the Robbers for some vegetables. Maybe I'd see Meryl Streep.

I didn't. I saw Wayne Morrison instead. It wasn't the same.

"How you doing, Fortune?" he asked.

"Okay," I answered. I didn't see any point in telling him I'd seen a kid who had everything to live for dead on a bathroom floor with a needle hanging out of his arm. "How about you, Wayne?"

He shrugged a pair of bony shoulders. "Could be worse. Channel Four was down here today, you see them?"

"I was out of town. What were they doing?"

Wayne ran a hand over his mouth as if he were performing a sleight-of-hand trick. "Interviewing and nosing around The Sweatshop Boutique. You know how they are. Jim Van Sickle was here so I guess it'll be on the six o'clock news. Vultures." He dropped a couple of oranges in a plastic bag.

"It's their job," I said. But I didn't like Van Sickle's style much. He sounded like the *Enquirer* read. I suddenly thought of the mysterious second postcard Patrick Baker had sent his sister. "Hey, Wayne. Does the Eurogallery have postcards?"

"Postcards?" He arched his thin eyebrows.

"You know, with a picture of the gallery on it?"

"Oh. Yeah, sure. They're by the door for free. Why?"

I thought fast. "A friend of mine made a bet with me. He said all the galleries down here had those kind of postcards. I said none of them did. Guess I lose."

"You both lose. Some do, some don't. Well, I'll see you, Fortune." He got on line at the counter.

I'd have to make the rounds of the galleries and see which ones had cards, then narrow it down.

When I got to my building I saw a big moving van being unloaded. I figured the apartment across from me was finally being occupied. It had been rented two months before but the tenant hadn't shown up. Whoever it was must have been paying rent on time; otherwise Mr. Bernardo, the landlord, would have rented it again.

Two burly moving men pushed past me on the stairs. Nice guys. The door to three-B was open and I looked in but I couldn't see anything except a lot of boxes and some pretty worn-out-looking furniture.

My apartment was quiet. No music. I knew nobody was home. I went into the kitchen and put my packages down on the counter. From the refrigerator I got a Coke, popped the tab and took a long swallow. Better, but not much. It was going to take more than a Coke to wash away the damage of the day. I had started putting away the groceries when the phone rang. It was Karen.

"You sound funny, Dad."

"I am funny, haven't you noticed?"

"Come on. What's wrong?"

"Nothing. Why're you calling?"

"Did you talk to Mom today?"

"Hey, enough of that, okay?" I snapped.

"Sorry." She sounded hurt.

"No, I'm sorry. It wasn't a good day, that's all. What's up?"

"I'm over at Tracy's and her mom asked me to stay for dinner. Okay?"

How did I know she was over at Tracy's? The Bakers didn't know their kid was climbing out a window every night. Maybe I didn't really know what my kid was doing either. "Tracy's, huh?" I couldn't ask her to prove it; it wasn't fair.

"Yes, Dad. You know her. Tracy Myron."

"Oh, yeah. Sure. When will you be home?"

"About ten."

"About nine," I corrected.

"Oh, Dad," she said, whining slightly.

"Nine's late enough to do everything you need to do."

"What's that mean?"

I wasn't sure. I remembered my mother fighting with my father about my sister staying out that extra hour. She made the mistake of saying Yolanda could be just as bad before eleven as she could before twelve. He'd slapped her across the mouth and I'd almost killed him. I was fourteen and Yolanda was twenty.

"Nine o'clock, honey, okay? I'm a little jumpy, so humor me."

"All right. See you later."

"Take a cab home, Karen."

"Dad, Tracy lives at Two Fifth."

It was only a few blocks away, but Washington Square Park was in between. "I don't want you walking through the park, Karen."

"I won't."

"Maybe I'd better meet you."

There was a beat and then she said, "You're flipping out, Dad. Please don't. I'll be okay."

I knew it would humiliate her if I met her, so I agreed. Parents in New York are constantly being torn between embarrassing their kids and protecting them from unknown harm. When we hung up I felt worse than I had before she called. It wasn't just that I'd worry about her getting home safely; it was also because I wanted her home *now*, with me. I felt lonely and I'd looked forward to being with the kids at dinner. Well, at least I'd have Sam.

I finished off my Coke, threw the can in my refund bag and went into the bedroom to change. I got rid of the tie, the pinstripe, the gun, took a quick, hot shower and put on my blue sweat suit. I didn't plan to do any sweating in it but I liked wearing it around the house. I got my exercise once or twice a week at Webster's Gym. I played racquetball, boxed a little and occasionally did some bench presses and curls. What I didn't do, never did, wouldn't do, was run. To me, running is the most boring thing you can do. I'd tried it a few years before and all it succeeded in doing for me was to make me not want to get up in the morning. Me, a guy who almost always looks forward to the day. During those three weeks I was running I hated every day that came my way. Depressed? You'd better believe it. I finally figured it was the running thing, and quit. It was like a miracle. The next day I jumped out of bed like a ten-year-old on Christmas morning. The truth is I'm not crazy about exercise in any form but if I have to do it I prefer it to involve other people.

Back in the kitchen I put in a call to Charles Horton. I wanted to know about that second postcard. I got an answering machine. At least the message was short and mature. What I couldn't stand were these messages that gave you music before and after. It made me feel I was wasting time. Besides, why should I be subjected to somebody else's taste in music? I left my name and asked him to call me back.

I clicked on the television to "Live at Five" and got out my cutting board and knife. Tonight I was making a mushroom curry. It was a recipe from the *Moosewood Cookbook* Karen had given me for my birthday. Even Sam admitted he liked this dish. I started chopping up the apples that went into it.

On the television Sue Simmons was giving us her braying laugh and I counted to see exactly how long it would go on. Six beats. And that was the tail. "Live at Five" hadn't been the same for me since Pia Lindstrom had taken a minor role. Pia was intelligent and attractive but she was at least forty. That Jack Cafferty, Sue's partner, was in his forties didn't matter; it was perfectly fine for the male reporters to be any age and look any way. It didn't escape me that there were no women on the air who looked like Irving R. Levine.

The show had also dimmed somewhat for me since Katy Kelly had left, but I looked forward to Liz Smith. She was the only one who seemed like a real person. Cafferty, with his ticks and twitches, gave the impression he thought his comments and interpretations were pure gold. I'd never heard anyone more banal. Or obsequious. He was interviewing a writer at the moment and I thought he might drool on his vest from the slathering he was doing. Why did I look at these creeps night after night? It was like watching an accident: I was mesmerized by the horror of it all.

The phone rang and this time it was Sam. He wanted to stay at his friend Bob's for dinner. I couldn't think of any real reason to say no so I told him he could. Nine o'clock for him, too. When I hung up I sat on a counter stool, my chopping knife in my hand. I felt like a kid who'd given a party and nobody came. Maybe I should invite a friend over, I thought. But who? There was Nina. We hadn't seen each other in three months; maybe it was long enough. Maybe we could be friends now. I dialed her number. When I heard her voice I hung up. I guessed it wasn't long enough for me. I still felt angry. I suspected if there had been someone else in my life I wouldn't have cared any longer. But then I wouldn't have been calling Nina. If only Meryl Streep would leave that damn sculptor!

I went back to my chopping. I'd make the curry for the next night and grab a slice of pizza for myself tonight. Jack and Sue were interviewing Morgan Fairchild again. It seemed she was on at least once a week. Mentally, I tuned out.

My mind drifted back over the day's events. I'd been purposely trying not to think about the case but I knew I had to. What did I know? A girl named Jennifer Baker had run away from home, ostensibly to find her brother who'd flown the coop himself. Both kids had lived like prisoners in their own home even though the girl had found a way to make her life bearable. Patrick had sent his sister at least one postcard and probably two. It was the second postcard that got Jennifer to leave her boyfriend Leo and her drug supply and come to New York to her uncle Charles Horton. She'd given the first postcard to Horton. Why hadn't she shown him the second? Or had she?

Assuming Horton had seen the second postcard, why hadn't he told me about it if he didn't have it? If Alison Gordon's memory served her correctly, that information was valuable. What reason could Horton have for keeping Patrick's message to himself? The second card told me a lot more than the first. It occurred to me now that it told Horton a lot more, too. It was the second card, not the first, that made him say Patrick was in trouble. Or maybe it was the combination. "If I live that long" in itself was nothing to cause alarm and I'd said that to Horton at the time. But, knowing about the second card, I could understand his concern. All the more reason it didn't make sense for him to have kept that from me.

So, if I believed Alison Gordon, and I did, Horton lied to me. Why? And what did Jennifer mean when she told her uncle that soon she'd have a lot of money? I didn't think she was talking about getting a job and I didn't think she was planning to stay in New York. I believed Alison Gordon's assessment of Jennifer's feelings for Leo so there was no way the girl wasn't going back to New Jersey. A job would have kept her in New York. No, it was a matter of getting money another way. I could only think of one way she could get money and not have to stick around. Selling something. What did a kid like Jennifer Baker have to sell? Dope? I doubted it. Besides, Leo was the connection. So what could she sell? Information. That was all she could have had. But what about? And who to? What did this kid stumble onto in just a week? It seemed crazy, but so was murder. I needed to talk to Horton badly. Maybe he'd killed his own niece. It wouldn't be the first time a client turned out to be the guilty party. I lifted the phone to try him again and there was a knock at my door. I put the phone back in its cradle and walked down the hall. I asked who it was, the way you do in New York.

"It's Nick," came the reply.

I opened up. He stood there looking dumb in his green polyester shirt that he wore hanging outside his rayon pants.

"I wanna talk to ya, Fortune."

"What about?"

He looked past me, down the hall. "Can I come in?"

"Okay."

Nick followed me to the kitchen where I took up my knife and continued chopping.

"Whatcha makin'?"

"Dinner. You wanted to talk?" I figured there was going to be a touch.

"Yeah. Listen, I'm thirsty. Could I have a drink a water?"

"Go ahead." I motioned him over to the sink with my head. I knew he wanted a beer or wine or something but I wasn't about to contribute to his habit. Reluctantly, he wandered over to the sink, ran the water, filled a glass and drank a few swallows before he spilled out the rest.

"Now that your insatiable thirst is quenched how about telling me what you want," I said.

Nick came back to the counter and stood across from me. He was frowning and his thick brows made a straight line above his eyes, giving him an angry look. "Yeah, well, I wanted to know could you use any help?"

"Help?"

"You're working on the case, ain't you?"

SoHo was getting to be worse than a small town for secrets. "What case?"

"Come on, Fortune, don't shit me. The case wit the broad in the window."

"Sounds like an Ellery Queen," I said.

"Huh?"

"Skip it. Who told you I was on a case?"

He smiled, revealing crooked yellow teeth. "I got my ways. It's true, ain't it?"

"What if it is?"

"So, like I said, maybe ya could use some help? Ya got a beer or somethin', Fortune?"

"No. What kind of help?"

"Ah, ya know. I could listen around, pick up stuff here and there. Ya never know what I might come up wit. Any wine, maybe?"

"No wine, Nick. What would it cost me?"

"Nothin' to start. If I give ya somethin', ya give me what ya think it's worth. You're a fair guy." He licked his lips showing how dry they were.

Sue Simmons's laugh cut through the air and Nick jumped.

"Nervous?" I asked.

"What the hell was that?"

"A woman laughing," I said.

"Sounds like my car door. What's wrong wit her?"

"Everything," I said.

"Yeah, well, what can ya expect from a nigger, anyways?"

His pinkie was on the edge of the cutting board and I brought my knife down hard, next to it, chopping a carrot neatly in two.

"Jesus," he yelled, jumping back. "Ya almost chopped off my finger."

"Almost, but not quite, because I didn't want to."

"What's wrong wit you?"

"In this house you don't call anybody a nigger. Got it?"

The blood had momentarily drained from his face but now it was rushing back in anger. He pushed out his stubborn chin as if it were a weapon. "Ya crazy or somethin', Fortune? Ya almost chop off my finger 'cause of a stupid nig—a stupid bitch on the TV?"

"I think it's time for you to be going, Nick."

"I come here in good faith, to try and help ya and ya almost cut off my hand and then ya wanna trow me out. What kind a friend are ya, anyways?"

"Whoever said I was a friend?" I moved toward him, around the counter, my knife still in my hand.

He backed up. "Hey, Fortune, we're *paisan'*, right?"

It was true, we were both Italians but that meant nothing to me. I wasn't one of those people who believed nationality came before honor or truth or decency. "Out," I said. I kept walking and backing him up, out of the kitchen and down the hall to the front door. The whole time he kept talking, telling me he could be of help to me and I was a jerk to let a good thing like him go. At the door I grabbed him by the collar and twisted it.

"For all I know you wasted the girl yourself. I wouldn't put it past you. But I don't have any proof. Not yet." I didn't really believe that but I wanted to scare him. "That doesn't mean I can't get proof, if you get my drift. Do you?"

His face was turning red and his dull eyes were watering. He made some choking sounds but didn't answer my question.

"Answer me, you scum." I twisted the collar a little tighter. He nodded and coughed. I let go and he fell back against the door. His hand went to his throat and he shook himself slowly, like a dog. I pulled him away from the door and opened it.

Nick stepped out into the hall and turned around to face me. He was still brick red and his eyes were filled with malice. "You gonna be sorry you done that, Fortune."

"I doubt it," I said and slammed the door. I shot the bolt and started walking back down the hall. I'd always hated the bum but... There was a knock. I couldn't believe it. What was it going to take for this guy to get the message? I turned back and covered the ground to the door in four bounds. I pulled the bolt and threw back the door, my knife thrust out in front of me as I yelled, "Beat it, punk!"

But it wasn't Nick.

It was Meryl Streep.

9

My mouth fell open and then I saw that she wasn't Meryl Streep but she might as well have been. She'd yelped and jumped away from me, her soft blue-grey eyes wide with fear. We both stood there staring at each other as if we were playing statue. Finally I dropped my knife-wielding arm to my side and she looked a little more relaxed. But not much.

"I'm not really doing this," I said stupidly.

"You're not? I guess I must be imagining it, then. Well, that's a relief."

"I mean, I don't always come to the door this way. I thought you were someone else."

"Not one of your all time faves, huh?"

"Did anyone ever tell you you look just like—"

"...Meryl Streep," she said, smiling. "A few people."

"Hundreds, right?"

"I've been told," she said.

"It must be very annoying. I know this guy whose name is Stuart Little and people are always making jokes about his name as if they were the first ones to ever make the connection." I felt like a jerk but I couldn't stop talking. I didn't want her to leave. "It drives him crazy. I guess it must drive you crazy, too. I don't know why I said that to you before. I knew as I was asking you if anyone ever told you you looked like Meryl Streep that, of course, thousands of people must have told you."

"Not thousands," she said.

I couldn't take my eyes off her. She was really a dead ringer for Streep. The mouth was a little smaller and maybe the chin was rounder but the rest was the same, especially the nose. She was wearing a red plaid flannel shirt, a wraparound denim skirt and blue sneakers. There was a touch of pinkish lipstick on her mouth but most of it had worn off. She had a tired look about her as if she'd been through something upsetting. "Who *are* you?" I blurted finally.

"I'm Cassie Bloomfield, your new neighbor. She motioned to the apartment behind her. The door was partly open. "My windows are stuck...paint...and, well, I hate being a helpless female and I'm not, but I just can't get the damn things open. I tried finding the super—"

"He's never around. I'd be glad to help," I said.

"Oh, thanks. We're dying of the heat."

We, I thought. Who was *we*? It couldn't be a man or she wouldn't have come looking for help. A roommate. Does a woman in her thirties have a roommate? Well, rents were high these days. I followed her down the hall. The apartment was a mirror image of my own.

"If you could just open a few of these in the living room. The place has been closed up since it was painted and it smells."

"It does." I was really getting in there with the snappy repartee. The last time I behaved like this was with Mary Ellen Ryan and I was fourteen years old.

When I got to the first window I started to reach up and I realized my knife was still in my hand. I put it on the sill and looked around to see if she'd noticed. She had. I smiled sheepishly and she smiled back, taking pity on me, I thought.

Putting the heels of my hands under the top of the lower window frame I gave a shove. Nothing. Strength, don't fail me now! I tried again. It didn't budge. Embarrassed, I turned to look at her.

"I see what you mean," I said.

"It's the paint," she said kindly.

I went back to my task a humbled man. But still no dice. "Listen," I said, "do you have anything we could use to sort of pry these edges away from the frame."

"What about your knife?"

"Hell no, that's my cooking knife."

"Sorry. I thought it was your killing knife."

"That too," I said, trying to get into the swing of things. "But basically it's a very expensive knife I use for chopping. I'd rather not use it on your windows."

"I don't blame you."

"Who's that?" a small voice came from what in my apartment was Sam's bedroom.

"Go to sleep, honey."

"I wanna see who's there? Is it Daddy?"

"No, it's not Daddy. Go back to sleep." She turned to me. "That's Zelda, my daughter."

We. I felt relief. But where was Daddy?

Cassie was rustling around in a box and finally came up with a screwdriver.

"Will this do?"

I reached over to take it from her and my fingertips touched her hand. For a moment I thought we'd gotten an electric shock but then I knew it wasn't that kind. We looked into each other's eyes and I felt that curling sensation down to my navel. I knew she was feeling it, too. You can tell those things. She broke the look and I went back to the window with the screwdriver. Was I feeling this only because she looked like Meryl Streep, or was it her? Whatever it was, I wasn't about to get involved with a married woman. I'd had that scene.

After a few minutes of prying I tried the window again and this time it gave an inch or so.

"Success," she said happily.

I didn't look at her. I was afraid to. I kept pushing on the window, moving it up inch by inch. Then, silently, I went to the next window and repeated the procedure. When I'd opened three she told me that was enough.

I handed her back the screwdriver. We were both careful not to touch. "Your husband can get the others when he gets home," I said.

Her smile caressed me. "I have no husband. Not any more."

I stifled a grin. "I'm divorced, too."

"Isn't everybody?" she asked in a world-weary tone.

"Sometimes it seems like that," I said. "Well, is there anything else I can help you with?"

She shook her head, the long blond hair shivering at her shoulders. "Thanks, I can manage now. I really appreciate your help."

"Any time," I said. I started to leave.

"Don't forget your expensive knife," she kidded.

I laughed. "I'm a very good cook," I said, retrieving the knife. "You and Zelda will have to come to dinner some time."

"We'd love to."

She walked me to the door and I could feel the heat of her body behind mine as though we were touching.

"Don't forget," I said, standing in the hall, "any time."

"Thanks. See you soon." She started to shut the door, then opened it again.

Something skipped in my chest.

"Hey, what's your name?"

"Fortune Fanelli."

"You're kidding?"

"I'm not."

"That's worse than Stuart Little. I mean, I like it but haven't you had to explain it a lot?"

"Some."

"Probably thousands," she said, eyes crinkling at the corners.

I smiled. "Not thousands."

"Good night, Fortune."

"Good night, Cassie."

I watched while she closed the door, then walked across to my apartment.

Back in my kitchen I returned to my chopping. The six o'clock news was under way and I figured they'd be talking about the Baker murder soon. But I didn't want to think about that; I wanted to think about Cassie Bloomfield. That wasn't quite accurate: I couldn't *help* thinking about Cassie Bloomfield.

Since Elaine and I had split up there'd been a number of women in my life. Some were more casual than others. Three had been meaningful. Teresa Bertelli I'd turned to because I wanted someone as different from Elaine as possible. I thought a woman who had no interest in anything but her man and children would suit me. It didn't. I was bored. Marilyn Van Iderstine was married. I didn't like the idea but I liked her; I really did. And, like so many men in my shoes, I was sure she'd leave her husband for me. She didn't. Nina Stamos was a totally different story. I found her sexually impossible to resist. But I didn't like her all that much. In fact, there was a lot about Nina I didn't like at all. I wondered why I'd even thought of calling her earlier. We fought all the time. I never figured out whether we fought because we always landed in bed afterward or because when we weren't in bed we fought! Whatever the reason it didn't prove to be a very satisfactory relationship. Relationship... God, how I hate that word. Anyway, none of the women I'd been involved with these last seven years had worked out. I thought I was gun-shy but the way I'd responded to Cassie told me I'd been fooling myself. Still, I should be cautious. Just because she was gorgeous, was obviously intelligent and had a sense of humor didn't mean I should go off the deep end. Right. Maybe I should ask her to dinner now. Wasn't that the neighborly thing to do when a person had just moved in? Nothing wrong with that. I put the knife down on the board and started to leave the kitchen when Jim Van Sickle's voice stopped me cold.

He was standing on Thompson Street in front of The Sweatshop Boutique, strands of his hair blowing in the April breeze, his microphone close to his mouth as if he wanted only you to hear what he was saying. And what he was saying and how he was saying it were predictable. I recalled his intoning voice during the Jean Harris trial and then the Von Bulow one. There was something about his presentation that made everyone seem guilty. I wondered how he'd make Jennifer Baker the perpetrator of her own murder.

He told us the owner of the shop was unavailable for comment. She'd been so upset by the murder that her doctor had advised complete rest for a day or two. But he was just lucky enough to have one of her saleswomen right here. He turned to a young woman with short hair, half of it dyed green, the other half pink. Her lips were a deep scarlet and her eyes were surrounded by green shadow. Most people would assume she was going to a costume party but I knew this was just the way she dressed for the workaday world. Van Sickle, in hushed tones, asked her what she thought of the murder.

"Far out," she said.

"Did you know the murdered girl?" Jim asked as if he were going to cry.

"Who me?" she asked as if he wasn't addressing her.

Jim nodded seriously.

"Not me. I never laid eyes on the chick."

"Why do you think whoever killed her put her in the window of your store?"

"I don't know. It's freaky, man, far out."

He thanked her as if she'd been profound, then turned to the people on the street. Nick Scola was in the background and so was Wayne Morrison. Mrs. Castelli, Mrs. Rauschenberg and Mr. Torterello were there too. He asked Mrs. Albetta what she thought.

"It's a sin. This was a good, clean neighborhood until they came here."

"Who's *they*?" Van Sickle asked, punching the word in such a way that the television audience might have expected her to answer anything from Mafia to Martians.

"The beatniks," she said.

I laughed out loud. Van Sickle, to his credit, didn't crack a smile.

"Do you mean the artists?" he asked.

"The hippies," she insisted.

I laughed again. I didn't agree with her sentiments but I liked her style.

Van Sickle persisted. "I believe you mean the new loft owners who are primarily artists, writers, musicians, don't you?"

"Bums," she said and walked out of camera range.

"Well, there you have it," Van Sickle said, practically swallowing the mike and moving into a close-up. "The long-time residents of this newly chic area are angry. A place they love, a place they call home has been defiled. And how? A girl from somewhere else has been murdered on their turf and no one knows who did it or why. This is Jim Van Sickle in SoHo."

Well, he'd succeeded in making Jennifer guilty of being in a place where she didn't belong. And I suppose he was right, in a way. She didn't belong here. She was too young to be on her own anyplace in New York. Looking for her brother she'd stumbled across something she shouldn't have and that knowledge had led to her death. But it was hard for me to believe any artist had anything to do with it. My experience with the artists in SoHo was that they just wanted peace, quiet and space to do their work. At least the real artists felt that way. But there were always the phony artists. A lot of people talked like they were artists. They thought it was glamorous to be a painter or writer; they didn't know it took a lot of hard work day by day, every day. And then there were the bad artists. They were the sorriest lot of all. They worked hard but it didn't do any good. No matter how hard they tried, they were lousy. Naturally they didn't get anywhere and that created a lot of bitterness and jealousy. You heard it all in the local coffeehouses or bars if you hung around them. It could be pretty depressing.

Suddenly I remembered Cassie Bloomfield and that I was going to invite her to dinner. But this time the phone stopped me. It was Charles Horton.

"I got your message, Fanelli. Did you find anything out?"

"I saw your sister and brother-in-law today."

"Charming, isn't he?"

"A real winner," I agreed. I wanted to ask him about the

second postcard but I wanted to see his face when I did. "Look, I'd like to meet with you."

"Oh?"

"I want to talk about something and I'd rather not do it over the phone."

"I see. Well, I don't think I can come down there tonight."

"That's okay. I'll come up there."

"I'm going out at eight-thirty."

"I'll be there in half an hour to forty-five minutes," I said. So long, Cassie Bloomfield.

"All right. I'm at the apartment. Fifth floor."

I thanked him and hung up. As much as I hated giving up a possible dinner with my new neighbor I wanted to see Horton in his surroundings. Seeing people in their own home always gave me a better idea of them.

I changed from my sweat suit into gray slacks, a black turtleneck sweater and a gray corduroy jacket. In the kitchen I left a note for the kids. If Horton was really going out at eight-thirty I'd be back before the kids got home, but just in case, I wanted them to know I'd be back soon.

When I opened the door to my apartment I saw that the light was out in the hall. I wouldn't have thought much about it because Doug Fanner was always letting the lights burn out and not replacing them. But when I looked over the banister, I saw that the lights were out on the floors below as well. Too much of a coincidence. I reached inside my shoulder holster for my .32. Holding it near my hip, I started down the steps next to the wall. The hall was silent; the only sounds I could hear were occasional street noises: a car horn, a dog barking. Each one of them stabbed me like an ice pick. Slowly, I kept moving, my eyes becoming more accustomed to the dark with every passing moment. I reached the second-floor landing, stopped and listened. There were only two apartments on each floor so there was nowhere for anyone to be hiding. The ground floor was going to be the trickiest because someone could be under the staircase or to the left of the stairs where the hall went back into an entranceway into Doug's apartment. I couldn't investigate both at the same time; I'd have to turn my back on one area while I searched the other. And if I turned to the right, to leave the building, my back would be to both areas. I had no choice.

Continuing down the stairs I kept listening for breathing. Everything was so quiet I was almost sure I'd hear it if someone was waiting for me. I didn't hear a damn thing. I reached the bottom of the staircase and waited. Nothing happened. I knew it was my move. The logical place for me to look first was under the stairs and if someone was waiting for me he knew that logic, too. Which might mean he'd wait in the other place so he could jump me when I went under the stairs. If I rushed the short hall near Doug's apartment I might have a chance. But if I guessed wrong and my friend was under the stairs, then I was lost. It was a gamble. There was no way to know my opponent's thinking. I had to take a chance. I decided to rush the short hall. I took a deep breath, let out a commando yell and ran, gun out in front of me.

The crack on the back of my head told me I'd guessed wrong. At first I didn't think it had done any real damage and I started to turn but my legs wouldn't go and only the upper portion of my body seemed to move. The floors in the halls of my building are made of small hexagonal tiles. Every one of them jumped up and hit me in the face, exploding and turning red, then purple, then white again. I heard a voice from far away say, "Lay off," and it echoed over and over and over until I didn't see or hear anything more.

10

The first person I saw when I came to was Mrs. Castelli. Her crimson lipstick was smudged and tears had made streaks on her powdered cheeks.

"His eyes are open," she said.

I turned to see who she was talking to and the back of my head felt like a crushed melon. I let out a small groan.

"He's dying," Mrs. Castelli said. "Call the priest."

"I'm not dying," I said, but no words came out of my mouth. It felt glued shut. Slowly, an awareness came over me that I was lying in the hall and then I remembered. The lights were all on now and I sensed that a number of people were surrounding me. "You fall down the stairs?" Mr. Rizzo asked.

"Nah," Mr. Segal said, "he got bopped on the bean. Right, Fortune?"

I nodded. It hurt.

"You want we should call the cops?"

Painfully, I shook my head.

"They get your wallet?"

I knew my assailant hadn't been after my money but I tapped my chest, felt my wallet and gestured no.

"Murder and muggings," Mrs. Castelli said, clucking her tongue. "What next?"

I wanted to know what had happened after I'd blacked out. How long had I been here? Who put on the lights? Who found me? Well, I wasn't going to get any answers just lying around like a slug. I tried to sit up, and a wave of nausea rolled over me almost knocking me back down. I fought it off while my friends and neighbors argued about whether I should be sitting up or not. At last I found my voice.

"It's okay, folks," I said. "I'm fine." I looked around me and saw that my gun was missing. I said nothing about it.

"You want I should get your mother, Fortune?" Mrs. Castelli asked.

"No, thanks. I'm okay, really." I started to get up and Doug Fanner reached down to help me. It occurred to me as I looked into his crafty brown eyes that he might have had something to do with the lights being out. "The lights were all out in the hall, Doug. What happened?"

"Beats me, Fortune. They were like that when I found you."

"You found me?"

"*I* found you," Mrs. Castelli said indignantly. "I'm over at Angie's with the girls, drinking coffee, and I come home and the place is pitch. So I creep in and then I get used to it, the dark, because I inch by inch come down the hall. And then I see the body. You. I scream. *Then* he comes out of his place and *then* he finds us both, me and you."

"Who put on the lights?" I asked.

"I did," Doug said.

"How?" I asked.

"How?"

"Yeah, how?" I looked at him hard.

"So don't be a dummy, Doug," Mrs. Castelli said. "Tell Fortune how you got the ladder and screwed back the bulbs."

"The bulbs were unscrewed?"

"Yeah," Doug said, and shrugged as if to say it was a mystery beyond him.

I didn't ask how he knew that that was the cause of the light failure, because I knew the answer. I'd confront him on it later. At the moment I wanted to get back upstairs, fix my head, call Horton and arrange another time. I heard the front door open and turned to see Father Paul loping down the hall.

We went through it all over again, the lights being out, me being hit on the head. Mr. Rizzo wanted to call the police but I discouraged him and said I'd do it when I got upstairs. Paul calmed them all down and the two of us went up to my apartment.

In the bathroom I sat on the closed toilet while Paul played nurse.

"Ouch," I yelled as he swabbed the cut with alcohol.

"Don't be a squirt," he said. "You don't even need stitches. Lucky man."

"That's me," I said. "My mama didn't name me Fortunato for nothing."

"Your mama took one look at you and knew she better do something to help you. That's why you got the moniker, kid."

"Paul," I said, "nobody says moniker anymore. I ought to introduce you to my parking attendant. *Ouch!* Hey, take it easy."

"What's your parking attendant got to do with anything?" he asked, ignoring me.

"Skip it. Stop pulling my hair, will you?"

"Done," he said, giving me a slap on the shoulder.

I turned around to face him. "Thanks. I'm glad you didn't become a doctor. You'd be fighting malpractice suits around the clock."

He laughed. Paul was one of the most handsome men I'd ever known. His large eyes were a cerulean blue and his nose was straight and just the right size for his face. He had a wide, full mouth with half-moon lines at the corners. There wasn't a sign of gray in his blond hair, which he wore full and slightly long in the back. Paul looked the way religious people were meant to look: serene and open but never superior as if he knew something you didn't know. In our school days girls and women went crazy for Paul but he'd always held back, knowing somehow what the future was going to hold for him. Women still went nuts over him and sometimes it caused him great embarrassment.

"You have anything to drink around here?" he asked. "And don't give me any of your Coke, thank you."

"You want a beer?" I stood up, swaying slightly.

"Hey, there," Paul said, grabbing my arm. "Maybe you should lie down."

"No, I'm okay."

We went into the kitchen where the labors of my earlier chopping still lay in a heap on the cutting board. I opened a beer for Paul and a Coke for myself. We sat across from each other at the counter.

"So what happened?" he asked me.

I told him.

"Any ideas?"

"A couple. When I saw the lights out I was pretty sure it was Nick Scola laying for me. I'd thrown him out of here earlier and he wasn't too happy about it. But now I'm not so sure."

"How come?" He took a long swig from the bottle.

"Doug Fanner unscrewed those lights in the hall. Or at least he knows who did. Mrs. Castelli said Doug got out the ladder and screwed the lights back in. How did he know to do that? The thing is, I can't see Fanner colluding with Scola. And then there's something else. The guy who hit me said something to me. He said, 'Lay off.' Why would Scola say that? No, I think this has got something to do with the case." I suddenly remembered Horton. "Jesus Christ," I said. "Oh, sorry, Paul."

He shrugged. "You said it; I didn't. What case?"

"The girl who was murdered yesterday." I reached for the phone. "I've got to call Horton. I was supposed to go up there."

"Who's Horton?"

"The uncle. The guy you sent to me."

"What uncle? I didn't send anybody to you."

Slowly I put the phone back in its cradle. "You don't know Charles Horton?"

"No."

"He came to see you last night about eight-fifteen. He said a friend of his recommended you, Robert Sheedy, I think his name was."

"I don't know that name either."

"I'll be damned. This guy Horton said getting a private eye was your idea."

"It might have been but it wasn't. You should have checked with me," he said seriously.

"You're right, I should have." I picked up the phone and dialed Horton's number. I got the machine and hung up.

"How about filling me in on this thing?" Paul asked.

I took a slug of my Coke, swished it around in my mouth and swallowed. I told him everything I knew and then I got out the pictures and the postcard. He studied the picture of Patrick for almost a minute; then he tapped it with his long index finger.

"I've seen this boy," he said.

"Where?"

"In the neighborhood."

"When?"

"I'm not sure. Not long ago, though."

"Was he alone?"

Paul shut his eyes. His long lashes fluttered against his skin as he tried to remember. Then he opened them. "I think I've seen him alone and then once with a man. I didn't know the man. I assumed it was his father."

"What did the man look like?"

The eyes closed again. "He was on the short side, chunky with gray hair. Fifties. Nice face, sort of craggy. Definitely an Irish type."

That certainly wasn't a description of Horton. "Where did you see them?"

"Just walking along the street. They seemed peaceful, happy together. I noticed them because the boy was so remarkable-looking. And then I thought the father must have looked like that as a boy. But it wasn't his father, was it?"

"No." I thought of Carter Baker and how much he didn't resemble his son. For that matter, neither kid looked like either parent. It happened sometimes. "And when you saw the boy alone, Paul, where was that?"

"In the neighborhood. Wait a minute. I think I saw him sweeping the sidewalk somewhere." He tented his hands under his chin. "In front of one of the galleries. I'm sorry, Fortune, I can't remember which one."

I pointed to the postcard. "Maybe that was the job he was referring to here."

"Could be. I wish I could remember."

I finished my Coke and stood up. "Sorry to make you drink and run, Paul, but I want to talk to Doug Fanner."

"Want me to come with you?"

"I think I can handle him."

Paul drained his bottle of beer and took it over to the refund bag under the sink.

"I'll be right back," I said.

In the bedroom I took off my empty shoulder holster and put on my hip holster with my .38. I'd have to report my .32 missing but I'd do that later. When I went back to the kitchen Paul was looking at the bulletin board. Karen had drawn a cartoon of a cat in dancing shoes.

"She's pretty good," Paul said.

"Yeah, I think so."

"Is that what she wants to do, be an artist?"

"I don't think so. She just does it for fun."

We left the apartment and when I was locking up I heard a woman's voice call my name.

"Hey, Fanelli?"

I turned. It was Cassie Bloomfield peeking out between the door and the frame. Right away I got putty knees.

"What's up?" I said.

"That's what I want to know. What was all the commotion before?"

Absently I touched my head. "It was nothing," I lied. I didn't want her to be sorry she'd moved into the building. Then I introduced her to Paul. She opened the door wider and shook his hand.

"Well," she said to him, "maybe you'll tell me the truth if your friend here won't."

Paul glanced at me, a desperate look in his eyes. He didn't want to betray me but he hated telling lies. I took him off the hook.

"I promise to tell you all about it another time but right now we're in a hurry. Don't worry about it, Cassie, you're perfectly safe. It was a personal matter."

"Okay," she said. "But I'm going to press you for details."

"You'll get them," I said. "How late will you be up?"

"About another minute. I'm beat."

"Moving day," I explained to Paul. "Tomorrow, then," I said to her.

"Okay."

We all said good night and Paul and I went down to the first floor.

"How long have you known her?" he asked me.

I looked at my watch. "Three hours."

Paul said, "You're in trouble."

"What's that mean?"

"You should have seen your face when she called your name."

"Yeah? What about it?"

"Red."

"Get out of here," I said, giving him a shove, like an adolescent.

"Fortune, I've known you all my life. You don't hide your feelings very well, never have. Anyway, she's a nice-looking woman."

"Nice-looking? She's beautiful. Doesn't she look like Meryl Streep?"

"Who's Meryl Streep?"

I forgot. Paul was deeply involved in his own community but popular culture escaped him. Even so, it amazed me that anyone could be unaware of her. "Don't you ever go to the movies or turn on your television or read a newspaper?"

"No. I hear enough about life in the confessional. I don't want to know anything more about the world."

"You're just afraid," I said. It was a running argument we'd had for years. I said he hid out in the priesthood from responsibility and intimate relationships and he said I hid out from God with responsibilities and intimate relationships. We'd never agree, but that was okay.

"Good night, Fortune," he said congenially. "Thanks for the beer. And watch your ass."

When he was gone I moved down the hallway to Doug's apartment. There was no light under the door but I knocked anyway. No answer. I thought about slipping the lock, then decided against it. Talking to Horton was more important than tossing Fanner's place. I didn't think there'd be much to find in there anyway. Somebody'd probably given Fanner a twenty or so to unscrew the bulbs and make himself scarce. That was probably all the punk knew. I'd talk to him later.

I went back upstairs and left a new note for the kids. I told them I might be out late and not to wait up for me. They were used to that, so I didn't worry about it.

When I left the building some of my neighbors were sitting in front on the stoop. The night was pretty warm for April.

"You going out, Fortune?" Mrs. Castelli asked, alarmed.

"Got some business," I said.

She clucked her tongue.

"How's the head?" Mr. Rizzo asked.

"Okay, fine." Actually it was beginning to hurt a lot.

I walked down the steps and turned toward Prince.

"You take care," she yelled after me.

"I will. Thanks, Mrs. C." I called back over my shoulder.

Then, in a stage whisper I heard her say to Mr. Rizzo: "What that man needs is a wife."

Maybe she was right.

11

I'd been waiting four hours when I finally saw Charles Horton getting out of a cab. My feet hurt from walking up and down Sixty-fifth Street and standing in various doorways. Surveillance in this kind of neighborhood wasn't easy: everyone who passed looked at me like I was a potential threat.

I crossed the street and when Horton got to the front door I called out to him. He turned, a frightened look on his face.

"It's Fanelli," I said.

"Oh. A little late, aren't you?"

I ignored that. "I'd like to talk to you."

"It's after midnight," he said.

"You going to turn into a pumpkin?"

His mouth turned downward. "I'm not in any mood for jokes, Mr. Fanelli. As I said, it's after midnight. We had an appointment earlier and you didn't show or call. I'm not used to that."

"Neither am I. I ran into a little trouble. I'll tell you all about it inside."

He sighed. "Oh, all right."

This guy was burning me up. He'd hired me to find his nephew, I'd been sapped on the head because of it and he didn't feel like talking because it was too late. I followed him up some carpeted stairs to the third floor where a steel, cagelike door was installed to prevent B&Es. He inserted a key and the door swung open. We went through and he clanged it shut. The door to his apartment was made of wood, oak maybe, and had a carved wooden knocker in the shape of a unicorn. He unlocked the door and snapped on a light to his left.

We were in a small Italian-tiled hallway and he motioned me to follow him to the right. Down three steps was his living room. I didn't know anything about antiques but I knew the place was loaded with them. Neither the chairs or the two couches looked like you'd ever want to sit on them. The surface of every table was covered with small objects made of marble, silver or gold and some stuff I couldn't identify. Heavy white draperies ran across an entire wall. A thick-piled white carpet matched the draperies.

"Sit down," Horton said.

I looked around trying to locate a chair that might hold me.

"They're not as fragile as they look," he said, guessing my dilemma.

I chose one of the couches. it was as uncomfortable as it appeared to be.

"You want a drink? Oh, no, you don't drink. I don't have any Coke," he said disdainfully.

"I don't want anything."

"I do." He went to a cabinet that was carved and inlaid with onyx. While he was pouring his drink, his back to me, he said, "So what happened to you tonight?"

"Somebody zonked me over the head and told me to lay off. Any ideas?"

He whirled around, some of his Scotch spilling over the lip of the glass onto his hand and the white carpet. "What's that supposed to mean?"

I shrugged. "I just wondered if you knew who it might be, that's all. No reason to panic."

"I'm not panicked," he said shrilly. "I thought I heard an accusation in your voice."

"You didn't." I took a good look at him again and saw how much Patrick resembled him. I hadn't really noticed before because a glass eye can throw you off a person's looks.

"You know," I said, "Patrick looks more like you than his father."

"So I've been told," he said abruptly. "I guess you got a picture from Rebecca."

I nodded. "Did you look like him when you were a boy?"

"Yes, a lot."

"I see."

"You see what?"

"Nothing. Look, Horton, I have a funny feeling you haven't told me everything. For instance, what about the second postcard?"

There was a beat before he spoke. "What second postcard?"

"The one Patrick sent to Jennifer by way of Alison."

"I gave you that."

"There was another one."

"If there was I never saw it."

I felt he was lying. "Alison says there was another. Why wouldn't Jennifer have shown you that one, since she showed you the first?"

"I don't know. Maybe Alison was lying." He sat opposite me on a chair with legs like bent, peeled twigs.

"I don't think she was lying. The card said something like 'All has changed. No friend, no place to live. Why isn't anybody or anything what they're supposed to be? I wish I didn't know so much. Knowledge kills.' Those may not be the exact words but that's the essence. What do you think?"

Horton's good eye darted around the room like it was looking for a way out. "What do I think about what?"

I was losing patience. My head hurt and I was tired. I stood up. "Okay, Horton, I guess you don't want to find your nephew."

"Where are you going?"

"Home to bed."

He rose, his glass still in his hand. "No, don't go. I want you to find him."

"Then stop jerking me around. What about the postcard?"

"I swear I never saw a postcard like that."

I still didn't believe him but I couldn't prove he was lying. "Okay. Let's just say, for the sake of argument, that such a postcard existed. Can you think of any reason Jennie wouldn't have shown it to you?"

He shook his head. "And I wouldn't have known what it meant either."

"You don't seem very alarmed by the message on that card."

He shrugged. "I can't be alarmed by a card that never existed. I would have found it among Jennie's things if it had."

I figured he probably had. "What things did she leave behind?"

"Just some clothes and jewelry . . . costume jewelry. A few books. Nothing much."

"Any drugs?"

"Drugs?" His thin lips became thinner.

"Your niece was a cocaine user," I said.

"I don't believe it."

"I don't care what you believe; she was. She tell you about Leo Schultz?"

"He was her boyfriend, I think." He took out one of his Nat Sherman's and lit up. "What about him?"

"He's dead. Killed himself today with an O.D. of cocaine."

"Good God." He sat down in his chair as if he'd been chopped at the back of the knees. "Well, just because this Leo took drugs doesn't mean Jennifer did."

"Horton, the girl took drugs; that's all there is to it. I don't know what that has to do with her murder but there might be a connection. She told you she was going to have money soon. I don't think she meant a job as a receptionist, do you? I think Jennifer found out something that was going to make her money. Or at least she thought it was."

"Are you suggesting that Jennie was going to blackmail someone?" he asked irately.

"Maybe. Or maybe she'd gotten in on a drug deal. I just don't know yet. And somebody doesn't want me to find out." I touched the back of my head.

"I'm sorry you were attacked, Mr. Fanelli."

"Me, too. I'd like to see Jennifer's things."

"All right. They're in the bedroom. I'll get them."

While he was gone I pulled out a drawer in an end table next to the couch. There were coasters, napkins, two decks of cards. Nothing else. I closed it just as he was coming back.

"It's all in here," he said, putting a blue leather suitcase with brown leather trim on the floor in front of me. "I don't think you'll find anything in there to help you."

"Maybe not," I said. I leaned over, put the case flat on the floor and opened the two brass catches. The inside was lined in a blue rayon. There were two skirts, two blouses, some underwear, some pantyhose, a pair of purple dancer's tights and a sweater. In a pocket on the side of the suitcase I found a necklace of red glass beads, a yellow plastic bracelet, and a toothbrush. On the inside of the lid there was another pocket. It held two books. One was *Garfield Weighs In*, about that damn cat, and the other was *Palomino* by Danielle Steele. I didn't think much of Jennifer Baker's taste in reading but then, of course, when you're taking drugs you can't deal with anything too demanding. I flipped through *Palomino* and then the Garfield book. Something fluttered out onto the rug. I knew what it was before I picked it up.

"Here's the second postcard," I said. I had a feeling that Horton had put it there only moments ago.

"Really?" he said.

"Yeah, really." I stood up and turned the card over to the front. It was a photograph of a painting. I couldn't tell which was the right way up because it looked the same no matter how I held it. It had a bright red background with streaks of purple and blue crisscrossing through the center. I turned it over to see where it was from. In the upper left-hand corner the print said that it was a painting by William Solomon called *Life with Mother* and that the exhibit was held from March tenth through March thirty-first at the Sarah Barber Gallery on West Broadway. I handed the card to Horton.

He read it, then looked up at me. "You remembered it pretty well."

"How come you didn't know it was there?"

"I didn't go through the books the way you did. I didn't want to deal with her things. I just put them all together in the suitcase and put it in a closet. Surely you can understand."

"I can," I said. But I still didn't believe he'd never seen the card before. "Well, what do you think of it?"

"It could mean almost anything."

"You don't seem concerned."

"Of course I am. I was concerned when I hired you. I just don't know what to make of the card. It could be serious, or it could be just the thoughts of a young boy. They're very dramatic at that age."

"I know. Nevertheless, your nephew is missing and your niece is dead. 'Knowledge kills.' I wonder if Pat and Jennifer found out the same thing."

"Do you think Pat's dead, too?"

"I just don't know. Have you checked the morgue?"

"Yes. And the hospitals. I've called every day since he disappeared."

"You mean since he left New Jersey?"

"No, just the last two weeks." He sucked in his breath realizing he'd made a mistake. "I mean, since Jennifer told me he'd been missing two weeks."

"That was on Saturday. This is Monday."

"You're getting me confused," he said, reaching for his drink.

"No, you're getting *me* confused. You said you've called every day since he disappeared. That would be two weeks. But you only found out three days ago that he'd disappeared. That's what I call confusing, Mr. Horton. So, have you been calling the morgue and the hospitals for the last three days or the last two weeks?"

"The last three days."

"You're lying."

"How dare you say that in my house?"

"Why didn't your nephew like you, Mr. Horton?"

He turned away from me, his shoulders slumping. "I don't know. He just didn't."

"Was it because you're homosexual and made a pass at him?"

Horton wheeled around so fast I didn't even see the right uppercut as it came my way. But I felt it. He got me on the chin and I fell backward over a small table, knocking everything to the floor. I looked up and saw Horton standing over me, his legs spread, his hands clenched in fists in front of him.

"Get up, you pig," he said.

I stayed where I was. "Hold it," I said, rubbing my chin. "It was just a question."

"Was it? In one so-called question you implied that I engaged in incest and that I'm a pederast." He was shaking with rage.

"I get the incest part but not the other."

"No, I'm sure you don't. You goddamn heterosexuals think homosexuals and pederasts are one and the same thing. Well, it's not the same at all. Now get up and get out. You're fired."

"Look, I'm sorry I insulted you. I shouldn't have said that."

"Just get out."

I stood up slowly, ready if he tried to hit me again. But he backed up, his fists unclenched at his sides.

"Get out," he said again.

"One more question. Why did you say Father Paul sent you to me? He's never heard of you."

"I don't owe you any explanations, Fanelli."

"I think you do."

He thought it over for a second. "All right, what difference does it make? I needed an entrée to you. That should be obvious."

"Who told you about me?"

"A friend. Now get out."

I remembered the painter he'd mentioned. "Robert Sheedy?"

Horton's good eye flashed with anger, or maybe fear. "He has nothing to do with this. Now get the hell out."

"You're not going to give up on finding Patrick, are you?"

"It's no longer any concern of yours. Please leave before I call the police."

I knew he wasn't about to call the police but there was no point in staying there irritating him. I started toward the door and when I got there he was right behind me. "Look," I tried again, "I'd like to stay on the case."

"You can keep the retainer I gave you," he said.

"It's not the money."

He laughed. "I'll bet."

"No, really. I'd like to try to find Patrick."

He hesitated for a second. "I can't stop you from looking for him, Mr. Fanelli, but I'm not going to employ you. Good night."

"Okay." I opened the door. "All the same, I apologize for what I said before."

He took a breath but said nothing.

I left feeling like a crumb.

I was too tired either to confront Doug Fanner or toss his place. I would deal with him first thing the next morning. Upstairs my kids were asleep in their beds with, I hoped, visions of sugarplums dancing in their heads. But for all I knew they could be having pot dreams. Was that really true? Wouldn't I know if either of them was on something? I liked to think I was an aware parent, not deep in some dumb denial about who my kids really were. Still, there was the possibility that the sugarplums were in *my* head. I would observe the kids more closely, I promised myself.

In my room I thought about taking a hot shower but my head and chin hurt too damn much and all I wanted to do was lie down. I stripped off my clothes and let them drop in a heap on the floor, then fell on the bed and slowly made my way under the covers. God, it felt good. I wanted my mind to go blank but it wouldn't. I kept wondering about that second postcard. Nothing could convince me that Horton hadn't known about it, but I couldn't figure why he hadn't told me or, more important, why he had shoved it between the pages of the book for me to find.

I supposed he realized that I knew he'd seen the card and decided he might as well let it turn up. But nothing explained his original concealment or his slip about knowing Patrick had been missing for two weeks. What it looked like to me was that Horton had known his nephew's whereabouts until the kid disappeared from SoHo, then had lost track of him and had been willing to let his niece see if she could come up with something. My guess was that he hadn't realized any danger was involved, so that meant he might have even known who Patrick's "friend" had been. But Horton wasn't going to tell me. Maybe Robert Sheedy would.

I got out of bed, threw on my robe and went into the kitchen where we kept the phone book. I looked up Sheedy. There were eight of them. Robert was at one-seventy-five Greene Street. I went back to bed.

I thought about my schedule for the next day. First I'd talk to Doug Fanner and then try to meet Tim Skelly, my only friend left on the force, for breakfast, to see what he had. Then I'd talk to Robert Sheedy and make a stop at The Sweatshop Boutique. After that I'd drop in at the Sarah Barber Gallery. In the afternoon I'd look up that kid, Price Allen. I remembered then that I'd been fired. It didn't matter. The case had gotten under my skin and I wanted to find Patrick Baker. Maybe it was because he was Sam's age, or maybe I wanted to make it up to Charles Horton. I was really sorry I'd insulted the man, and even though I knew he was keeping information from me, I didn't believe he had anything to do with his niece's death or his nephew's disappearance. There was another reason he was keeping quiet and now I had a hunch I knew why. Robert Sheedy, I thought, would confirm my thinking.

I looked at the book on my night table, thought about reading, changed my mind. I snapped out my light, pulled the sheet up to my chin, careful not to touch it, and closed my eyes. Almost at once I started to drift down into sleep and when the phone rang it shot through me like a .44 mag.

It was Elaine.

"Sleeping?" she asked.

"Trying."

"Well, this is the first opportunity I've had to get back to you," she said as if it was my fault.

I looked at the clock. "It's almost two."

"I *know* what time it is. Don't you think *I'm* tired? Christ, I've been going since six this morning. You can't imagine what it's been like in the office. We're trying to get Dustin Hoffman for an episode on the show and it's like trying to get Reagan."

"Why?" I asked.

"Why what?"

I yawned. "Why are you trying to get Dustin Hoffman?"

"You're kidding."

"I am?"

"Fortune, the man's hot and it would be the biggest coup in the business."

"Oh."

There was a moment of hostile silence and then she said, "What did you want, Fortune?"

"I wanted to know when you're going to see your son and daughter?"

"You just can't stand it that I'm independent, can you?"

I closed my eyes and held the phone away from my ear. I knew she was good for a five-minute rap, at least. Elaine was convinced that I resented her having a career and giving me custody and no matter what I said or did I couldn't convince her that that was not the issue. I understood perfectly why a woman would want a life of her own, a career, and no children for a while. But what I didn't get was why she *never* wanted to see them, why I had to badger and fight to get her to see her own kids. The only thing I could figure was that they reminded her of me and she wanted to think of me as little as possible.

"Hey, Elaine, enough, okay?"

Silence again.

I said, "Can we please talk about this like adults?"

"Do you expect me to leave my work to be with them?"

"No."

It was as if I hadn't said that, because she said, "You wouldn't leave yours if you had any real work. Two working people are raising children and one of the kids gets sick, who do you think stays home from work with the kid? Who, huh? Who? The father? Not on your life."

I decided she was feeling guilty. "Elaine, please. Nobody's asking you to stay home from work. The kids go to school. They're not going to stay home to see you. But how about a Saturday or Sunday?"

"This is a seven-day-a-week job, Fortune."

It sounded like she was crying and I wondered if she was having a breakdown. "Well, if that's true it's pathetic."

"What's that mean?"

"It means that no job is worth seven days a week." I was ignoring the fact that when I was on a case I had no days off either. But that was different: cases never lasted more than two weeks.

"I can't talk to you," she said. "You have no understanding of what it is to try to get someplace, to be somebody."

I got the implication because I'm real quick on the uptake. "Look, I don't want to talk about who is and who isn't somebody. Are you going to see the kids next weekend or not?"

"It'll all depend on Dusty. I may have to fly out to L.A."

"You going to take a meeting?" I couldn't help myself.

"What?"

"Yes or no on the kids, Elaine?"

"I'll have to let you know. Don't call me at the office anymore this week because you won't get me. I'll call on Friday and let you know what's happening." She hung up.

I put the phone back in its cradle and fell down on the pillow again. Inside I was burning. She hadn't even asked about them. How they were, what they were doing. I didn't know what to tell them. The last thing I wanted to do was turn them against their mother but she was managing to do that herself.

I turned over on my stomach and shoved my arms up under the pillow. If things went as usual I'd be awake for hours stewing over Elaine's call. She always had that effect on me. There was never any satisfaction in talking with her. Nothing was ever resolved and she always managed to piss me off. I ground my teeth and shut my eyes tight.

At first I saw jagged pieces of light, the way you do when you push on your eyes, and then the light spread out and formed an image. It was of a woman. It was Cassie Bloomfield. I started to untense, my body letting go of the grip it had on itself. The acid in my gut receded.

I turned over and lay on my back. Cassie Bloomfield, I thought. I hadn't put her on my list of things to do the next day. That was an error. One I'd correct. I wondered if she liked Italian food and started planning a menu. As she lifted a homemade gnocci with tomato sauce to her lips, I fell asleep.

12

I got up at seven, showered, shaved, put on a green turtleneck sweater, gray slacks and my tweed jacket. I called Skelly and we planned to meet at Angie's for breakfast. In the kitchen I told Karen and Sam we might be having company for dinner.

Sam said, "Will they taste good?"

"A regular riot, you are," I said. "So go ahead, correct your old man's grammar. *To* dinner, all right?"

"Who?" Karen asked.

"A new neighbor. Finally moved in across the hall."

"Man or woman?" Sam asked.

"Woman and child," I said, looking down at the sheet of paper in front of me. I was writing a note to Cassie.

Neither of them said anything. I looked up. They were staring at me with eyes of hundred-year-old sages.

I said, "What's the matter?"

"Is she pretty?" Karen asked.

"I didn't notice," I lied. "Okay, I gotta go. You're all right?"

They nodded. I kissed them both good-bye and got their solemn words that they'd be home *to* dinner that night.

In the hall I stood in front of Cassie's apartment listening to see if anyone was up. I couldn't hear anything. I reread my note.

Dear Cassie,

I thought it might be nice if you and Zelda would come for dinner tonight. If you like Italian food, I'm a good cook. I can't give you a time now but I'll try to be back around five to see if it suits you. If you can't make it we'll try another time. No big deal.

Fortune

Stupid. It was the stupidest note I'd ever composed. I'd even written *for* dinner instead of *to*. And it sounded as if all I could cook was Italian food. What if she didn't like Italian food? But everyone did, and if she didn't, who needed her? Why did I have to put "No big deal," like some kid. I started to shove the note in my pocket when her door opened. She yelped and jumped back.

"We have to stop meeting this way," I said.

She laughed. It was the greatest laugh I'd ever heard, like bells and ringing crystal.

"What were you doing?" she asked.

I held up the note in my hand and gestured with it. "I was going to slip this under your door. It's an invitation to dinner."

"Let's see," she said.

I shoved it in my pocket. "No need now. I'm asking. Tonight at my place. You and Zelda."

A small dark-haired girl with huge brown eyes peeked out from behind her mother's hip. "Me, too?" she said.

"This is Zelda," Cassie said.

"I guessed." I offered my hand and she took it. "Hi, Zelda."

"Hello. Are you the man who fixed the windows?"

"The very one."

"Thank God, it was an inferno."

I laughed. Zelda wasn't more than five or six.

Cassie said, "She's given to hyperbole. We'd love to come to dinner."

"Terrific. Let's say about seven, okay?"

"Fine." She pulled the door shut and locked it. "We were just going down for some milk. Where's the best place?"

"M & O on the corner of Prince."

We started down the stairs together, them in front. Cassie was wearing a pair of worn jeans and a gray blazer with a light blue turtleneck underneath. Her hair was covered by a red bandanna tied in the back. My heart was playing a mambo in my chest.

At the bottom of the stairs I said, "I've got to see the super about something."

"Okay," Cassie said. "We'll be by at seven. Can I bring anything?"

"Nope. Just yourselves." I smiled, hoping there weren't little beads of sweat above my lip.

We waved good-bye, Zelda continuously, and then they were gone. I couldn't believe how this woman made me feel; I wasn't sure I'd ever felt that way. Was I kidding myself?

I walked down the short hall and knocked on Doug Fanner's door. He should have been up by now attending to his super's duties. I knocked again. No answer. I called his name a few times but there was no response. I decided to go in anyway. I could see that he had one simple lock so I took out my American Express card, which I never left home without. It only took about fifteen seconds until the tongue depressed and I was able to open it up. I stepped inside and closed the door behind me, my hand ready to grab my gun from my hip holster.

This was a smaller apartment than the others in the building, three rooms and a bathroom. I was standing in the living room, or what was supposed to be the living room. He used it as a studio. I had no idea he painted. There were canvases stacked around the place and one on an easel. I quietly moved into the room and slipped in front of the easel. It was, I suppose, a work in progress. I admit I don't know a damn thing about art, but like Eisenhower, I know what I like. I didn't like this. Maybe it was the greatest thing since Michelangelo but somehow I doubted it.

The canvas was fairly large, maybe four feet by five, and the background was mostly brown with some yellow near the bottom. In the foreground there were circles. Blue ones. Lots of them. That was it. Nothing about it appealed to me but what did I know? There's this gallery in SoHo called the Mary Boone and Mary'd discovered some guy named Julian Schnabel who everybody said was the greatest thing since sliced bread. I thought I'd check him out one day. I couldn't believe it. There were these huge canvases painted in a muddy brown with broken crockery pasted all over them. I think a pair of antlers were sticking out of one. And this guy was hot. So maybe Doug Fanner was the next Julian Schnabel for all I knew. Still, I had the persistent feeling that Fanner was a loser.

I moved away from the canvas toward the bedroom. The door was ajar. I stood to one side and slowly pushed it open with my foot. I listened for breathing but heard nothing. I eased my way into the room, reached around the door, felt the light switch and snapped it on. There was no one there. The bed hadn't been slept in. I left the bedroom, checked out the kitchen and bathroom just to make sure, but the place was empty.

Back in the bedroom I looked through the closet and found nothing but clothes. There was a small chest against one wall but that was a disappointment, too. I didn't know what I was looking for but I was sure there was something to find.

Next to the bed was a small wooden night table with one drawer. I opened it and hit pay dirt. Among the pens, a pad and some dirty tissues was a teaspoon. I picked it up and examined it closely. The back had been wiped down but I could see that it still had some black on it where a lighter had charred it while cooking the dope. I thought of Leo Schultz. I pulled the drawer out farther thinking I might find a syringe and needle, or maybe the stash itself, but there was only a blank postcard. I turned it over and saw that it was William Solomon's painting from the Sarah Barber Gallery, the same one Patrick had used to send his second message.

I pocketed the card and started looking through everything again. This time, in the closet, I found another postcard in a jacket pocket. This one was from the Eurogallery and had a photograph of another painting on the front. It was of two cows in a field. I looked at the dates of the show and found that it was running currently.

But I wasn't looking for postcards, although the one from the Barber Gallery might link Fanner with Patrick. I was looking for heroin or cocaine and I found it in the heel of a shoe. It was a cowboy boot and the heel was hollow. Seven glassine envelopes were stored inside. I tried the other boot. Same thing. This one had six envelopes. I figured this little cache was worth about seven hundred bucks. Where did a super get that kind of scratch? I doubted that he sold his paintings and I didn't think this was a private cache. Fanner was obviously dealing. I didn't know whether this was coke or heroin; they looked the same to me. I took an envelope to get it analyzed, although it didn't matter much which it was. I went through the rest of his things but I didn't find anything else.

It was getting late and I didn't want to keep Skelly waiting. I let myself out, snapped the door locked, and left the building.

Outside the day was getting under way in gray tones. It looked like rain. I walked up Thompson to the corner of Houston where Angie's luncheonette held out against high rents and chic eateries. Her place was almost the last coffee shop in SoHo where you could get a decent breakfast for a buck fifty, and a bowl of spaghetti at lunch or dinner for three dollars. And it was good, too. She'd been there for more than twenty years and I'd been coming in that long.

"Hey, Fortune," she said from behind the counter, flipping an egg, "I hear ya got a headache!"

Nothing was sacred. "Small one," I answered, giving her my three-finger salute.

She smiled and saluted back. Angie was pushing fifty and you could see it in her tired face. She'd been working long hours, supporting her kids alone for as long as I knew her. But she was always impeccably groomed. Her dyed red hair curled around her face with a big pompadour on top and her makeup was thick but even, covering her face in a pinkish hue. She wore a white dress, like a nurse's uniform, and over it a long white apron.

"You want your usual?" she asked.

"Right."

I looked around the room, saw a lot of regulars, waved and spotted Skelly at a table near the back.

"You're late," he said in greeting, a piece of bagel hanging from his Zapata mustache.

"Couldn't help it." I sat down opposite.

"You think I got all day, Fanelli?" Cardboard containers of milk were on all the tables in Angie's and Skelly poured some into his coffee turning it almost white. I never understood why he bothered with the coffee. "You want to talk or what?"

"Talk," I said.

Francesca, Angie's daughter, put my breakfast in front of me. Two eggs over easy, home fries, sausage, a cup of coffee and a Coke. I thanked her and looked back at Skelly.

We were the same age but the job had aged him around the eyes. Or maybe *in* the eyes. Skelly looked like he'd seen his own funeral. He was a thin guy, long nose, creases in the cheeks. The mustache gave him a dashing look and detracted from the sparse hair above his narrow forehead. He was wearing a glen plaid suit, worn a bit thin at the elbows, a flowered tie and a white shirt. A silver ball-point pen stuck out of his breast pocket.

"So what have you got?" he asked.

"A bunch of stuff that doesn't add up . . . yet. Maybe when you tell me what you got it will."

He smiled, the mustache rising. "We gonna play that kind of game?"

I smiled back. "Whatever." We were friends. We'd gone through the Academy together and helped each other out while I was on the force. We were even partners for a few months before I quit. The other guys used to razz us about our names. Like a vaudeville team: Skelly and Fanelli. He'd never held it against me that I quit the force. We liked each other.

"Tell me what you got," he said.

"Okay. Some of it." I drank down my Coke. I told him what I'd learned about Jennifer, the Bakers, showed him the picture of Patrick and the postcards. I continued on about getting sapped, and what I'd found in Fanner's apartment. But I didn't mention Horton even though technically I could have because he was no longer my client. I don't know why I wanted to protect him; I just did.

"So you're not telling me who hired you, huh?"

"No."

"Why not?"

"Skelly, you know I can't do that."

"You and friggin' priests. Okay, it doesn't matter. What do you wanna know?"

"What was the autopsy on the girl?" I pushed an egg around on my plate.

"Hit with a blunt instrument, two, three times. She died somewhere between two and six, Sunday morning. There were traces of cocaine in the nasal passages."

That didn't surprise me but all I said about it was that it might connect Fanner to the murder. Skelly stayed mute on the subject, sphinx that he was. "Any prints?" I asked.

"You kidding? The place was loaded. No prints worth shit. No weapon either. There was some blood in the back room, so we think the girl was wasted there then carried to the window where somebody played his idea of a joke."

"How'd they get in?"

He shrugged and I could see his collar move around his neck like it was too big for him. "Walked in. All locks in place."

"What about the people who work there?"

"There's three. A girl about twenty named Sandee who's got an alibi tighter than a gnat's asshole, and no key."

I figured she was the one I'd seen with Jim Van Sickle.

"A guy named Rory, who doesn't have a key either and was with his mother and sister sewing sequins on a dress all Saturday night." He rolled his eyes upward. "And the third one is Sable, the owner. Her name's really Thelma Sable but she just calls herself Sable."

"What do you call her?"

"Loony Tunes, but she's clean. She was being interviewed on a cable station from two to three and then partied with the crew until seven."

I said, "What about the kids who discovered the body?"

"What about them?"

"They know anything?" I asked innocently.

"Nah. They were just Sunday sightseeing. All the girl was afraid of was that her mother was going to go crazy because she was down here."

He was slipping but I decided not to tell him just now. I wanted to interview Price Allen myself.

Skelly said, "So who do ya figure sapped ya, Fortune?"

"I don't know. I want to find Fanner and ask him a few questions. Incidentally, I borrowed this from his place." I slid the glassine envelope across the table. "Coke or heroin?"

Skelly moved it to his lap and I could hear him undoing the package. Then he wet his forefinger, went down to his lap with it, came back up and tasted the white powder with his tongue.

"Coke."

I'd had it analyzed! "So what do you think, Skelly?"

He slipped the packet of cocaine into his pocket. "I think somebody doesn't want you nosing around because maybe this murder's got something to do with drugs. Or maybe this Fanner and his coke have nothing to do with the murder."

"I thought Fanner was just a patsy, making an extra buck to turn out the lights and turn his back, but now I'm not so sure. And what about Patrick Baker?"

He pointed to the second postcard. "'Knowledge kills,' the kid said. Maybe it did."

I didn't want to think that. "You going to pick up Fanner?"

"On what charge?"

"I'll find him," I said.

"'Course I can tell the drug boys about him; then they can keep their eyes open." He popped in the last of his bagel, chewing while he talked. "So Fortune, you know the rules, huh? You come across any pertinent info while you're looking for this kid Baker and you tell your old pal, right?"

"Right," I said. "And the same applies to you, right?"

"Naturally. How could you think otherwise?" He washed down the bagel with his cold milk-coffee. "Hey, you didn't eat anything."

I'd lost my appetite somewhere along the way and my plate was half full, the eggs congealing, the sausage collecting beads of fat. "Not hungry," I said.

He stood up. "Gotta go. So, call me you find out anything."

"Will do, Skelly."

He left and I stared into my coffee cup as if it might reveal some answers. All I saw was a hair floating on top. I pushed the cup away. I needed to find Doug Fanner. I went to the counter and sat on a stool at the end. Angie was scooping some bacon onto a paper towel. I watched her plop some eggs on a plate, take toast from the toaster, slop some butter on it, flip the bacon onto the plate and bang it down in front of Mr. Torterello who was sitting three stools down.

"Eat," she said.

The crowd was thinning out and Angie lit a cigarette. I called her over.

"You want coffee or Coke or what?" She fluttered her black false lashes at me.

"Nothing," I said. "I wanted to know if you've seen Doug Fanner around this morning."

"Don't mention the bastard's name."

"Why not?"

"He's supposed to sweep up last night and open up today. So where is he, huh? You seen him? I'm still waiting."

"Wait a minute, Angie. What do you mean, open up?"

"What do I mean open up? What are you? Open up is open up!"

"You mean Doug opens up your place with a key?"

She cocked her head to one side. "Nah, he does it with his teeth."

I laughed. "Thanks, Angie." I paid my check and left. Walking down Thompson to Prince I couldn't believe what a dope I'd been. Fanner was practically the neighborhood super. He worked for lots of places besides our building. It was how he made his living. I'd never noticed him around Angie's place because, obviously, he was there late at night and very early in the morning. But I'd seen him sweeping in front of the Eurogallery and three or four other places. And then there was the work he did inside stores and galleries where no one saw him. He couldn't have worked for The Sweatshop Boutique because Skelly would have known. But maybe he had at one time. And maybe he'd kept a key.

13

There was another apartment house on Thompson where I knew Doug Fanner worked, one on Sullivan and one on Prince. I stopped at all of them, asked around but no one had seen Fanner since the day before. I was beginning to think maybe he'd skipped. But if he had why would he have left his cocaine behind? He would have done that only if he'd been in a big hurry, like maybe having somebody after him. Could he have thought that somebody was me? He'd known immediately that he'd blown it and that I knew he was connected to my attacker. But it didn't make sense. If it was me he was afraid of he still would've had time to take his drugs and some clothes. That was the other thing: I couldn't be positive about his wardrobe but it didn't look like much of anything in that line was missing. The guy was probably shacked up somewhere, flying high on his drugs. Whatever it was, I didn't have a lead on his whereabouts so I had to put him on the shelf for the moment.

The galleries didn't open until around noon so my next move was Robert Sheedy. I called him from a pay phone. Horton had obviously warned him because he was defensive and tried to put me off. I convinced him he'd prefer talking with me rather than to the police.

Sheedy's building on Greene Street was small, about seven stories, and the facade had recently been sandblasted. Iron grillwork scaled the front, like hard ivy. I pressed the buzzer and in a moment his voice came over the intercom. I said who I was and he buzzed me in.

I stepped into the small elevator and waited for Sheedy to pull me up to the top floor. The first time people get into a loft elevator they have the illusion that when they push the floor button they're doing something. But the thing won't move unless you have a key; either it's unlocked or your host brings you up from above. Most elevators in loft buildings open into small lobbies or foyers but this one opened right into the loft. It was spectacular.

Floor-to-ceiling windows spanned the front, filling the place with light, even on this dull day. White Doric-type columns stood between beamed ceilings and parquet floors. The main area was open and half of it served as a living room, the other half as a studio. Doors at the back probably led to bedrooms. I could see part of a kitchen to my right. Plants, both standing and hanging, were everywhere. Large paintings hung on all the walls. From where I stood I could see they were not all by the same artist: some looked interesting, others left me cold. I wondered which were his.

Looking at Robert Sheedy I was almost positive he was the man Father Paul had seen with Patrick. He was not more than five eight, and had a stocky build. His hair was totally gray, although he couldn't have been more than fifty, and he wore it full but not long. He had a good face, very Irish, craggy, as Paul had said. His eyebrows hadn't turned yet. They were very black and stuck out like two small shelves over sad brown eyes. Robert Sheedy looked like life had walked on him more than once. He was wearing chinos and a blue-striped button-down shirt under a navy crew-neck sweater. A cigarette curled smoke between the fingers of his left hand.

"I don't have a lot of time, Mr. Fanelli," he said.

No one ever did. "I won't take much."

He drew a deep breath. "All right. Let's sit over here." He motioned to a conversation pit of gray velour. I followed him over and we sat opposite each other, a large, square redlaquered table between us. He stubbed out his cigarette in a clear glass bowl. "I think you should know I've spoken to Charles Horton and I know he fired you."

"I think you should know that I know you recommended he hire me. How come?"

"How come what?"

"First of all, how'd you know about me? And how'd you know that mentioning Father Paul's name was the way to get me to listen?"

"Mr. Fanelli, how long have you lived in this neighborhood?"

"All my life."

"Then surely you know that there are no secrets here."

"There are to outsiders," I said, nodding his way.

He smiled but he still looked sad. "Do you remember Sheedy's Drugs? No, you're probably too young."

I thought about it. "I think I've heard my mother mention it. It closed during the war, didn't it?"

"Near the end. My father ran it on Vandam Street until he enlisted and left my mother to try to raise six kids by herself. He was killed at Parry Island. I was ten. She had a breakdown, my mother." His eyes misted over and he got a cigarette from a pack in his shirt pocket. "It's funny but people don't think about Irish ladies of that era having breakdowns. They did. She did.

"We were all shipped around the country to different relatives. The ones who lived here, on MacDougal and Sullivan streets, had too many kids of their own and couldn't take any of us. I grew up with my grandmother in Boston." He laughed and blew a plume of smoke above his head. "Not on Beacon Hill either. She cleaned offices, my grandmother. She'd bring paper home for me to draw on. I thought it was the greatest gift anyone could have. If there's anyone responsible for my success as an artist it's that lady." He shook his head, remembering with fondness.

"Anyway, a number of years ago, before SoHo began getting popular, I had dinner with an aunt of mine who still lives on Sullivan and she told me she'd heard that a number of artists were buying loft spaces to paint in. She thought it was terrible, subversive practically, but it sounded like a good idea to me so I looked into it and . . . *viola!*" He made a sweeping gesture with his hand.

"It's very interesting, Mr. Sheedy, but what's this got to do with the price of salt?"

"Oh, sorry. I do drift, don't I? The point is I'm not totally an outsider. Well maybe I am but I have inside contacts. My aunts, uncles, cousins."

"They must be proud of you," I said.

He laughed, a bitter tinge to it. "Hardly. They don't understand what I do. They think it's . . . well, peculiar for a man to make his living painting pictures. Still, we're related and they feel it's their duty to have me to dinner once every six months. That's how I heard about you and Father Paul."

"How come Father Paul doesn't know about you?" I asked.

"Why should he? As I said, the relatives don't bandy my name about."

"Because you're gay?" I asked, hoping I wouldn't insult him but needing to get to it.

He took a beat. "We've never discussed that. But I suppose they know. They're not stupid people. Still, I've noticed most people only know what they want to know."

"I've noticed that, too." I reached into my pocket and took out Patrick's first postcard. I looked at the front. It had always bothered me that a fifteen-year-old boy would have chosen a card like this. Now I knew he hadn't. The boy in the chair, the man framed in the painting above, the shadow of another man: all of it could have been a metaphor for Robert Sheedy's life. I put it on the table and slid it across to him. "Did you buy this card for Patrick or did he just take it from your desk?"

He ran his fingers across the front of the card as if he were reading braille. "I *gave* it to him," he said.

"You want to tell me about it?" I asked.

"No, but I will. I guess I don't have a choice, do I?"

"Not much."

He stubbed out his cigarette and immediately lit another. "Charles Horton and I are very old, close friends. We're not lovers, if that's what you're thinking. We were once, a long time ago when we were both very young and dumb." A shadow of remembrance crossed his face and caused his eyes to light for a moment. Then they quickly faded back into their hurt centers. "Anyway, we've stayed friends all these years. I guess there isn't much we don't know about each other. I've always known about Jennifer and Patrick, for instance. I've seen their pictures, heard about their lives and listened to Charles rant against Carter Baker. Naturally I knew about Patrick running away.

"About three days after the boy disappeared I was coming home from the theater. I got out of the BMT on Prince and Broadway and started walking down Prince. At the corner of Mercer, in the doorway of that building that's being worked on, I heard a sound, like crying, and I stopped. I saw that someone was curled up there and I assumed it was one of the bums who hang around down here. You know who I mean, don't you?"

"Sure." There were three regulars, two old, one young.

"But something made me look more carefully and I could see that the person's hair was light in color. None of the bums have blond hair. Besides, the form seemed very small. Still, I felt cautious and didn't go too near. If it wasn't a bum it might have been a mugger. But that didn't seem too likely. I asked the person if he was all right and the sound stopped. I stepped closer. The person turned and I could see from the streetlight that it was a child. I went right up to him."

"Even children can mug," I said.

"True enough, but I just knew this child wasn't a criminal. I had a gut feeling, the way you get sometimes."

I nodded.

"I bent down and started to ask him again what was wrong and I saw at once that it was Patrick. I almost said his name but something stopped me. We'd never met, of course, but he's an incredible-looking boy and if you'd ever seen a picture of him you'd recognize him."

"I *have* seen a picture of him," I said. I laid the photograph of Patrick on the table, then slid it across to Sheedy.

He picked it up and studied it. "Yes," he said softly, "that's Pat."

It was as if he were talking about his own child, someone special. A lover? I wondered. I was afraid to broach that subject again. I'd wait to ask any provocative questions.

"Don't you think he's beautiful?" Sheedy asked, looking up at me.

"Unusual for a boy."

Sheedy sighed. "Yes. It caused him no end of trouble."

"How so?"

"Oh, you know, sexual trouble. There are men who like beautiful young boys."

I let that go and urged him to go on with his story.

"Well, I pretended not to know who he was and simply asked him if I could help. At first he kind of curled away from me, in a fetal position, but then he looked over his shoulder, into my eyes. I guess I must look safe or something because he said that he was hungry."

"You look kind," I found myself saying.

"Thanks," he said, surprised. "I told him I'd feed him if he came with me. He asked if I meant a restaurant and I said I had food at home. He shook his head. So I said I'd take him wherever he wanted to go. He chose Ben's Pizza." Sheedy laughed. "Kids. He could have had a gourmet meal. But what do fifteen-year-olds know about gourmet food?"

I thought of Sam. "Not much," I said.

"Well, we went to Ben's and he wolfed down about five slices. He hadn't eaten for almost two days. He'd left home without any money. Not that he told me he'd run away. I didn't question him too closely because I wanted his trust. Charles was frantic about his disappearance and I thought if I could get the boy to come home with me, well, something might be worked out. I mean, Lord, I just couldn't let him go back to wandering the streets." He twirled a diamond ring on his pinky finger. It was identical to Horton's. "Do you have children?"

"Yes, a boy and a girl. The boy's about Patrick's age."

"Is that why you're pursuing this case even though you've been fired?"

"Partly."

"What's the other part?"

I didn't want to explain about having insulted Horton, which I was sure he knew about, because I was going to have to ask him certain questions along those lines. I hoped I could think of a way of putting it that wouldn't be too incendiary. "Oh, professional reasons. What happened next?"

Sheedy smiled. "Detectives are like psychiatrists, aren't they? They like to ask a lot of questions but don't want to answer any. So, what happened next? I convinced the boy he should stay at my place but not until I assured him that there were no strings."

"How'd you do that?"

"He came right out and asked me if I was straight. I lied and said I was. I never do that, but under those circumstances I thought it was best. I knew Patrick's sentiments about homosexuals that he'd learned from Carter Baker. I told him I was divorced, which is true. I tried to be straight right after college but, of course, it didn't work. It never does. I didn't tell Patrick how long ago I'd been married and he didn't ask. Still, he said, 'Marriage doesn't mean a damn thing.' I asked him what he meant by that but he just shook his head. Anyway, he was right. Plenty of married men indulge in homosexual activity." He looked in my eyes as if he were asking me a question.

"I'm not married," I said.

He laughed. "I guess that lets you out, then." He lit another cigarette. They were unfiltered and he pulled a piece of tobacco from his bottom lip. "For whatever reasons, Patrick believed me. I think he was desperate and needed to, and I think on some level he knew I wasn't going to hurt him. I took him home with me and we went to bed. Separately. I have three bedrooms here." He pointed to the back part of the loft. "I waited until I was sure he was asleep and then I called Charles. You can't imagine how relieved he was."

"I can," I said.

He nodded. "Well, we agreed not to tell the Bakers, even though Rebecca should have been told. But Charles felt she might tell Carter and, although he said he didn't want the boy back, Charles didn't believe him and was afraid for Patrick."

"Afraid of what?"

"I don't think he really knew. Carter Baker was an abused child and although, as far as Charles knew, he'd never abused Patrick I think Charles was afraid he might just start. It wasn't based on anything real."

"What did Horton plan to do about the boy? You couldn't have kept him forever."

"Naturally we didn't think it through that first night. But after that, one thing just followed another and I liked having Patrick here. He was helpful and considerate and good company. And he had some very definite artistic talent. I'll show you." He got up and walked over into the studio part of the loft. I followed.

Sheedy pulled a canvas from a compartment built into the wall. He brought it over to one of the large easels and put it up. It was unfinished but I thought it was pretty good. Of course it was my kind of painting: it had figures I could recognize and shapes I understood.

"The kid did this?"

"Yes. Not bad, huh?" He looked like a proud father.

"Looks good to me."

"With proper training I think he might just be an artist. He loves to draw and paint. He's just like I was as a kid." Sheedy turned away from the canvas and looked at me. "I want you to find him, Mr. Fanelli. I'll pay you."

I thought I'd take the opening. "Mr. Sheedy, I don't want to insult you but why are you so interested in Patrick Baker? I mean, is there another reason besides the fact that he's your friend's nephew?"

He shook his head slowly, as if it were almost too heavy to move. "I'm not going to punch you the way Charles did but I'm going to try to explain something to you. I've been honest with you; in fact I'm always honest. I'm gay. That's a fact. I like other men sexually. Not *all* other men. Not you, for instance."

I felt a momentary sting, as if I'd been rejected and it made me laugh inside. I stopped myself from asking him why but he anticipated the question.

"You're a very attractive man but not my type. People have the idea that homosexuals will go to bed with anyone but we have our preferences just as you do. I'm sure you're not attracted to *all* women, are you?"

"No."

"And tell me this, Mr. Fanelli, are you attracted to little girls?"

"Of course not," I said, offended.

"Nor am I attracted to little boys."

"What about this man-boy thing?" I asked.

"I think it's outrageous," he said. "Saying that a six-year-old has the right to choose a sexual partner is absurd. Those men are *not*, I repeat, *not* homosexuals. They're pederasts."

"People get confused," I said defensively.

"I know. It's enraging. I'd like to blast those man-boy love maniacs off the face of the earth."

"A lot of people would like to blast you off the face of the earth," I said.

"That's true. But we're consenting adults. Can't you see the difference?"

"*I* can, but many people can't. Look, Sheedy, I have nothing against homosexuals, and I happen to agree with you about the man-boy people, but try to understand that when a homosexual your age takes in a beautiful boy like Patrick, well, it makes a guy wonder. Or it did. I didn't really get it, I guess."

"And you do now?"

"Yeah, I think I do."

His shoulders drooped slightly as if he were relaxing. "How about some coffee?" he asked.

"Got any Coke?"

"As a matter of fact, I do. Patrick likes it. Come on in the kitchen."

I guessed he had more time than he'd thought.

14

We sat at a marble counter drinking coffee and Coke, and Sheedy told me more about his life with Patrick.

"I took him to plays and movies and, of course, the museums. He was overwhelmed. The Bakers never bothered with that sort of thing, it seemed. By this time he'd told me about his family but not what his last name was. He said he wanted to use my last name, so around the neighborhood he was called Patrick Sheedy. I kept Charles informed daily."

I pulled out the second postcard. "Did you know about this?"

Sheedy picked it up and read the message on the back. His eyes lost the sheen they'd had when he'd been talking about his life with Pat. "I didn't know about this card until Charles showed it to me. Patrick wrote it after he left here."

So I'd been right in believing Horton had known about the second card. I had a thousand questions now. "Let's go back a minute. To the first card. Okay, now I know about the place where he lived, and his friend . . . you. But what was his job?"

"I don't know."

I was surprised. Sheedy had painted a picture of two people who were very close. "How come?"

"It was his little stab at independence. First of all he didn't like taking money from me. He didn't mind my buying him things like food and clothing but for everyday stuff he wanted his own pocket money. Secondly, he told me a guy had to have some secrets, some privacy. I gathered he had had none at home. So Pat chose to keep this job his secret. I never asked him anything about it but I gathered from little things he said here and there that it was in a gallery."

I tapped the postcard from the Sarah Barber Gallery. "Could it have been this one?"

"It might have been. Most of the galleries use people to sweep or help install shows, things like that."

"Did he have working papers?" I asked.

"No, but lots of gallery owners look the other way when it comes to that."

"So now I know the job. Maybe. By the way, what were you planning to do about school?"

"Charles and I discussed that. Pat seemed to need a reprieve from structure so we decided to let him skip the rest of the semester. If he'd gone on living with me . . . Well, I don't know. We didn't think that far in advance."

"He might have been picked up as a truant."

"We were willing to chance that."

"Okay. Now tell me why he left here?"

He pulled at one of his bushy eyebrows, then took a sip of coffee. "I'd been very careful about not letting Pat see much of my life. I'd told my gay friends I was working on a big project and not to call for a while. Nobody thought anything about it, because I do that from time to time when I get involved in a painting."

I turned on my stool and looked into the studio part of the loft. "Which are yours?" I asked.

He pointed to a very large canvas directly behind me. It was of an open closet packed with all sorts of stuff. It was very realistic looking, like a photograph. I liked it because I could identify with it.

"I'm a photo-realist," he said. "We're not in vogue right now but I still make a very good living."

"I like it a lot."

"Thanks. Do you know much about painting?"

"Nope. What do you think of Julian Schnabel?"

He laughed mirthlessly. I had my answer.

I turned away from his painting and told him to go on.

"Well, I turned off my gay friends and encouraged my straight ones to come around. I said Pat was my sister's son, he'd agreed to that deceit, and that I didn't want him to know I was gay. It all worked wonderfully for a while. Then he discovered the truth." He looked as if he'd been punched in the gut. "I came in one day and Pat was sitting here waiting for me. I could see at once that he was upset. I asked him what was wrong and he threw a photograph at me. It was of Charles. I had a box of photos in the studio that I used for work and Pat knew about them. He'd decided to look for one to paint from. I'd completely forgotten about the picture of Charles but he'd found it."

"And he felt betrayed?"

"Exactly. And then one question led to another and I admitted to him that I was gay. I suppose that was an even bigger betrayal. I tried to point out that I was still the same man he cared for before he knew, but he wouldn't have any of it. He ran out of the house and I haven't seen him since."

"So the second postcard referred to you?"

"Yes. That was why Charles didn't give it to you. He didn't want to involve me. And if he'd shown it to you and not explained, it might have put you on the wrong track."

"Or the right track."

"What do you mean?"

I read the card out loud. "'No place to live, no friend.' We know what that means. And 'Why isn't anything or anybody what they're supposed to be?' That's probably you, too. I'm not sure about the 'anything' part of it. It could just be an expression or he could have meant something else. 'I wish I didn't know so much.' Do you really think he means about you?"

"I assumed. So did Charles."

"Could be, but not necessarily. 'Knowledge kills.' I don't think he meant knowledge of you and Charles."

"What, then?"

"I don't know. My hunch is that Patrick stumbled on something he shouldn't have and he knew he was in danger. I think Jennifer might have found out the same thing."

"But what could it be?"

"I wish I knew but I don't have all the pieces yet. If I'd had this postcard right from the beginning I'd probably be further ahead. Have you told me everything now?"

"I can't think of anything else." He looked down at the counter, blinking several times.

I knew he was lying. "There *is* something, isn't there?"

He pressed his lips together and shook his head.

"You're lying, Sheedy."

"Please," he said. "It's not for me to tell you."

"I thought you were hiring me."

"I am but this has no real bearing on the case and it's not my business."

"Maybe you don't know what has bearing and what doesn't."

"I know this doesn't. I just can't break a confidence. Please don't ask me to. Maybe when Pat's found, the truth will come out."

I decided to believe him. "You're that sure he's alive?"

He touched his chest over his heart. "I feel it in here."

I did, too, but I didn't want to give him any false hope. Besides, it was unprofessional. Stupid, really. I might as well have been going by astrology for all those kinds of feelings were worth.

"I'm sorry Charles didn't show you the postcard Mr. Fanelli. It's his natural inclination to be secretive."

"I'm a funny guy to get involved with, then."

"He thought it would be safer than going to the police. Charles leads a double life. He always has. You have no idea how damaging that can be and how confusing it can get."

"I can guess." I rose. "You've been a real help."

We walked to the elevator. I gave him a card. "Call me if you think of anything else."

"Do you want a retainer?"

"I still have Horton's. I'll let you know about money."

We shook hands. He looked so wounded, so defeated I wanted to put my arm around the guy, pat him on the back and give him a pep talk but I didn't. I have a little trouble being affectionate with men. Maybe it's because my father always gave me a smack when I tried it with him. Instead, I gave him my three-fingered salute and told him I'd do my best. On the way down in the elevator I decided Sheedy was a really nice man and I hoped for his sake, as well as Patrick's, that I could find the kid. I would if he was alive. And maybe even if he was dead.

The sky was looking more threatening than it had before, a definite pewter cast to it. April showers. But no May flowers to follow, not in Manhattan's cement garden. I looked at my watch and saw that it was quarter to ten. The Sweatshop Boutique was supposed to open at ten so I headed up Greene to Spring; I'd take a fast run through the lot, check with Julio and be at The Sweatshop Boutique when it opened.

A runner with headphones passed me, his eyes like somebody on smack. I wondered what the hell he was listening to or if the glazed look was just due to the running. At the corner of Wooster and Spring I looked in at the window of a dress shop. Mannequins filled the space and I couldn't help checking them closely. They were all real dummies.

A little way in from the corner I could hear squealing tires. When I got to the lot I saw Julio jockeying a Buick into a space that looked to me like a spot for a Honda. He got it in. I went up into the shack and waited for him.

"Hey, boss," he said, touching the brim of his porkpie hat.

"Julio, you don't have to race the cars that way. How many times do I have to tell you?"

He grinned sheepishly. "Not too many, boss. Other boss, Mr. Sklar, here lookin' for you. He say to call him at Mercer. Nothin' else to report. Everythin' fine. More checks in the box."

"Thanks." I reached for the phone and Julio left. My brother-in-law took care of the Mercer Street lot and we seldom crossed paths unless something went wrong. We had a meeting once a month to go over things. I wondered why he wanted me to call him. I hoped I didn't have to play landlord. There wasn't time. Roy answered on the second ring.

"It's Fortune," I said.

"Oh. Yeah." He sounded terrible.

"What's wrong?"

"It's your sister. I had to put her in again."

I felt my stomach dip. "What happened?"

"What happened. What do you think happened? She got into the booze is what happened. It's what always happens. I hide it, she finds it, then she drinks it."

I wanted to ask why they had it in the house at all but I knew it wasn't my business. Besides, it was a game they played and even though Roy complained it was obviously a game he needed to play. "Where is she?"

"St. Vincent's. I don't want to tell Mama."

He meant my mother. "You want me to, is that it?"

"It'd be better, Fortune."

I hated telling my mother that her daughter was in the hospital again because she was a drunk. Mama really didn't understand. She thought Yolanda could stop it if she wanted to, thought it was a moral issue. I tried to explain that Yolanda was sick, that alcoholism is a disease, but Mama didn't get it. She was the kind of woman who cured herself of anything that went wrong and she couldn't understand why others didn't do the same. "Okay," I said, "I'll tell her."

"No visitors for a few days," he said.

"That bad?"

"Pretty bad."

I didn't want to hear the story so I asked if there was anything else. He said no and we hung up. It wasn't that I didn't love my sister but I'd heard it all before. The details might be different but the essence would be the same. Yolanda was an alcoholic and whether she drank Thunderbird or Chivas she was not much different from the bums who hung around the streets when she got the stuff into her. I'd seen her in action enough. I didn't have time to see my mother now; I'd deal with it later.

I took the checks from the box to deposit and left the shack. Julio was leaning against the hood of a Pinto.

"You leave now, boss?"

"Yeah."

"Okay, see you. I keep thin's runnin' fine and dandy."

"You do that," I said.

I left the lot and walked up Wooster to Prince where I turned toward Thompson. I felt sick about my sister. It was the third time in a year she'd been hospitalized. The last time she'd been gotten down from the edge of the roof of her building, naked. We all knew that if she kept up the drinking one day no one would be around to stop her from killing herself. Of course the booze itself might kill her first.

I passed the M & O Grocery and thought of Cassie. I wondered if she had any skeletons in *her* closet. Who didn't? Just thinking about her, remembering that great laugh, made me feel a little better. I realized I could hardly wait to see her again. I hadn't felt that way about anyone for a very long time.

The lights were on in The Sweatshop Boutique. I opened the door and was immediately assaulted by blasting music. It had a very unpleasant sound and I longed for the dulcet tones of Old Blue Eyes, or even Simon and Garfunkel would do.

The interior of the store was painted orange; walls, chairs, racks, mirror frames, everything. Klieg lights, hung from the ceiling, provided the illumination. On the walls, in metal frames, were sets of iron bars, like pieces of jail cells. All the clothes had chains or keys or bits of metal on them. Sable was covered in the stuff.

She was a tall woman with short, spiky orange hair and orange eyebrows. She had close-set gray eyes that made her look mean and her lips were covered in a thick orange gloss. On each wrist was a handcuff worn as a bracelet. Around her waist she wore a heavy-link chain and from her neck a Medeco lock hung like a pendant. Her dress was made of orange burlap and looked like the potatoes hadn't been thrown out of it too long before.

"Sable?" I asked.

"Yeah, that's me." Her lids fell, hooding her eyes, and I noticed that they, too, were orange.

I gave her my card.

"I told the police everything I know, which is nothing. You know what this has done to my business?"

Another compassionate soul. "Helped it, I'd guess."

"Helped, schmelped, it's killing it."

You could take the Thelma out of Sable, I thought, but you couldn't take the Sable out of Thelma! "You've just re-opened, haven't you?"

"Do you see any customers? Are you a customer?"

"No, but it's only ten after ten."

"What do *you* know?" She made a gesture with her hands like I was a washout.

"Look," I said, "I only have one question."

"He only has one question," she said to a mannequin near her. "The man only has one question. Is this supposed to make me feel better?" She turned back to me. "I'm not a well woman. I may look in the pink but I'm not."

I thought of saying she looked in the orange but I skipped it.

"I've worked hard all my life, fought and clawed my way up, so to speak. All through the years at F.I.T. do you know what I ate? I ate salami on rye. For years, every day, I ate salami on rye. And that was not lunch. That was my dinner. For lunch I had water. That's right, water. Sometimes a glass of tea if somebody was buying because I'm not a schnorrer. Just because somebody else is buying I don't order steak, if you know what I mean."

"I do," I said.

"So then school's over, I get a job...You know, up there in the Thirties with the men. I have to put up with plenty, if you get my meaning."

"I do."

"I'm not a prude or anything, but this stuff, yuck. So anyway, finally I get out of there into a nice place but I have to do very conventional stuff, when inside," she pointed to her head with both hands, the nails painted in orange, "there's magic dying to get out. But I'm thwarted at every turn. This is when the illness begins, in here." She touched her heart. "So I realize I gotta get out. Out of the muck and the mire of conformist clothing. I leave. What then? I go to my old father and I beg for a loan. But do I get it from the cantor? Of course not. If I was his son it'd be a different story, if you understand my implication."

"I do."

"I try the banks. Nothing. Friends. No dice. The sickness is getting worse." Her shoulders drooped and she held her hand over her breast as if she was pledging allegiance. "So then one night I'm invited to a party and I see I have nothing to wear. A joke, right? A designer with nothing to wear. So I pull off a slipcover from an old chair, cut a hole in it for my head, wrap it around me and take my dog's chain leash and tie it around the waist. Gorgeous, I'll have to admit. My nephew had left his toy handcuffs behind when he was visiting so I clip them apart with a wire cutter and put one on each wrist like this." She held up her hands. "These are real ones. So I go to the party and this guy is there. He sees me, flips over the outfit and in an hour we have a deal and here I am. Within two months this place is a success. And now this happens." She placed a hand on either cheek and shook her head. It reminded me of that old movie actor, S. Z. "Cuddles" Sakall.

I wondered if she gave a damn that a young girl was murdered but I didn't want to get into that. "A lot of people who wouldn't ordinarily know about you do now. I saw this place on the news last night."

"Tell me about it. That moron girl who worked for me really showed herself for what she was. I fired her. An opportunity like that and she blows it."

I wondered what Sable would have had her do.

"I was sick because this thing has gotten to me." She touched her middle, and her orange brows came together in a painful frown.

I felt Sable was a woman who couldn't be comforted easily so I didn't try. "Could I ask you my question?"

"One question he has. So ask."

"Do you know Doug Fanner?"

"Yes. Good-bye."

"What do you mean, good-bye?"

"You said, one question. You asked, I answered."

"Look, Sable, it's more than one question. I should have said it's one topic. The topic is Fanner."

She looked at me quizzically, then clanked her way over to a little orange table, opened a drawer and took out a pill bottle. She unscrewed the top and popped one into her mouth. A small orange chair was behind the table and Sable fell into it with a crash of metal. "I'm not a well woman. So what do you want to know for about Fanner? The police didn't ask me about him."

"Did he ever work for you?" I asked.

She rolled her eyes in disgust. "I suppose you could call it that. I employed him, let's put it that way. He was supposed to sweep outside and vacuum in here. He was a schmutzadicka bum as far as I'm concerned. When he did show up, he didn't do a damn thing. I fired him after three weeks."

I felt a clicking inside me. "He had a key, I suppose."

"Naturally. But I got it back when I fired him."

I didn't say Fanner could have had another one made. "You still have the same locks now that you had then?"

She raised one orange eyebrow. "What're you getting at?"

"Do you?" I insisted.

"Yeah. Well, no. I mean, I had them changed yesterday but up until then, yes. You saying Fanner killed the girl?"

"I'm not saying anything."

"It wouldn't surprise me," she said, her lips turning down.

"Why not?"

"I don't think he likes women too much."

"Why do you say that?"

"Just a feeling. I saw him with a girl once at the disco on Prince Street. You know the one?"

I nodded. Nobody in the neighborhood wanted the place there, didn't like the element it attracted, but so far we hadn't had any luck in getting it shut down.

"He just seemed to be treating her like dirt. I don't know, it's something a woman can tell, if you get my meaning."

"I do. Well, thanks, Sable, you've been a big help."

"Help, schmelp," she said despairingly.

"I hope business picks up."

"How about a nice dress for your wife?" She pointed to a little number that looked like something I might clean the stove with. I thought of sending it to Elaine anonymously but gave it a pass.

"I don't have a wife," I said.

"So maybe you should get one."

"I'll give it some thought. So long."

It seemed even strangers wanted to get me married.

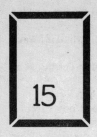

15

It was still too early to hit the galleries so I decided to pay a call on Nick Scola. I wanted to check out if he knew anything about my crack on the head or about Doug Fanner. I crossed the street. Nick's building was two up from mine.

The hall smelled of onions and garlic and I felt my salivary glands give a tug. If there's a better food smell around I don't know what it is. Nick lived on the fourth floor with his mother. She answered the door.

"Oh, Fortunato," she said, "come in, come in. I make you a nice cup of espresso, okay?"

"No, thanks, not today, Mrs. Scola," I said.

She was a tiny woman with short pearl-white hair. She wore no makeup and no jewelry except tiny gold circles in her pierced ears. Her once pretty face was seamed and she had a crushed look, probably from the weight of carrying her son.

"You want a nice cannoli, Fortunato? I make myself."

"No, thank you. I don't have time today. I need to see Nick."

Her face grew dark at the mention of his name. "He still sleep," she said. "I hear him come in late. Four in the morning."

"You were up?"

She sighed. "It's hard to sleep when the boy's out. You know how it is?"

I knew. But this boy was in his thirties. I wondered which

it was: had the mama kept him a boy or had the boy needed to keep mama? Maybe both.

I started toward the back of the apartment. "Mind if I wake Nick up?"

"Fortunato," she said, her wrinkled hand at her throat as if it was sore, "Nicky's in trouble?"

"No, don't worry. I just want to talk to him."

She quickly blessed herself. "Nick a good boy. Second door down there his room," she said, pointing.

I walked down the hall. On the wall to the right of his door was a statue of the Virgin Mary in a curved white mounting. When we were kids we called them the Lady in the Bath. I knocked but there was no answer. I tried the door and it was unlocked. I opened it.

The room smelled stale; there were whiffs of alcohol, tired smoke and dirty feet. I felt the wall for the light switch and snapped it on.

Nick was lying across the bed in his clothes. His mouth hung open and saliva ran down his chin. He was snoring. I moved closer and saw the empty glass in his hand, lying on its side. A large wine stain bled into the sheet. Mrs. Scola wouldn't get that one out. A jug of red, a quarter full, stood on the night table. On the other side of him was an ashtray overflowing with butts. There was one in the groove, burned down to nothing but a perfect cylinder of ashes. He could have killed them both. I wanted to kill him.

I took out my gun, kept the safety on, got up on the bed and sat on him, my knees on his chest. He grunted, expelling air. I slapped him hard across the face and put the gun under the point of his chin. His eyelids fluttered open, the eyes unfocused.

"Wake up, Nick," I said.

"Huh?" He tried to move but I kept him pinned.

I pressed the gun harder into his chin. "Know what this is?"

He clicked his dry lips together and tried to focus. The whites of his eyes were streaked red and his breath stunk of old wine. My finger kept sliding over the trigger.

"I've got a gun under your chin, Nick and I'd love to use it." It was true. I could feel my heart volleying in my chest from the thought of killing him. I blotted out any feelings of decency or compassion and slapped him again.

He woke up. "Hey, wha's tha'?" His eyes grew round as he took in the situation.

I said, "What it is is a gun. You know about guns, don't you, Nick?" I pushed it harder into the fleshy part behind the chin bone.

He tried to move his head. "Tha' hurts."

"What a shame."

"Fortune," he said, as if he'd just recognized me.

"Right."

"What d'ya want?" His voice was hoarse.

"Some truth." I pressed down into his throat with my knee and he began to choke. His face became red, eyes bulging and I found myself watching dispassionately, as if he were a specimen on a slide. I realized, when the choking stopped and he was turning a bluish color, that I was cutting off his air. I suddenly came out of wherever I'd been, pulled back and sat on my haunches.

Tears leaked from the corners of his eyes. "Why?" he asked in a whisper.

It was then I understood and a rush of shame, like a blast of hot air, pushed through my body. It wasn't Nick I was abusing; it was my father and my sister Yolanda. All the anger I'd felt for both of them had merged and focused itself on this poor slob. And wasn't Nick just as sick as they? He was.

I eased off his chest and stood next to the bed, my gun at my side. "Sit up, Nick," I said softly.

He slid up on the bed, rubbing his throat, his eyes never leaving the madman he saw in his room.

"I want to talk," I said.

"What about?" His eyes shifted toward the bottle of wine and he unconsciously licked his lips.

"Go ahead," I said.

"Huh?"

"Have a drink."

His eyes lit up with gratitude and my shame deepened. I watched him fumble for the glass, pick up the bottle with shaking hands, pour the wine. He tried to pick up the glass but couldn't; his hands were shaking far too much. I reached out to help and he jumped back in fear. It made me sick at myself: the bully in the schoolyard.

"I'll help you," I explained. I took the glass and held it out to him.

His eyes searched mine for tricks. After a moment, when he'd decided I was sincere, he cautiously moved away from the wall, closer to me. I lifted the glass to his lips. He opened his mouth and I carefully tipped the glass. A rivulet of wine ran down his chin but enough got in so that he could take the glass from me and finish it off himself. He wiped his face with the sleeve of his shirt. Another stain for Mama.

"Thanks," he said. He began to look around the bed.

"Your cigarettes are on your left near the pillow."

He found them and lit up. "So whatcha want, Fortune?" He was all mine now, my abuse put aside if not forgotten.

I'd try to put it aside, too. "I want to know why you sapped me last night?"

"Me?" he said, jabbing a thumb into his chest. "Not me, Fortune."

"Who, then?"

He shrugged. "How should I know?"

I brought my gun to waist level and Nick moved back.

"Honest, Fortune."

"You've never been honest a day in your life. Don't make me start in on you again." I knew I wouldn't, couldn't, but he didn't know that.

"I left your place I didn't see nothin'. I heard about it, sure. Later, in Barney's."

"You see Doug Fanner last night?"

"Ya mean after you was conked?"

"Yes."

"No. I only seen him before, when I was leavin' your place."

"Doing what?"

"I dunno, fixin' a light or somethin'." He eyed the bottle again. There was a mouthful left.

I motioned for him to drink it. He poured it into the glass, his hands fairly steady, and swallowed it down. "What do you mean, fixing a light?"

"I dunno. He was up on the big ladder and screwin' around wit the bulb in the ceilin'." He laughed, showing a gap between his two front teeth. "Hey, that's funny, screwin' around wit the bulb. Get it?"

I ignored his joke. "Did Fanner say anything to you?"

"Nah. Hey, ya thought I zapped ya?"

"Maybe."

"Not me, Fortune. I wouldn't do that."

"'Course not," I said. "Nick's a good boy."

"Listen, I got mad but I known ya all my life. I ain't about to zap ya."

"My gun got taken, Nick. Hear anything about that?"

"Nope."

"You hear about anyone with a hot gun you let me know, okay?"

"Sure, thing. Hey, Fortune," he said and then his sentence trailed off.

"Yeah?"

He shook his head and his brown eyes glistened with unshed tears.

"What is it, Nick?" I asked gently.

"I'm a bum. Ya think I don't know it?"

"You're a drunk, Nick, not a bum. You're sick."

"Yeah, sick. I wanna get off but . . ." He shrugged. "Maybe I could, huh? Maybe today."

"Why not?"

"Yeah, why not?" He looked longingly at the empty wine bottle. "That's it. No more."

"Good," I said, but I didn't believe him.

"Yeah, no more. Hey, ya want I should help ya on the murder thing, Fortune?"

I don't know whether it was guilt or not but I told him he could. What the hell difference did it make?

I said, "You know anything much about Doug Fanner?"

"Like what?"

"Like who does he hang out with?"

"I dunno. I seen him at Barney's with some guys."

"What guys?"

"I dunno, just guys."

I holstered my gun and took out Patrick Baker's picture. "You ever see this kid before?"

His cigarette was clenched between his teeth and he looked at the picture through mists of smoke.

"Take the cig out of your mouth," I ordered.

He did. "Yeah, I think I seen this kid around. Why?"

"Where?"

"I dunno, around."

I was losing my patience. "Look, Nick, you want to help you have to try to be more specific. Think. Where have you seen this kid?"

He brought his black, bushy brows together in a thinking frown. He looked like an ape.

"I dunno, Fortune, I can't remember where. Ya want I should ask around?"

"No. Just keep your ears open."

"For what?"

"The kid's name is Patrick Baker...or maybe Patrick Sheedy. You hear anyone talking about him don't do anything, you understand? You come to me."

"Okay."

"And anything else you hear that sounds fishy. Maybe about drugs, cocaine. You see Doug Fanner today you find me and tell me where he is." I started to leave.

"Hey, Fortune?"

"Yeah?"

"Don't tell my mother, huh?"

"Don't tell her what?"

"Ya know, about the wine and all."

Did he actually think she didn't know? I told him I wouldn't and left the room. Mrs. Scola was drinking espresso at the Formica kitchen table.

"Everything okay?" she asked.

I said, "Just fine."

"You sure you can't eat?"

"Not today, Mrs. Scola, thanks."

She walked me to the door. "Nick awake now?"

"Yeah, he's awake."

She nodded several times and I could see she wanted to say something. Then she changed her mind and unlocked the door for me. "Come again, Fortunato," she said.

"I will." I started down the stairs, stopped and turned back to look at her. She looked old and frail as if she were made of dry timber. I thought of the mess she was going to find in her son's room and how she'd have to look the other way, pretend. "Mrs. Scola," I said, "Nick's a good boy."

"*Grazie*," she said and closed the door.

I went down the stairs and out to the street. It had started raining. Not hard but thin, like an ocean spray. I walked up Thompson toward the Eurogallery. I felt that I wasn't getting anywhere. I had a lot of pieces but none of them fit together. For instance, I couldn't put Doug Fanner together with Jennifer or Patrick. It was clear now that he'd been involved in my crack on the head. Whether he'd actually sapped me himself I couldn't be sure, but he surely knew who had. I thought if I could find Fanner and get that information out of him, things might start to make sense.

The Eurogallery was in a building that had once been a mill. The windows on the upper floors were two stories high and arch-shaped. The gallery, on the ground floor, had rectangular windows of normal size. They were covered with vertical aluminum blinds. The door was open and I went in.

I'd been in this gallery a few times because it was on my block and it often had the kind of paintings I liked. The paintings and sculptures were all from various parts of Europe, thus its name. Like all the galleries in SoHo the walls were white, the floor polyurethaned wood. Wooden columns went floor to ceiling.

To the left of the door was the office, which was empty. Above the white desk hung a large painting of ducks. I recognized it as the work of Joyce Mayer, George's wife. A small room off to the right of the gallery housed a permanent show of Joyce's paintings. They were almost all of ducks and they were godawful. Even I knew that.

A counter with some desks behind it was to the right of the door. A young woman with long black hair and blue eye makeup sat typing at one of them.

I said, "Excuse me."

She looked up but continued typing.

"Is Mr. Mayer in?"

"Who wants to see him?"

"Fortune Fanelli." I gave her my card.

To take it she had to stop typing. "You kidding?" she asked after reading it.

I wondered why everybody was always asking me this. "About what?"

"A private investigator? Gimme a break."

"Look, is Mr. Mayer in or not?"

"Does this mean you're like a private eye?"

"Yes."

"God, it's so interesting down here. I live in the Bronx," she said sadly. "Are you like Columbo?"

"Exactly. Is Mr. Mayer in?"

"I'll see." She picked up a red phone and pushed a button. We waited, staring at each other. "Mr. Mayer, there's a man here to see you. Fortune Fanelli, a private investigator. . . . Okay." She hung up. "He says he'll be right out."

"Thanks." I moved away from the counter and found a piece of sculpture. Usually the pieces here were representational but this wasn't. It was fairly large, about six feet high and maybe four feet in diameter. It seemed to be made entirely of lead pipes, the kind that are used in plumbing. I took a closer look. Each pipe was screwed into things that looked like oversized washers and in that way the pipes became connected. I couldn't imagine what it was supposed to be so I looked down at the gray pedestal it was resting on and read its title: *Life Is Just a Bowl of Cherries.* I looked up at the sculpture again. Well, you could have fooled me!

"It's a piece of shit, isn't it?" a voice behind me said.

I turned and saw Wayne Morrison. He wore his usual work shirt and jeans.

"Why is it here, then?" I asked.

He laughed derisively. "Because that's what they like. Shit."

"Who?"

"The public. The crummier a work of art is the better they like it. Most collectors wouldn't know a good piece of sculpture or a beautiful painting if they fell over it."

I figured I fell into that category but at least I wasn't a collector.

"Take this painting over here, for instance," he said, pulling me by the sleeve.

We stood in front of a medium-sized canvas in an aluminum frame. It was like the one I'd seen on the postcard. But this painting was a landscape and in the background were two horses. It was pleasing and technically well done. At least to my eye. Maybe it was dull but at least it was understandable. Next to it on the wall was a red circle, which I knew meant it had been sold.

"What do you think of this?" he asked.

I knew the answer he wanted so I gave it to him. "Not much."

"Right. But you know what it went for? Thirty thousand."

I wasn't surprised; I knew what paintings sold for. I wondered why Wayne was so amazed. I kept staring at the painting while he went on talking. Something about it bothered me but I couldn't put my finger on it. Then he pulled me along to look at another. The next one was a still life by a different artist: apples, oranges, a blue and white pitcher on a table in an aluminum frame. This one bothered me, too. Still, I couldn't grasp what was wrong. He took me down the whole line and kept pointing out how lousy they were and telling me how much they sold for or what the gallery was asking. Every one of them bothered me. It was as if I was staring at one of those kid puzzles that asked, "What's wrong with this picture?"

Wayne said, "Well, this show's closing today but the new

one will open next week. The paintings are still crated down-stairs but without looking I could tell you what they're like. More shit."

I looked at him then and saw that his face was flushed and his brown eyes were wider than usual.

"Good artists are starving," he said stridently, "but worse than that they're not being shown and you know why? Because assholes have the money and the power, that's why. Real artists don't have a chance in this market."

I wondered what and who he meant by *real* artists. It was true I wasn't any art critic but none of the paintings here were trash. I knew my question would enrage him but I wanted to know exactly what his gripe was?

I said, "Tell me, Wayne, what's wrong with these paint-ings?"

"Jesus Christ. Everything. Look at them. There's no imag-ination, no innovation, no real intent. People have been paint-ing like that for thousands of years. Anybody with a little training can do it."

"Really?"

"It takes a real artist to do something new, unusual."

"Like Julian Schnabel?" I asked.

His eyes narrowed and he stared at me suspiciously. "You like Schnabel?"

"Actually I don't, but I wondered if that's the kind of art you were talking about."

"That's not art," he said bitterly, "that's hype. Mary Boone invented Schnabel. He's like Frankenstein's monster. In the old days artists had patrons; today you have to have friends...friends in high places, if you know what I mean."

"In other words, talent has little to do with it?"

"Precisely. You have to know the right set. Hang out with the beautiful people, be a darling of the rich."

I'd heard this kind of talk before. There were writers, musicians and actors who said the same thing: "I didn't get published because I don't know anybody in publishing" or "My music isn't performed because I don't have the right connections" or "You have to sleep with somebody to get a part." They were angry, frustrated people who spent their whole lives complaining and hating. And they were usually not very talented; it was their way of excusing themselves.

"Tell me something, Wayne, are you an artist?"

"I try," he said modestly.

"Surely you know the right people."

"Because I work here? Don't kid yourself. We sell like crazy but this gallery is not in a league with Leo Castelli, or Boone, or Barber or any of the rest. You have to remember we don't show any Americans."

"But don't you know the other gallery owners?"

He shook his head and laid a fatherly hand on my shoulder. "You just don't get it. I'm not one the 'darlings.' I won't sing for my supper or dance for my dinner. I'm my own person and I pay a high price for that."

"Like not getting shown?" I asked.

"That's right." He leaned closer to me and lowered his voice. "George could show me in the back room where he keeps that trash his wife paints, but he won't do it."

"Why not?"

He shrugged. "I've never asked; he's never offered."

"What kind of stuff do you do, Wayne?"

"I make art," he said. "That's all you need to know."

"Could I see it sometime?"

"Sure, sometime." He looked over my shoulder and I saw his mouth twitch. "Here they come," he said, "Mr. and Mrs. Culture."

16

Mr. and Mrs. Culture were the Mayers, of course. They walked toward us, her arm through his.

"See you later," Wayne said and went off toward the rear of the gallery.

George was a medium-sized man in his late forties. His dark hair had been styled and curled just below his ears. Brown eyes were set far apart and he had a cleft chin below a worried mouth. He was wearing an elaborate cowboy shirt in red and white satin which was open to mid-chest. Salt and pepper hair filled the open space. Three thick gold chains hung around his neck. He wore designer jeans with a wide belt, the buckle of Mexican silver. His stomach fought to stay above the belt and lost the battle. He extended a wide hand, rings on the three middle fingers.

"Fortune, how you doing there, pal? You know my wife, don't you?"

We'd met at block association meetings. "Sure. Hello, Mrs. Mayer," I said.

Joyce Mayer said hello. She was a short woman with very long, straight dyed blond hair that looked like she spent a lot of time ironing it. I couldn't tell how old she was but she was a lot younger than her husband. Her face was wide but her features seemed pushed together in the middle and she had small, angry eyes. She was wearing a cowboy shirt that matched her husband's and very short red shorts. On her feet were red plastic shoes with one-inch heels. Bracelets jangled on her wrists.

"Come on into the office," Mayer said affably.

We followed him in and he took his place behind the large desk. Joyce sat slightly to his right and I sat in front. I noticed that the yellow ducks in the painting on the wall were the same color as Joyce Mayer's hair.

"So what's up, Fortune?"

I put the picture of Patrick on the desk. Joyce Mayer grabbed it.

"Who's this kid?" she asked.

"I thought you might tell me," I said.

"Let's see, babe," Mayer said holding out his hand.

She passed him the picture and he studied it for an inordinately long time.

"I don't know this boy. Do you, Joyce?"

"Never seen him before." She crossed her short arms in front of her as if to say that was that.

"Who is he?" Mayer asked.

"His name is Patrick Baker, also known as Patrick Sheedy. He's the brother of the girl who was murdered at The Sweatshop Boutique on Sunday."

"Listen," Joyce said suddenly, "what are you coming around here for? We don't know anything about that."

"Now, Joyce, don't get excited," George said, reaching over and patting her arm.

She pulled away. "Why shouldn't I get excited? I'm an artist. I don't have time for this crap."

It seemed a lot was being said in the name of art. I said, "I'm not accusing you of anything, Mrs. Mayer. I just wondered if you'd ever seen the boy."

"We told you no, so what else do you want?" She tugged at her hair, then smoothed it down, stroking it as if it were a pet.

"Patrick worked for a gallery," I said.

"He looks pretty young," George said.

"I've heard gallery owners look the other way when it comes to that."

"Might be. But not this owner. I stay strictly within the law in everything I do, pal. Never had a parking ticket, never even had a garbage summons. Everybody else around here gets them all the time, but not me. I say on top of things."

It was true that everybody got summonses for garbage that overflowed on to the sidewalk. The fault was that of the tourists who threw stuff wherever they wanted. But the sanitation department didn't ask who threw what where. I wondered how George Mayer kept his sidewalk clean.

"How do you manage that, George?"

"Oh, I always have some kid who cleans up." His face flushed and little beads of sweat appeared above his lip. "They're always the right age, though. You can bank on that," he quickly amended.

"You have a kid who works for you now?"

"Sure I do. Comes before school. He's seventeen. His name's Pete something. You know his name, babe?"

"No." She was sulking.

"Well, anyway, he comes early in the morning and sweeps up, makes sure all the garbage is in the bin."

"Is that his only job?" I asked.

"Jesus, what're we talking about Pete for?" Joyce said. She reached over to the desk, opened a black enamel box and took out a cigarette. George lit it for her. She blew a huge puff of smoke into the room. "If you have a point I wish you'd get to it so I could go back to work."

"You mean painting?" I asked.

"Yeah, that's work," she challenged.

"I'm sure it is."

Mayer raised a hand above his head. "That's one of Joyce's," he said proudly.

I said, "Very nice."

She smirked. "Thanks."

"Joyce is very successful," Mayer said. "Sells all over Europe."

"Really?"

Mayer said, "It's like we have a cultural exchange. I sell their art and they sell ours."

"Do you send them other artists besides your wife?"

"Oh, sure, we represent plenty of—"

"Look," Joyce said standing up, "I don't have time for a lesson in the business of art."

"Now, toots," he said, "take it easy."

I handed her the camp picture of Jennifer Baker and pointed her out. "Ever see her before?"

She studied it a moment and I thought I saw a flicker of recognition. "I don't know. Maybe. Who looks at kids?" She handed it to George. "She ever around here?"

George stared at the picture while he fingered one of his gold chains. "She doesn't look familiar. Kids this age all look alike to me." He smiled showing large white teeth. "Who is she?"

I told him.

"Any leads on that thing?" he asked.

"I wouldn't know. But they'll get the killer.... It was too outrageous a crime... like the murderer was signing his name."

Mayer waved a dismissive hand at me. "Come on, pal, we all know most murders go unsolved."

"Do we?"

"Listen, I don't give a damn who solves..."

"Neither do I," Joyce interrupted angrily. "I have paintings to paint, so is there anything else?"

I wanted to tell her she *should* care because when a killer is loose you never know who might be next, but instead I said, "One more thing. Do you know Doug Fanner?"

She blinked. "Yes. He used to work for us but he's a fuck-up. We couldn't ever count on him."

The consensus about Fanner seemed to be a hundred percent. "How long ago did he work for you?"

"Oh, let's see, two, three months ago, I think," Mayer said. "Isn't that right, darling?"

Joyce Mayer seemed to flinch at his endearment. "I suppose." She turned to me. "Is that all?"

I couldn't think of any reason to keep her even though her hostility fascinated me. I stood up and offered my hand. "Yes, that's all, thanks."

She looked at my hand like it was something beneath contempt, but then she took it. Her handshake was firm, hard, almost crushing. She left without saying anything.

"See you later, babe," Mayer said, following her departure with loving eyes.

I sat back down and looked a little harder at Mayer. I could see now that his hair was touched up on the sides and that maybe he'd even been lifted. There was something too definite about the chin line.

"Oh, that Joyce," he said chuckling. "Artistic temperament, you know. She's something, isn't she?" There was a pride in his eyes, like a father with a recalcitrant daughter.

"How long you been married?" I asked.

"Eighteen years."

I was surprised and he could see it.

"I married her when she was sixteen. I'm a bit older." He stroked his throat as if to make sure none of the wattles was slipping. "She had a crummy home life, if you could even call it a home life. Mother ran around, no father to speak of. All Joyce wanted to do was paint her pictures."

"And all you wanted was Joyce," I supplied.

He smiled, remembering. "That's right. It was an even trade." Something sad touched the corners of his mouth. I think he knew his bargain hadn't been the best. Where did love come in?

"You been happy with her?"

"Happy? Sure. We get along."

"You have any children?"

"Nope. She'd like to have one but I don't want any. I like it the ways things are. Besides, we can go out and boogie all night if we want. We couldn't do that with a kid around. Joyce takes care of me. I mean, I take care of her; she has everything she wants, but she takes care of me, too. You know, sometimes in the middle of the night I want something special to eat and

Joycie, she gets up and makes it for me. If we had a baby she'd be waiting on him all the time. No, that's not for me. I like to know I can have my midnight snack if I want it."

I'd heard a lot of reasons for not having children but this one was tops.

"Besides," he went on, "Joyce doesn't really want a kid. She just thinks she does because some of her friends have them. She's perfectly content with me and her painting. You saw how she wanted to get back to her work. . . . Well, what the hell would she do if she had some baby she had to change and feed? She'd flip her lid, that's what."

I for one was very glad Joyce Mayer didn't have a baby to change and feed. I couldn't see the little darling as a mother. Something about her reminded me of Elaine.

"You're positive you've never seen this girl?" I asked, pointing to the photograph of Jennifer. "Or this boy?"

"Positive," he said. "I'd remember him. He a faggot?"

"He's fifteen," I said.

"There are faggots at twelve, younger even."

I knew giving George Mayer a lecture about homosexuals wouldn't do him or me any good. I stood up. "He's a missing boy," I said, an edge to my voice.

"Hey," he said, "you're not one, are you? Hell, I didn't mean to offend."

I found myself about to say that I'd been married and had two children but I stopped. Why was it so important that a jerk like George Mayer know I was straight? Let him think what he wanted. "I don't think my sexual persuasion's any of your business."

"Listen, pal, don't get uptight. Some of my best friends are faggots."

I laughed. "With friends like you, George . . ."

"Huh?"

"Nothing. Listen, I forgot to ask Wayne about the boy. Could you get him here?"

His hard, hooded eyes peered at me for a moment and then he reached for the phone. He pushed a button and waited.

I noticed that the tiny beads of sweat dotted his upper lip again.

"Wayne, come on up here. Mr. Fanelli wants to ask you something."

"I'll be in looking at your wife's paintings," I said.

"He'll be in the Joyce Room," Mayer said into the phone then hung up. He came around the desk and gave me a pat on the back. "Listen, if you're interested in anything we can work out something."

"Meaning?"

"Payments," he said. "We'll let you pay on time. We do that for certain people." He gave me a big wink as if to say I was special and that it didn't matter a damn to him that I was a faggot.

"I'll let you know," I said.

We parted company at the back of the gallery. He went off to the left and I to the right where I knew the "Joyce Room" was. The paintings were even worse than I remembered. It wasn't just the subject matter, which was one damn duck after another; the execution was clumsy and amateurish. Karen's little drawings were a thousand times better and I didn't think that was just fatherly pride.

But I hadn't come back here to look at the paintings. I'd come to look at the frames and I wasn't surprised at what I saw. They were all aluminum, just like the ones in front. On the duck paintings they looked okay and besides, they were all by the same artist. But on the paintings in front they didn't work. It was the thing that had bothered me. I didn't know any more about framing than I did about painting but I instinctively felt the European paintings should have been framed in wood. And in different woods. Why would various artists have their paintings framed exactly alike? I supposed that they could have gone through the same dealer who had them framed but that still didn't explain why they were done in aluminum and not wood of some type. I needed to talk to somebody about this but not anybody in this gallery.

I suspected that the Mayers had seen both Baker children before I showed them the pictures. George had been more obvious about Pat than Joyce had, but her denial had come too quickly. Why were they hiding the truth? Did these damn frames have anything to do with Pat's disappearance? I stepped closer to one of the paintings and reached out to touch the frame.

"Want to touch the fuzzy wuzzy?" came Wayne's voice.

I jumped up and turned around forcing a laugh. "You've got to stop coming up on me like that, Wayne."

He wasn't smiling. "You wanted to see me?"

"Yes." I took out the picture and handed it to him. "Do you recognize this boy?"

He kept his head bent over the picture. "No, I've never seen him." He handed it back to me, his eyes focusing to the right of my nose so I couldn't look into them.

"You know Doug Fanner?"

"Sure."

"When's the last time you saw him?"

"Let's see." He gazed up at the ceiling, his head cocked to one side. "Maybe last week some time."

"What do you think of him?"

"I don't know. He's all right."

"Did you ever see his paintings?"

"Once."

"And?"

"Not bad."

"Has he ever had a show?"

He snorted. "Of course not. Weren't you listening earlier?"

"You mean Doug Fanner doesn't know the right people?"

"You got it."

"How about Robert Sheedy? Do you like his work?"

Something shifted in his eyes. "Hey, is Pat related to him?" The color drained from his face. "Oh, Christ."

He realized I hadn't mentioned Patrick's name. "Okay, Wayne, why don't you tell me about it."

"Holy Christ. Look, George'll kill me."

"A lot worse than that's going to happen to you if you don't talk. This boy has been missing for weeks and he's the brother of the girl who was murdered on Sunday."

"No shit? Look, don't go getting funny ideas, okay? George

told me to keep my mouth shut because the kid was underage and didn't have papers."

"You mean he *did* work here?"

"Sure. Listen, you don't have to tell George I blew it, do you? You might think he's a nice easygoing guy but when he gets crossed, watch out. He'd never believe I slipped."

"When did Patrick work here?"

"He started at the beginning of March. He was a good little worker and then one day, about two weeks ago, he just didn't show up." He shrugged. "We didn't think much of it. Kids come and go."

I took out the picture of Jennifer. "Did you ever see her?"

He studied it. "No, I don't think so. That the sister? The one who got killed?"

"Yes."

"No, I don't think I ever saw her." He handed me back the picture. "You going to tell George?"

"Not unless I have to."

"What's that mean?" He jutted out his fleshy lower lip like a baby about to cry.

"It means I'm not interested in whether or not gallery owners are hiring underage kids. It depends where this information leads me. For now your secret is safe with me. Is there anything else I should know?"

He scratched his head trying to act like the shit-kicker he wasn't. "Can't think of anything."

I didn't bother to tell him to let me know if he thought of anything because I knew he wouldn't. We left the Joyce Room together and he walked me through the gallery to the door.

"Listen, thanks," he said.

"Yeah."

The rain was coming down in a more serious fashion but it wasn't pouring yet. I could have run up to the house for an umbrella but I didn't want to bother. I trotted down Thompson to Prince, turned left and made it over to West Broadway where I took a right. The Sarah Barber Gallery was in the middle of the block. But before I got near I could see that there were three police cars in the area.

When I got to the gallery Skelly was standing in the doorway.

I called to him. "What's up?"

He walked over to me, his Zapata mustache sleek with rain. "It's your friend Doug Fanner," he said.

"What about him?"

Skelly said, "Deader than a doornail." And then he laughed.

17

I'd been surprised at Skelly's laughter but as soon as I saw Doug Fanner I understood why. "Deader than a doornail," Skelly had said, and then he'd laughed at his own unconscious joke.

There were two huge rooms in the Sarah Barber Gallery and Doug's body was in the second one. Someone had hung him on the wall where a painting had been and then hammered huge nails through his hands and into the paintings on either side of him. He was in a Christlike pose and I wondered if that had any significance. But I suppose when your arms are outstretched and nailed, your head automatically hangs down. At least his feet weren't crossed or nailed. The top of his head was bloody and was the same kind of mess Jennifer Baker's had been. Blood covered his palms and ran down his arms and over the frames. Stuffed into his belt was a gun. The handle looked familiar.

"Cute, huh?" Skelly said.

"Very."

"Any ideas?"

"I think the gun is mine."

He arched an eyebrow.

"I told you somebody got it when I was knocked out in my hall." I moved closer to Fanner and pointed to the handle. "See that mark? Mine has the same mark."

"You report it?"

"No. I forgot."

"Jesus, Fortune."

"I know, I know."

"Stupid," Skelly said.

"Right."

"Hey, Fitzhugh. You finished with the pictures?"

"All done, Skelly."

"Is the M.E. here yet?"

"Not yet."

Skelly said to me, "Goddamn M.E. takes his goddamn time. Well, he doesn't need to examine the gun." He took a handkerchief from his pocket and pulled the gun from Fanner's belt. "Moss," he called to a cop, "dust this; then get it to ballistics." He gave the gun to the young policeman; then he turned back to me. "Far as I can see this bozo wasn't shot. And it doesn't look like his head was made into meatloaf with the gun either. Lucky for you."

"What was used?" I asked.

"Beats me. Nothing around here. Looks like the same kind of wound the Baker kid had."

"How'd he get in here?"

"Don't know. No forced entry. Mrs. Barber, the lady who owns this joint, said he used to work for her, so maybe he had a key but there were no keys on him."

I was surprised. I thought we'd find a key to every place in the neighborhood. "No keys at all?"

"No. Nothing in his pockets."

"So whoever killed him took his keys."

"Or he didn't have any."

"There were no keys in his apartment," I said.

"You sure?"

"Positive. Who found him?"

"The owner."

"Where is she?"

"In her office."

"Can I talk to her?"

"What about?"

"Art," I said.

"You shucking me, Fortune?"

"No. I got an idea and I want to check it out."

"An idea about this murder?" Skelly asked hopefully.

"Not exactly."

Skelly pulled on his mustache with both hands. Then he said, "You know, if there's one thing I hate it's 'not exactly.' I never know what that means. Either you do or you don't."

"Okay, then I don't. I want to ask her about something else."

"What?"

"I don't want to waste your time."

"What? I said."

"Frames."

"Frames?"

"Yeah, frames that go around paintings."

"You becoming an art collector or something?"

"No."

"So what do you want to know about frames?"

"Look, Skelly, what do you care?"

"I care because I don't trust you. Frames. You want to hear about frames I'll tell you about frames. 1971 Henderson frames Balkian for first degree."

"I'm not interested in that kind of frame. I just want to ask the woman one simple question about picture frames."

"You never asked anybody one question in your life. Ahh, go ahead. What do I care? I don't have time to waste with this shit."

"Right. Where's the office."

He pointed to a blue door in the back. I started to go and he called to me. I stopped.

"What I want to know is, you have any ideas what kind of nut case would hang a guy up on a wall like this?"

"An artist," I said and walked to the blue door.

The door was opened by a cop. "Yeah?"

"Skelly sent me. I'm going to talk to the lady."

He eyed me suspiciously, then stepped back to let me by. He started to come in.

"Alone," I said.

"Yeah?"

"Yeah."

He didn't like it but he left.

Sarah Barber was sitting in a brown Eames chair. She was a small woman with short ginger hair. Round tinted glasses sat on the bridge of a small pug nose and her face played host to a light sprinkling of freckles. She wore a tan jacket, dark brown pleated pants, a cream-colored shirt and a brown and yellow polka-dot bow tie. On her feet were brown and white spectators. Rings were on eight of her ten fingers. She was about thirty-five and looked like a woman who'd never seen violent death before. Not many had.

"Mrs. Barber?"

She looked up at me but said nothing.

"I'm Fortune Fanelli, a private investigator, and I'd like to ask you some questions."

"I told the other one everything I know."

She had a great voice, sultry, like a radio voice from the forties.

"It's not about the . . . the murder." I felt clumsy even mentioning it. "It's about frames."

She looked at me quizzically.

"Picture frames."

"I don't sell frames," she said definitely.

"I know. I just want to ask you a question."

"What is it?"

"Do artists frame their own paintings or do the galleries do it?"

She waited a moment, then took off her glasses. Her eyes were gray. She took a lace handkerchief from her inside pocket and began wiping the glasses. "Mr. Farelli . . ."

"Fanelli," I corrected.

"Mr. Fanelli, I can't see what this has to do with anything. Haven't you got any sense of decorum? A man was killed in here. In *my* gallery. And you want to talk about frames. I guess life is cheap to you people."

I felt a sting of irritation. "I don't know who you mean

by 'you people' but life is *not* cheap to me. If it was, I wouldn't be trying to find out...Let's skip that. Would you please answer the question?"

She put her glasses back on. "I knew him, you know."

Obviously she wanted to talk after all. "He worked for you, I understand."

Her laughter had a sarcastic ring to it. "I suppose you could put it that way."

"I've heard from other people that he—"

"You've heard what?" she interrupted, a hint of alarm in that silky voice.

I had been going to say that I'd heard Fanner wasn't much of a worker but her reaction made me change it, take a risk. "That you and he were very...close friends."

"Who told you that?" Her face stained red, the cheeks like fall apples.

I took another shot in the dark. "Wayne Morrison."

"That bastard." She jumped up and stormed across the room to a desk where she snatched up a crumpled pack of Pall Malls. After watching her make several tries with a box of wooden matches, I took them from her and lit her cigarette. She didn't thank me.

"Why is Morrison a bastard?" I asked.

"He's scum," she said.

"Okay, I'll buy that, but why?"

"Look, I think you'd better go, Mr. Farelli."

I didn't correct her this time and I ignored her suggestion that I leave. "Why don't you tell me about you and Doug?"

"Why should I?"

"Because you'll feel better."

She considered this, blew a cloud of smoke over her head, then paced the room twice. "Doug Fanner and I were once lovers." She stuck out her chin as if to defy me. "Well, at least I thought we were."

I wondered how you could think something like that if it wasn't true. "What do you mean?"

"I was in love with him but he was just using me. So we

were lovers in the sexual sense but that was all. To be real lovers you both have to feel the same way, don't you think?"

"Yes, I do."

"What an ass I was. And Morrison put him up to it, too."

"Put him up to it?"

"Oh, God," she said, "it's so humiliating." She flopped into the Eames chair again.

I pulled out the white plastic desk chair, turned it around to face her and sat down. "Go on."

She said, "I can't believe he's dead. I wished him dead so many times and now he is." Her eyes filled and she took out the handkerchief again.

This might have been a good ploy, to throw me off the track, had she killed him, but I didn't think she had. Getting Fanner up on the wall would have been difficult for a woman her size. Still, it was possible. I'd have to stay open. "Why'd you wish him dead?"

"Because he made a fool of me. He and Morrison. I thought Doug loved me and then I found out what he really wanted."

"And what was that?"

"A show. I didn't even know he was a painter. If I had I might have been more cautious. We'd been together two months and then he sprang it on me. He wanted a show for himself and Morrison. Well, God, if you could see their work." She shook her head in despair.

"I've seen some of Fanner's."

"Morrison is worse. I couldn't give them a show. I would have lost all my credibility. Well, I tried to get out of it diplomatically. I didn't want to hurt Doug." She laughed in an angry spasm. "What a joke. I told him I was booked for years ahead but then he found my schedule and confronted me with it. I made all sorts of excuses and finally I just had to tell him the truth. I was as gentle as possible. But he became enraged and then he told me that he'd never loved me, that it had all been Wayne's idea...to soften me up. Oh, God." She stubbed out her cigarette in an ashtray shaped like a pelican.

I said, "I'm sorry you were hurt, Mrs. Barber."

She looked surprised that anyone would care and tried to smile but couldn't.

"Do you think Wayne killed Doug?" I asked.

"Why would he?"

"I don't know. But Morrison told me he'd seen Doug's work only once. Why would he say that if what you say is true."

"Are you doubting my story, Mr. Farelli?"

"No, it was just a figure of speech. What do you think of the Eurogallery, Mrs. Barber?"

"It's all right. Occasionally they have some very nice work. George and Joyce Mayer are idiots, however. They might as well be in lingerie for all they know about art. They're strictly business people. We all are to some extent, but some of us care about art. They don't. If you'd ever seen her duck paintings you'd know what I mean."

"I have," I said. "Mrs. Barber, the question I came in here to ask you was about frames. Have you ever noticed anything funny about the frames in the Eurogallery?"

"I didn't mean to give the impression that I go there all the time. In fact, I don't think I've been in there for over a year. Not since . . . well, since everything happened with Doug."

"And when you went in there you didn't notice anything about the frames?"

"No, I don't think so. What do you mean? Wait a minute, you asked me if the artists framed their own paintings or the gallery owners did?"

"That's right."

She said, "Some galleries frame their artists' paintings; some don't. I always leave it up to the artist."

"There are many ways of framing, aren't there? I mean, every artist wouldn't frame his paintings the same way?"

"No."

"How are most oils framed?"

"How?"

"Wood, plastic, aluminum?"

"Oh, I see. Oils are usually framed in wood or something that looks like wood, depending on the quality of the painting."

"But not aluminum."

She wrinkled her nose in distaste. "That would be very unaesthetic."

"Can you think of any reason why anyone would frame an oil in aluminum?"

"Only one; bad taste."

I stood up. "Thank you, Mrs. Barber, you've been very helpful."

"Are you going to tell that detective with the mustache about Doug and me?" She lit another cigarette.

"I think *you* should. These things have a way of getting out. You wouldn't want it to look like you were hiding something."

"No, I suppose not."

"One more thing," I said. I showed her the pictures of Patrick and Jennifer. She said she'd never seen either of them. I believed her.

"Poor Doug," she sighed, "I can't believe he's dead. And he never had a show." Her face changed, everything drooping downward.

"Not many of us do," I said.

"How right you are, Mr. Farelli, how very right you are."

I said good-bye and left her sitting in her chair blowing smoke into the air and thinking about her dead ex-lover and his nonexistent show.

Skelly was still in the front room, so I told him Mrs. Barber wanted to talk to him. He told me to be available and I said I wasn't going to Acapulco for at least an hour.

The rain had stopped, leaving the smell of wet dog in the air. Sometimes I toyed with the idea of moving to the country, getting that fresh country air, never having to worry that my kids might get mugged or that I might be sapped. But what would I do there? I knew I'd go crazy in two weeks. I was a city person. Always had been, always would be. Wet-dog air was okay by me.

It was one o'clock and my stomach was sending me signals to feed it. I went over to Angie's, sat at the counter and ordered a bowl of minestrone and a Coke. Tucci, the bookie, was moving from table to table picking up bets from his regulars. The place was jammed and a kid played a video game in the corner like his life depended on it. Maybe it did.

I thought about Fanner and how he'd died and why. I didn't think he killed Jennifer because the same M.O. was used on him. Besides, why would he have been killed if he'd been the original killer? The fact that his keys were missing seemed important. Maybe Jennifer's killer had borrowed Doug's keys and Doug knew it. And maybe Doug also knew who'd sapped me and told me to lay off. The man who knew too much. Would Wayne Morrison kill his buddy? I thought he might. It was the hanging him up on the wall that made me think so. I'd flippantly said to Skelly that an artist had done it but when I thought about it it wasn't so farfetched. A frustrated artist. If Doug knew about the murder, that was plenty of reason to get him out of the way. So why didn't I just tell Skelly and go on about my business of finding Patrick?

Because Patrick's disappearance fit in with all this and I didn't know how. And then there was the thing with the picture frames. Something was fishy with them. Patrick's disappearance, Jennifer's murder, Doug's murder and the picture frames were all of a piece, I was sure. And I was beginning to think that there was less and less chance that I was going to find Patrick Baker alive. The thought put me off my feed and I pushed my unfinished bowl of soup aside. Angie was on me like a piranha.

"Why ain't you eatin', Fortune? Soup bad?"

"No, 'course not, Angie. Soup's great. I'm just, I don't know, not as hungry as I thought."

She leaned over and whispered conspiratorially. "I heard," she said. "Fanner all hung up like that. He was a bum but I mean." She shook her head, long silver earrings twirling. "It's funny, you was just askin' about him this A.M. You didn't do it, did you, Fortune?" She laughed and it sounded like a lot of ice cubes falling.

"Not my style." I stood up and she wrote out my check. As I was fishing in my pocket for money she whispered in my ear again.

"Sorry about Yolanda." She tsked twice. "Connie know yet?"

I looked into her eyes, which were almost obliterated by the lashes. "If *you* know, she might. I'm going over there now."

"Anything I can do, Fortune, you let me know, huh?"

I thanked her and went to the phone on the wall. I looked up the number of the Chambers School and dialed it. I told the woman who answered that I was the uncle of a student I had to pick up and I didn't know what time the school let out. She told me two-thirty and then realized she shouldn't have and was screaming "What student?" when I hung up. I didn't have a whole lot of time but I had to see my mother before I did anything else.

There were two customers in the store when I went in but I didn't know either of them. Bruno growled at me as I sat in one of the straight-backed wooden chairs that had been there as long as I could remember and waited, praying nobody else would come in for a while. Nobody did.

When we were alone my mother finally looked at me and I knew she knew.

"Who told you?" I asked.

She shrugged. "Who knows? Everybody."

I went to her and put my arms around her. She laid her head on my shoulder. "I'm sorry, Mama."

"Everybody's sorry. What I want to know is why Yolanda has to take off her clothes all the time?" She looked at me, her brown eyes hurt, scarred.

"I don't know." I wondered where Yolanda had done it this time but didn't want to put Mama through the pain of telling me. The stripping was almost more humiliating than the drunkenness to my mother. The idea of her daughter exposing her body to strangers was anathema to her. I didn't like it much myself.

She extricated herself from my embrace and went back to her work, making lamb chops.

"You going to go see her, Mama?"

She sighed, her shoulders heaving. "I go, I go."

"Want me to go with you?"

"We see."

I looked at my watch. "I have to be somewhere now," I said.

She stopped stripping fat and turned to look at me. "You okay?"

"I'm fine." I leaned down and kissed her cheek. "Try not to worry, Mama."

She looked at me like I was crazy. I couldn't blame her. I said good-bye and left the store. As Sam said, sometimes life just sucked.

18

The Chambers School was in the East Seventies. It was a
brick structure built in the thirties, I guessed. A tall iron fence
surrounded it and I stood waiting to the left of the gate. I felt
a little bit like Woody Allen watching the young girls come
out of the school and it made me uncomfortable. I'd never
understood the interest some men have in younger women,
sometimes girls. Nothing would bore me more than to spend
an evening with somebody who didn't know who Betty Grable
was or who thought Phil Rizzuto had worked for the Money
Store all his life. I wanted a peer. How old was Cassie? I
wondered. My guess was she was somewhere between thirty
and forty. I hoped she was closer to forty, because even thirty
was too young for me. I'd been through my thirties and I didn't
want to go through them again.

I almost missed Price Allen as she came through the gate
because her hair was loose, more like the picture, but she
looked much older. Maybe seeing death had aged her. She
wore a white cotton turtleneck with little roses on it and a gray
corduroy skirt. The same blue Adidas I'd seen her in two days
before were on her feet. Tennis socks with red tassels in back
hung over the sneakers. I walked up to her.

"Excuse me," I said.

She sucked in her breath, startled to see me.

"I'd like to talk to you for a minute, Price."

She glanced around her as if she were looking for someone. "What do you want? Who are you, anyway? How do you know my name?"

"Which question do you want me to answer first?" I said.

"None. Leave me alone." She started to walk away, her books wrapped in her arms and held tight against her chest like a shield.

I followed and caught up with her. "Look, Price, I'm a private investigator and I'm trying to find out who killed your friend Jennifer."

"I don't know what you're talking about," she said, and kept walking.

I dug out the camp picture and thrust it in front of her. She stopped abruptly then whirled around to face me. Her face had drained of color, her blue eyes lit with apprehension. "Where'd you get that?"

"From Jennifer's mother," I said.

She said, "Oh, God," and her head dropped, her chin resting on the edge of her books. "I'm in so much trouble already."

"I don't want to get you in trouble, Price. I just want to talk. Can we go somewhere for a Coke or something?"

"I can't go anywhere. I'm grounded for the rest of the year. I have to go right home."

"Are you grounded because of what happened to Jennifer?"

"In a way. I wasn't supposed to be down there. I really have to get home now," she said and started walking.

"Let's talk while we walk, okay?"

She didn't answer me but she didn't say no either. I walked next to her. "Why weren't you supposed to be in SoHo, Price?"

"My *mo–ther*." She drew out the word with distaste. "She thinks anyplace below Sixtieth Street is a hellhole. I've always been forbidden to go down to the Village or around there."

"So why did you go?"

She looked at me suspiciously. "I thought you knew."

"I only know that you and Jennie went to camp together."

"I don't see how talking to me is going to help. I think you'd better go." She quickened her pace and I grabbed her arm. Her books fell to the sidewalk. "Oh, God, now look what you made me do."

I bent down to help her pick them up and my face was only inches away from hers. Softly I said, "You lied to the police, Price. You could get into a lot of trouble for that."

"My mother made me," she said.

We stood up and I put a book of Millay's poetry on top of the pile she held. "Why?"

"Because she didn't want me involved, why do you think? She said admitting I knew Jennie wasn't going to bring her back to life and she was right."

"Yes, she's right about that, but you might be able to help find her murderer."

"How?"

"By telling me everything you know. Like why you went down there to meet her. You did, didn't you?"

She began to walk again. "Yes. She called me the day before and told me she'd left home. The thing was, we weren't really friends, hadn't ever been. I wondered why she called me and then she let me have it." Remembering, her face seemed to wilt like an old bouquet.

"Have what?"

"Jennifer could be mean. I guess I shouldn't say that about a dead person, but it's true. She liked picking on people."

"And she picked on you," I supplied.

She turned away and nodded, ashamed to have been a victim.

"How did she pick on you, Price?" I asked gently.

"Oh, you know, she said I was a nerd because I never did anything bad. She said I was a mama's baby. I guess it's true. Anyway, she was always trying to get me to do stuff."

"Like what?"

"I don't know, just stuff."

"To smoke pot?" I asked.

"Yeah, like that."

"And did you?"

She didn't answer.

"I'm not going to tell your mother, Price."

"How do I know?" She looked at me, her eyes pleading for understanding.

"You don't. You'll just have to believe me because if you don't talk to me you'll have to talk to the police again and I can't guarantee what they'll tell your mother."

"That's blackmail," she said astutely.

I felt a wave of shame. "You're right," I said. "But I don't have any choice. So, come on, tell me about the pot."

We were at the corner of Seventy-ninth and Madison and Price started to cross the avenue.

"Where do you live?" I asked. I wanted to know how much time I had.

"Seventy-ninth and York."

A fair amount but not a lot. "The pot," I urged.

"You swear you won't tell my mother? She'd ground me forever if she found out."

"I promise."

"Well, Jennie had some at camp and I tried it."

"And?"

She shrugged. "And I got high. But while I was high I guess I said a lot of stuff I wouldn't ordinarily have said."

"Like what?"

"I said I'd take cocaine if she had it. I guess I was trying to be a big shot. After I came down I was scared because I didn't really want to. But I guess Jennie never forgot it."

"Is that why she called you? Did she have some cocaine?"

"Yes."

"Tell me exactly what she said to you."

"She said she had some good cocaine and that it was time I tried it. I felt like an awful fool. I didn't want to but I said I would."

"Did she say where she got it?" I asked.

"Some man. I think what she said was that she'd met this neat older guy and she was going to have all the cocaine she wanted and lots and lots of money."

I thought of Wayne. "Did she mention his name?"

She screwed up her face, thinking. "No, I don't remember any names."

"How about the name Wayne? Does that sound familiar?"

"No. She didn't mention any names."

I said, "So you told her you'd meet her. Where?"

"We were supposed to meet in front of a gallery. The Eurogallery across the street from where...where, you know."

I nodded.

"At four in the afternoon. We were so stupid. We should have left when she didn't show. But Jimmy was determined."

"Your boyfriend. The boy who was with you?"

"My *ex*-boyfriend," she said. "I never want to see him again." She pressed her lips together in determination. "The whole thing is his fault. I wasn't going to go. I mean, I told her I would, just to get her off the phone, but I really didn't plan to go. And then I told Jimmy about it and he got all excited. He sounded just like Jennifer. He said we never did anything exciting and we should meet her."

We'd reached York Avenue. I stopped walking. "So you went down to SoHo, waited in front of the Eurogallery and then what?"

"And then nothing. We walked around, had a cup of cappuccino, looked into the store windows and then...Oh, God." Her eyes clouded with the memory of seeing Jennifer in the window. "I had to lie. I thought I'd get out of it and my mother wouldn't ever know. And my father, God! When he gets back from Europe it's going to be even worse. The thing is I see now why they didn't want me going down there. I never will again but I'm not going to tell them that. I mean, I'll have to say I won't but I don't want them to know they were right all along."

"Naturally," I said.

"Do you live down there?" she asked as if SoHo were truly another planet.

"Yes, right down the street from the Eurogallery."

She shuddered. "That must be awful."

"I manage," I said.

"Hey, look, I have to get going. The Hag will give me hell if I'm not home before three twenty-five."

I didn't need to ask who The Hag was and I wondered if Sam and Karen had a nice name like that for me. I thanked Price, assured her her secret was safe with me and watched her as she disappeared into a high-rise on York.

As I walked back toward the subway it all started to fit. Wayne had gotten involved with Jennifer, fed her cocaine and promised her more, plus money. Then somehow Jennifer had discovered something he didn't want her to know, so he'd had to kill her. But what had she found out? I was convinced that the Eurogallery was a front for something, maybe drug dealing. Was that what Jennifer had discovered? Or something else? Was it where her brother was? Or that he was dead . . . murdered?

And what about Fanner? Maybe he'd found out about Jennie's murder, having lent Wayne his key to The Sweatshop Boutique, and he had to be eliminated, too.

I knew I should call Skelly and tell him what I had but I also knew I wasn't going to. Not yet. Wayne would stay on hold for a bit. I didn't think he was going to kill anyone else at the moment and I had to get into the Eurogallery when no one was there. I'd do it tonight, after midnight. After my dinner with Cassie Bloomfield. And Zelda. And Sam and Karen. Ah, romance.

Back downtown, on the planet SoHo, I stopped at Dean and DeLuca, the most expensive food store around, and the most beautiful and delicious, and bought a half-pound of Ligurian sun-dried tomatoes. They were eighteen dollars a pound. I was going to use them for an appetizer with Brie on Bremen crackers. It was an extravagance but I wanted to impress her. I didn't even try to pretend to myself that there was any other reason.

I had my mother cut me some special veal chops, which I would saute with lemon and butter. She wanted to know if my neighbor was pretty and I said she was. Mama's eyes had a moment of brightening, like they'd been infused with light, but they faded back to sadness again when I had to say no, she wasn't Italian.

At the Robbers I picked up broccoli, watercress and some potatoes, which I'd pan-fry in oil and butter. I didn't see Meryl Streep and I didn't care. Vesuvio supplied me with bread sticks and pepper twists. I stopped at SoHo Wines and bought a bottle of Burgundy. Cassie would be the only one drinking unless Zelda was a drinker! I hoped my not drinking wouldn't put Cassie off. Some women found it intimidating. I felt she wouldn't. Wishful thinking?

It was after five when I got up to my apartment. The kids were in their rooms doing homework. I took a quick shower, dressed in gray slacks and a blue shirt, changed to tan slacks and a cream-colored shirt, put the gray slacks back on with a pink shirt, ended with the blue shirt and tweed pants, then started my preparations. When Cassie and Zelda arrived, everything was ready and the Fanelli family was calm and collected. Like hell!

But it all went off without a hitch until I sent Sam to my room for some cough drops for Zelda who was developing a cold. Before that everybody seemed to get along, and Karen especially took to Zelda. Cassie was terrific with my kids. She treated them like adults and I could see that they both liked her. Dinner was, naturally, wonderful and Cassie drank two glasses of wine and said nothing about being the only drinker. Zelda passed on the Burgundy.

It was during coffee that the kid started coughing and that's when I sent Sam to my room. He didn't come back for a very long time and then when he did his face was ashen as if he'd been sick or heard some terrible news.

"What's wrong, Sam?" I said, taking the cough drops from him.

"Nothing."

"You look awful," Karen said.

"Thanks," he said.

"No, really, Sam," she went on, "what happened? You were gone forever."

"Nothing happened," he snarled. "Drop it, okay?"

I handed Zelda a cough drop. "Just suck on it, honey. Don't chew it."

Zelda said haughtily, "I know about cough drops, Mr. Fanelli."

"Sometimes you forget, Zel," Cassie said.

Karen said, "Did you get sick, Sam?"

He threw down his napkin and stormed from the room. We heard his door slam.

"I just wanted to help him," Karen said.

"Sure, honey," I said and patted her hand. "I'll just go see what's up. Will you excuse me?"

They both said they would. I knocked on Sam's door and there was no answer. I knocked a little harder and said, "Sam, it's me. I want to talk with you."

"Come on in," he said, meaning anything but.

He was lying on his bed, his arms under his head. He still looked sick but now there was a frightened glaze to his eyes. I sat on the edge of his bed.

"What's up, sport?"

"Nothing, Dad."

"Come on. You're perfectly normal, laughing, talking, even scarfing down the food, and you leave the room on an errand, are gone ten minutes for something that, tops, might have taken a minute, and you come back looking like you'd seen Darth Vader in my bedroom or something. So don't tell me it's nothing."

He shrugged.

"Sam, something happened in those ten minutes you were gone. Now what was it?"

"I can't tell you. Okay, Dad?"

"No, it's not okay. Something happened in my house and I want to know what it was."

"Jesus, can't you stop playing detective for five minutes?"

"No."

We stared at each other for a few seconds. Then I could see anger and fear in his eyes. I reached out to touch him and he rolled away from me onto his stomach.

"Sam," I said softly, "please tell me what's wrong." I put my hand on his back and kept it there until he slowly rolled over to face me again. He looked as though his world had ended. I brushed the hair back from his forehead.

"Whatever it is, Sam, we can work it out."

He shook his head.

"What happened when you went to my room?" I tried to picture my room and I saw the top of my bureau where the cough drops had been. On the right was a small square box where I kept collar stays and a few old cuff links I never used. On the left was a bank in the shape of a cow that Karen had given me for Christmas one year. Next to that was my change, keys, a handkerchief. And beside those things were the postcards Patrick had sent and the pictures. One of Jennie and her friends at camp and one of Patrick.

"Sam," I said, "did you see something in my room, on my bureau?"

He closed his eyes and turned his head away from me. I turned it back.

"Open your eyes." I demanded gently.

He did.

"Sam, was it the pictures?" I couldn't understand what they could mean to him but it was the only thing that made sense.

Almost imperceptibly he nodded.

"You've seen someone in the pictures before?"

"Yes," he whispered.

"Who?"

"The boy."

"Where?"

"Oh, Dad, I feel so crummy."

My heart was socking the wall of my chest. "What do you mean, Sam? Where have you seen that boy before?"

He moved up on the bed so that his head and neck were against the wall. From his pocket he took a handkerchief that looked like it hadn't been washed in the last decade and blew his nose. Then he said, "Dad, that boy...that boy in the picture is the one you're looking for, isn't he?"

"Yes. Patrick Baker."

"I saw him.... Jesus, Dad, you're going to be so mad."

"Sam, I won't be mad. Just tell me where you've seen Patrick. Please. This is serious."

"I know. I know it is. I saw him in another picture." His face flushed and he turned away from me again.

I was beginning to feel queasy, like I was in a rocking boat. "What picture?"

He kept his head turned away. "I know you're going to be disgusted with me, but all these guys were looking and, God, they let me look, too. I mean, mostly they don't let me hang around with them or anything. They call me a runt even though we're all about the same age. So, when they said I could see the pictures...I wanted to be like the other guys, Dad.... You know how it is?"

I squeezed his shoulder. "Yeah, I know. It's okay. Sam, was what you saw a pornographic picture?"

He nodded and faced me. "It was disgusting. I mean, they were just kids."

"Kiddie porn," I said.

"Yeah, I guess."

"And the picture you saw was of Patrick?"

"Patrick and a girl. She looked even younger than him."

Now I was starting to feel furious. "You're sure it was him?"

"You can't mistake him, Dad."

That was true. His angelic face was easily identifiable. "When did you see it?"

"Yesterday."

I hoped it meant that Patrick was still alive but, of course, the picture could have been taken any time since his disappearance. Or his abduction. I couldn't believe he'd be doing this of his own volition.

"Who had the picture, Sam?"

"Ah, Dad, he wouldn't know where the kid is."

"We don't know that. Who?"

"A guy from the neighborhood but, Dad, come on. He bought them from another guy."

"Okay. Who was the seller, then?"

"Some guy named Mat the Rat."

I knew the creep. He lived down around Canal but I didn't know where. He was a two-bit hustler into petty thievery, selling pot, making book. And now kiddie porn. I couldn't feature him kidnapping a kid but maybe he knew where the pictures were made.

"Sam," I said, "you want to help?"

He sat up straighter. "Sure."

"I want you to find Nick Scola and bring him here."

"Nick? I thought you hated his guts."

"I'm trying to learn to love my neighbor," I said. "So go find Nick, okay? Don't tell him anything except that I need him." I stood up. "And when you get him here don't bring him into the kitchen. Just have him wait in the hall by the door; then come tell me."

He swung his legs over the side of the bed and sat on the edge. "Are you mad at me, Dad?"

"No, I'm not mad. I've looked at pornography myself in my lifetime."

"That kind?"

"Only when I was on the force. But I've looked at grown-up porn on my own. It's pretty gross."

"Yeah, I guess." He stood up.

I put my arm around him. "Thanks for telling me, sport."

"Thanks for not being mad."

We parted ways in the hall. He left the apartment to find Nick and I went back to the dining room. Karen and Cassie had cleared the table and were having coffee in the dining room. Zelda was looking at television. We sat around for about fifteen minutes and then Sam appeared in the doorway. I excused myself again.

Nick was waiting in the hall. I thanked Sam and told him to keep the women company.

"You know Mat the Rat?"

"Sure."

"Can you find him?"

"Why not?"

"That's what I'm asking you, Nick." I felt myself starting to lose my temper already. He looked bleary-eyed, as if he'd been drinking for hours. "You sober?"

"I had a couple. I needed it, Fortune," he said apologetically. "Look, I can find him. Whatcha want him for?"

I debated whether I should tell him or not and then I remembered there was a code among crooks. Not the old one where they wouldn't sing about each other and all that stuff, but a new one. Better. Most bums didn't like other bums who raped or hurt kids. I told him.

He slammed a fist into his palm. "The fucker. You want I should bust him up?"

"Not unless you have to. I want you to find out where he got those pictures. If he needs a little persuasion that's okay. But I want him able to talk."

"You got it, Fortune."

I handed him a ten. "There's another one when you get the info."

"Don't worry, I'll get him." He walked to the door and opened it, then turned. "And thanks, Fortune."

I knew he meant for trusting him. "Get going," I said and gave him a three-finger salute. He smiled and I returned it.

If I could get Mat the Rat to tell me where he got the pictures I might be able to find Patrick. I started down the hallway, then stopped. Could Wayne Morrison actually have sold Patrick to some kiddie-porn ring? If he was capable of murder, then he was capable of anything. But if Pat had found out something, why had Wayne let him live? Knowledge kills, Patrick had written to Jennie. Had he meant knowledge of Sheedy's homosexuality? I didn't think so. Patrick Baker had found out something that was going on at the Eurogallery and Morrison had discovered the kid knew. Then the same thing had happened with Jennifer. If I could find out what was going on there I'd have my wedge and I could nail Morrison. I blanched at the awful image.

I looked at my watch. Quarter to nine. I hoped Nick could find Mat the Rat soon. By two o'clock I'd be inside the Eurogallery and God only knew what I'd find there.

19

I sat in Cassie's living room while she put Zelda to bed. Most of the cartons were gone but there were still some stacked against a wall. The furniture was in good taste but shabby, as if she'd picked up pieces here and there: divorce furniture. I'd seen it in other homes. It had been different when Elaine left me; she hadn't taken anything, as though she wanted no reminders at all. Once I'd visited her at her apartment and I noticed she'd even changed her brand of soap and toothpaste. I was completely expunged from her life.

"Well," she said, coming into the room, "she's finally quiet. Can I get you anything?"

"No, thanks. How long've you been divorced?"

"Not long, eight months." She sat across from me on the blue couch. "You?"

"Seven years."

"Then you're used to it."

"Kind of. You're not?"

"No." She smoothed down her pale yellow skirt.

"Maybe you don't want to talk about it."

"I don't mind." She looked at me, her eyes like two burned-out stars.

"You got a lousy deal, huh?"

She nodded. "My married name was Bertino. I was married to Al Bertino, the film director."

I'd seen all of his pictures. I thought he was good. I tried to remember if I'd read anything about him, and some vague gossip about him and a movie star filtered back through pages of print. I waited for her to go on. Finally she did.

"He dumped me for Donna Dukes."

"He must have been crazy," I said.

She smiled and I felt it against my cheeks, like a caress.

"Thanks," she said. "He is a little crazy but not because of that. Anyway, he doesn't remember much about child support so Zel and I are pretty much on our own."

"That guy must have millions," I said angrily.

"At least two," she said.

"And he won't give you child support?"

"He forgets."

I wondered if she was defending him, if she still loved him. I asked. "You still love the guy?"

She answered without deliberation. "No, not anymore."

"How long were you married?"

"Eight years." She lit a Marlboro. "I had Zelda when I was thirty-two."

I mentally calculated that that would make her about thirty-eight. Good enough. But would someone who'd been married to Al Bertino be interested in me?

I said, "I guess you've had a pretty exciting life."

"I suppose...if you call cocaine parties and malicious gossip and playing power games exciting."

"Actually, I was thinking about making movies."

"Making a movie is very boring. Mostly you wait."

"For what?"

"The light to be right, the sound to be perfect, the star to be sane, the weather to be sunny or not, the director not to be stoned, the makeup person to be...oh, just everything. You wait and wait and wait."

"You're right; that doesn't sound very exciting, especially if you're not directly involved."

She said, "Oh, but I was. Not that anyone would know it. Al didn't see any reason to give me credit, but I basically wrote his last two pictures. That's what I do. I'm a writer."

I liked that. "Screenwriter?"

"That and other things. I do articles, too. If I ever get settled I'm going to go back to a novel I started years ago. Al said it was lousy but I'm not so sure."

"He sounds like a real supportive guy."

"He's just about perfect," she said sardonically. "But I guess I wanted that kind of pain then. I don't anymore. What about your ex-wife? What was she like?"

I didn't feel like talking about Elaine but I knew it wasn't fair since she'd told me about Al. So I told her. Once I got going I couldn't seem to stop. I went on for a long time. When I was finished my mouth was dry.

"You have any Coke...to drink?" I asked.

"Sorry. I have Tab."

"No, thanks."

"You're not against Elaine having a life of her own, are you?" she asked warily.

"No, it's not that. I understand that a woman could want to do something other than raise kids. But I can't understand how a parent can be so neglectful."

"Neither can I," she said.

We were silent then, staring at each other. I could feel the electric charge between us as if it were palpable. I wanted to go to her, sit next to her at least. I couldn't move a muscle.

She said, "Why is it I'm always attracted to Italian men?"

"Because," I answered, "we're hunks!" I smiled and she smiled back.

"At least you're tall," she said. "The others were short."

I wondered how many others? Did I dare ask? She read my mind.

"There were two before Al. Boyfriends, not husbands. But they were short Italians."

"The tall ones are different," I said. "Very nice. Intelligent, sensitive, and we don't forget child support."

"You certainly don't."

Again we stared and now I felt a rippling along my arms and legs and across my stomach. I leaned forward. She didn't move. I got up and crossed to the couch. I sat next to her.

"Can you feel it?" I asked.

"Yes," she whispered. "But there's something I have to tell you."

I touched her face with two fingers and drew them down her cheek. Soft. "What?"

"I'm not going to go to bed with you tonight."

"That's all right," I said.

She looked surprised. "It is?"

"I'm a very old-fashioned guy." It was true. "I only kiss on the first date."

"Me, too," she said.

We leaned toward each other, our mouths meeting. Gently we let our lips respond. Then slowly our tongues found entry, intertwined. Together we broke the kiss, pulled back and tried to read each other's eyes. We were both breathing heavily and neither of us said anything for moments. Then she touched my lips with her fingertips, which I kissed.

"This is scary," she said.

"Why?" I asked, but I knew. It was for me, too.

"It feels very intense and that's the last thing I want."

"I understand. Should I leave?"

"What good will that do?"

I laughed. "None. Maybe it'll make you feel better if I tell you that I'm scared, too."

She said, "It's nice to hear but I don't feel any better."

"Oh," I said.

We kissed again and it lasted a long time. I felt myself whirling down into a black velvet vortex of pleasure, drowning in the warmth of her lips. Eventually we stopped. I knew I had to move away from her and when I did she understood. I went back to my chair.

"You're something," she finally said.

"You, too."

"No, I mean the way you just went over there." She pointed to where I was sitting.

"I had to."

"Most men wouldn't."

"I'm not most men."

"I can see that."

"And?"

"It's okay with me."

I said, "It's okay with me, too, that you're not most women."

She said, "We have something in common, then."

"It's a start," I said.

"A start," she repeated.

We sat in silence for quite a while and then she said, "Tell me about your life. What do you do? It's something dangerous, isn't it? I told you I'd ask about what happened in the hall last night. So, what happened?"

I considered playing the detective part down but Cassie was too smart and I had no desire to con her in any way. I told her the truth: that it could be dangerous but that so far I'd never been hurt seriously and that it was something I just had to do. Then I told her about the Baker case, every last detail. She listened the way no other woman I'd ever been with had.

When I was finished she asked, "What's your next move?"

I only debated a moment as to whether I should tell her or not, because I had an odd feeling I'd be sharing a lot more than this with Cassie Bloomfield. "I'm going to find out what's going on in the Eurogallery, what those paintings have to do with everything. And then I'm going to find Patrick Baker."

"When?"

"Tonight."

A look of concern crossed her face. It made me feel good.

"How are you going to do all that?"

"I'm not sure about all of it but the first thing I'm going to do is to get into that gallery."

"How?"

I smiled. "I have my ways."

"Professional secret?"

"You could call it that, yes."

"I wish I could come."

I was stunned. "You do?"

She nodded.

"You wouldn't be afraid?"

"Of course I would. Aren't you?"

"Yes."

"Well, then, what's fear got to do with it?" she asked.

I thought about it. "Not much, I guess. For me."

"But for me, because I'm a woman, it should inhibit my interest and curiosity?"

"You could get hurt."

"So could you."

"It's my job," I insisted.

"Because you want it to be." She laughed that wonderful way she had and my heart gave an extra thump. "Fortune, you're pretty good but you're a man and your sexism's ingrained. It's okay; you can't help it."

"Am I hopeless?" I asked.

"Perhaps with my help..." She shrugged.

"I'm a willing student," I said.

"Good."

We were quiet then, looking at each other across the room, wanting to touch but resisting. Time passed and then she rose.

"I think we'd better call it a night," she said.

I got up and we walked from the living room down the hall to the door.

"It was a great dinner," she said. "And your kids are terrific. You must be doing something right."

I thanked her for the compliment, then kissed her, softly, almost chastely. She unlocked the door and I went out into the hall.

"Fortune," she said as I was unlocking my door.

"Yes?"

"Be very, very careful, will you?"

"I will," I said.

She shut her door and I opened mine.

At one-thirty in the morning I left my apartment with my small bag of tools and my .38 on my hip. I hadn't heard from Nick so I assumed he'd either used my ten for a gallon or two or he simply hadn't found Mat the Rat.

It was a very dark night, the moon was not in sight and no stars were available. The air was stale, as if it had just been let out of a bar. I walked up the block to the corner of West Houston to see if the street was quiet and then took another tour down to the other corner at Prince. I crossed Thompson and did the same thing on the other side. Nobody was around. Nights in SoHo were fairly quiet, unlike the Village. I crossed back to the other side and entered the small lobby of the loft building next to the Eurogallery. A part of the gallery belonged to that building and it was my best way in. I took out a set of skeleton keys and after trying six I got in. Just inside the front door a staircase led up, but I could see a wire gate at the first landing. I wanted to go to the basement anyway. At the back of the short hall another staircase led down. It was dark and I couldn't see what was at the bottom. I went down the steps and ran smack into another wire gate. I tried a dozen keys but none of them worked. I had been afraid of this. I was going to have to get to the basement via the elevator. It was the riskiest entry of all. The elevator was at the back of the hall. I pushed the button and watched it come down from five.

The door opened and I got on. The moment the door closed I opened my tool bag. I had to pray that everyone who lived in this building was in. The elevator was not going to move until I found a way to make it do so. I was stuck here on the first floor until I could get to the basement. If anyone came home from a late night date I was cooked.

There was no use trying to fit any of my keys into the basement lock on the elevator panel because I knew from experience that that wouldn't work. I had to remove the panel and then play with the wires until I got it unlocked.

There were four hex screws holding the panel, two at the top and two at the bottom. A normal screwdriver, or a Phillips, wouldn't do the trick. I needed an Allen key and discovered several on a chain at the bottom of my bag. I tried three before I found one that fit. The screws were in there as if a machine had tightened them. My key wouldn't budge the first one so I moved on to the second. After a few moments it began to turn. I got it out. Sweat made my scalp feel cold and some of it ran down my cheeks and forehead. I stopped to wipe it away with my sleeve before I went on to number three.

Fifteen minutes later I had all four out and was able to remove the panel. Quickly, I manipulated the wires for the basement lock and got a shock. I knew I'd have to endure that so I pushed them together again, felt the electric shock, jumped and smiled as the elevator began to descend. When it reached the basement the door yawned open. I placed my tool bag across the door track to keep it open while I replaced the panel. I accomplished that in six minutes, got off the elevator and let the door close. I stood there for a moment and, as I did, I heard the unmistakable sound of someone buzzing for the elevator. Staring at the lighted panel I watched as it stopped at one. I listened to the door open and then close and prayed whoever it was didn't find it odd that the elevator had been at B at one-thirty in the morning. There was a washer and dryer to my right so perhaps the person would assume someone was doing a late night wash. Nothing happened for a moment and I found myself holding my breath. Then the elevator engaged and for several beats, between floors, I didn't know which way it was going. My hand was on my gun. And then Two lit up. I expelled my breath and relaxed my gun hand. I watched the panel as the elevator went all the way to seven. I heard it open, close, and saw the light go out. I waited five minutes and nothing more happened.

It had been a very close call and the tension in my back and neck began to pain me. I stretched, arching my back, then hunching my shoulders forward. I stood, listening. The basement was lit so I had no trouble in that area. What I had to do was find my way up to the gallery. A large steel door was to my right. I tried it but it was locked. Putting my ear against it I heard the sound of machinery and assumed it was the boiler room. I turned to my left. In front of me were cubicles stuffed with various things. They were obviously storage bins for the tenants. I passed by them on my way toward the back and found another steel door. This one was unlocked. I couldn't believe my luck. I carefully pulled it open and found it led to a short set of stairs, which I took. The door at the top was also unlocked. I turned the handle slowly and pushed it open. It was very dark on the other side but I knew I was in the gallery because the light from my side spilled into the room. Although this was not the main area it was certainly part of it. I reached into my bag for a flashlight, flipped it on, then aimed it at the floor. I stepped into the room and closed the door behind me.

Listening, I heard nothing but the frightened sound of my own breathing. I slowly panned up with the flashlight and found myself looking at a packing crate. I moved closer and studied the outside. The address was the Eurogallery and the return was someplace in France. I remembered Wayne telling me the current show was closing so I figured these were more paintings for a new show. From my bag I got a small crowbar and began to pry off the top of the case. It wasn't difficult and it came up in a minute. I flashed the light in and saw what I expected. The edge of an aluminum frame. I went back to work on another corner of the crate and then the last two. I took off the top of the case and laid it on the floor. Carefully, I pulled out a painting. It was a still life of pears next to a plate of cheese. The look of it was very classic and old and I knew it didn't belong in this frame. I squatted on the floor behind the crate and laid the painting flat. Running my hand around the frame I found the connecting joints. I beamed the light on the upper right-hand side. Examining it, I could see that the side piece fitted into the upper and lower as if it were on a track. I pushed from below and watched it move up. When it almost got to the end of the track I pulled it out and laid the painting down. Turning over the piece of frame that had come out, I saw that there was another piece of aluminum that fit perfectly inside the first. I pushed that up from the bottom and it, too, slid out. I grabbed it before it fell to the floor.

I turned it over to inspect all four sides and couldn't find an opening. But the top and bottom were not closed and I stuck my finger inside and felt something pliable. I gave a push and watched as some tinfoil peeked from the other end.

I pulled the packet out of the hollow rectangle and even before I opened it I knew what I'd find.

That one length of tinfoil held probably four thousand dollars' worth of cocaine and when it was cut and out on the street it would bring in about twenty-four thousand. I reached for the painting and quickly pulled the frame apart. Each side held the same thing. I stood up. If my quick calculations were right, and if every frame contained sixteen thousand dollars' worth of uncut coke, then the box I'd uncovered, which had ten paintings in it, was worth nine hundred sixty thousand on the street. I flashed the light around the room and saw that there were six other cases. I stopped calculating; it was too much for me. I had to get out of there and get help. I didn't have time to put the painting back together and replace it in the crate. Besides, I figured nobody else was going to be doing anything tonight.

But I was wrong. As I started for the door I heard voices and noticed a spill of light to my right. I couldn't make out the words; they were just mumbles, so I moved away from my escape route and toward the heart of the gallery. When I got to the open door I stepped through and saw that the light was coming from across a hallway. I took out my gun and set my tool bag at my feet. I didn't want both hands full. Then I got my bearings and realized I was looking at the Joyce Room. The sounds of voices grew louder but not any clearer. I took two large steps and crossed the hall then edged my way toward the door, which was ajar. Inside the room were Joyce and Wayne. Why hadn't I guessed? Joyce and Wayne, a perfect match. They were taking her paintings down from the wall and putting them in a packing crate.

"You sure he's out?" Wayne asked.

"Don't be such a worrywart," she said, "I doped his hot chocolate."

"You saw him drink it?"

Joyce whirled on him. "Listen, Wayne, you'd better get over this. What's an old fart like George going to do to us anyway?"

"I don't know. It just gives me the creeps. I'll feel better when we get out of here. You think we have enough money?"

"Jesus, you're getting on my nerves." She pulled a painting from his hands and gingerly put it in the crate as if it were a baby. "I told you we have no money problems. You should know that."

Considering that the stash in the other room was certainly not their first, he sure should have known that. But maybe four hundred thousand, or thereabouts, wasn't enough for Wayne Morrison. Well, he wouldn't need four cents where he was going. I stepped into the doorway.

"Hi, kids," I said.

They looked up, terrified.

"What the fuck?" he said.

She opened her mouth to speak, too, but her eyes looked past me as if she saw something behind me. I wasn't about to fall for that old chestnut...but I wish I had. At the moment I felt the presence behind me I turned, too late, and the crack echoed in my ears as I went down and out for the count.

20

I felt squeezed. Something was pressing on either side of me as I struggled to open my eyes. My vision was blurred and the pain on the side of my head was excruciating. I fought not to vomit. This time, I was sure, I wasn't going to get off so easy. I was bound to have a concussion. I blinked a few times and things started coming into focus. I saw my own legs stretched out in front of me and realized I was sitting on the floor, leaning against something. A wall. I turned to my right to see what was pressing against my shoulder. It was Wayne. He was staring straight ahead. By the set of his mouth I could tell he wasn't pleased. Little things mean a lot. I turned my head, which felt like it had gone through my mother's meat grinder, looked to my left, and there was Joyce. She wasn't happy either. I wanted to ask her what was going on but I couldn't get the words to hit my lips. My head fell down on my chest and I thought I might go under again. I forced myself to lift it up and when I looked straight ahead I saw a pair of boots and then a pair of legs. They seemed to be dangling in the air but then I realized my POV. I traveled up the legs with my eyes and came to the Mexican belt buckle. George Mayer was sitting on a table swinging his legs. In his right hand was a Colt .45 Magnum. My .38 was on the table next to him. Our eyes met.

"Hello, pal," he said. "You've been a busy schmuck tonight, haven't you? Messing around with my new shipment of coke and all."

"What shipment of coke?" Joyce asked.

Mayer's eyes narrowed and the hardness that had always been lurking beneath his tucked skin shone through. "You shut your trap," he said. "I've got nothing more to say to you."

"Listen, George," she said.

"I said, shut it." He raised the gun and I felt her push closer to me.

A few beats passed and then Mayer looked back at me. "I tried to warn you off, Fanelli, but you wouldn't take the hint."

"You?" I got out in a croaky voice.

"Well, let's say my protégé."

"Fanner?" I asked.

"The very one. But as my wife so delicately put it yesterday, he was a fuck-up. I should have dropped him long ago. After he couldn't even get Sarah Barber to give him a show I should have known he wasn't much good for anything. But I'm a softie at heart."

"I can see that," I said, looking down the barrel of his gun. I'd found my voice now but my eyes kept going in and out of focus. "Why'd you want him to have a show there?"

"I thought it would be nice for the Barber broad to be humiliated. Fanner was a lousy artist. But he didn't know that and he thought I thought he was good. I told him how to go about getting a show from that bitch because I could see she was hot to trot. All these SoHo shits think they know so much about art and culture and don't give me the time of day. Well, I have my own ideas about things and I thought it might be fun to have Sarah Barber laughed at for a change." His mouth set in a hard, thin line.

"How'd you explain not giving him a show yourself?" I asked.

"Blamed it on Joycie. Said she couldn't take the competition from another American artist." He laughed, loud and long, the sound bouncing off the walls as the three of us sat staring at him, watching the gun jiggling in his hand.

"You shit," Joyce mumbled.

He didn't hear. When he was finished laughing he wiped the tears from the corners of his eyes and his face fell back into his earlier mean expression.

"Did you kill Fanner?" I asked.

He stared at me, debating whether to answer or not. Then he smiled and ran a finger of his left hand up and down the cleft of his chin. "You gotta go, Mr. Fanelli, you just gotta go. Know what I mean?"

I didn't answer. I couldn't because I *did* know what he meant. I thought of Karen and Sam and tried to clear my head. I had to keep him talking while I figured a way out of this.

"Did you kill Fanner?" I asked again.

"Nobody thinks gallery owners are creative," was his reply.

I knew for sure then that he'd done it. I'd thought it was Wayne because he was an artist, a frustrated one but Mayer, it seemed, was even more frustrated.

"And you *are* . . . creative?" I asked.

His eyes widened and appeared to twirl in their sockets like the eyes in a movie cartoon. "You'd better believe it, buddy boy." He glanced at Joyce. "Unlike some hacks."

"What's that supposed to mean?" she said.

"It's means that you, my pet, are a mediocre talent. No, I take that back. You're lousy. Trash."

"Listen, George—"

"Shut up," he ordered and again aimed the Colt in her direction.

I looked at Joyce and saw that her face was florid. I knew her anger was because she'd been told she was a rotten artist and not because she was going to be killed at any moment. Unlike Joyce, I knew what the priorities were here. My life was at stake and I had to do something about it. I wanted to see my kids again, my mother, Cassie. I had a lot of living left to do.

George interrupted my thoughts. "Even your boyfriend here thinks you stink. Don't you, Wayne?"

Wayne's chin was on his chest and he said nothing.

"I asked you a question, asshole." Mayer's face was gray in its intensity as he directed the gun toward Wayne.

"I don't know what you want me to say, George."

"I want you to give Joycie a critique of her work."

Wayne looked up at his tormentor with pleading eyes. I wondered if he was more afraid of Joyce than he was of the gun?

Joyce started yelling: "Wayne thinks I'm a genius. Go on, Wayne, tell him. Tell him what you think of my work."

"Yeah, tell me, Wayne," Mayer said.

There was a moment of silence while Wayne weighed which was more lethal, gun or Joyce. Then he said, "It sucks."

Simultaneously, George laughed and Joyce screamed. Wayne folded his arms across his raised knees and rested his head on his arms as if he might go to sleep.

"You bastard, Wayne," Joyce yelled. "You goddamn bastard. What did you want from me? Huh? What?"

His voice was muffled against his arms but the word was clear enough. "Money," he said.

She screamed again in pure rage. George Mayer just kept laughing. I was beginning to feel better but I didn't want him to know it. I was sure at some point he'd make us get up because I didn't think he was going to kill all three of us sitting there. And when he got us up I wanted him to think I was still groggy. I touched my head where I'd been hit and groaned. Mayer looked at me.

"You got a boo-boo?"

I said nothing. Joyce was still grumbling and Morrison was silent.

"So what did you think of my sculptures, Fanelli?" George asked.

"You mean Fanner and Jennifer?"

"Smart boy."

"Why?" I asked.

He smoothed down one side of his styled hair. "Well, what the hell? It doesn't matter much now. Fanner knew too much and I was sure he'd give me away first chance he got. He was a cruddy artist and a wimp."

"How did you get him over to the Barber gallery?"

"You know," George said, "revenge is a fascinating thing. Give a person that kind of opportunity, they jump at it."

"What kind of opportunity?"

He twirled a jade ring on his finger. "As you can imagine, Sarah Barber had bruised Fanner's artistic pride so he was eager to, shall we say, bruise her back? Anyway, I told him I'd help him torch her place and he was happy as a pig in shit. See, I'd already heard through the grapevine that he'd given himself away to you about dousing the lights, so I thought some speedy action was in order."

"And he still had a key?"

"Naturally."

"So when you got there you bashed him, with whatever it was you used on Jennifer."

"Right."

"And what was that?"

"I'll get to that later. Don't you want to hear how I hung him up like a painting?"

"I can skip that," I said.

"You'll have to admit it was a brilliant touch. My second creation in living-dead art! Jennifer was my first."

"Tell me about her." I swallowed hard, thinking about that poor kid at this maniac's mercy.

"Now there was a tasty morsel. Too bad I had to get rid of her. But it was fantastic, wasn't it? I watched you pass that store window about six times that day, Fanelli." He laughed and it sounded like a dentist's drill. "I liked that little girl. She was just my type."

"You pig," Joyce said.

"You old whore," he said. "Yeah, Joycie, you're over the hill, far as I'm concerned." To me he said, "I like them real young. The Baker girl came around here looking for her brother. Well, at first I didn't know who she was talking about because

I knew him as Patrick Sheedy, but I told her I'd keep my ears open. Then I gave her some money, some coke and a poke." He laughed again. "Hey, that's good."

I wanted to strangle him. "Then what happened?"

"She came across a picture of the boy, her brother. He was in, shall we say, a compromising position?"

"Where'd you get the picture?" Silently I prayed that Patrick was alive.

He ignored my question. "See, when she saw the picture I made a little slip and said, oh, you mean *that* Patrick, so the jig was up, so to speak. Well, she kicked up a fuss, said if I didn't tell her where he was, she was going to go to the police, so what could I do? I said I'd take her to the boy that night. I told her to meet me around midnight. She did. Well, first we went to the disco on Prince, boogied until about three, and then I told her it was time to go see Patrick. She was all coked up by then, hardly knew where I was taking her. I'd borrowed Doug's keys earlier and had decided to give Thelma Sable a treat." His face hardened into a mask of hatred. "That phony bitch had given me the cold shoulder once too often." He looked at Joyce. "By the way, babe, I doped *your* hot chocolate that night."

"You swine," she snarled.

He smiled and I thought I'd never seen such pure evil.

"Go on," I said.

He adjusted his position on the table, like a man settling down to tell a good story. "Earlier I'd unscrewed a pipe from the *Life Is Just a Bowl of Cherries* sculpture. You know the one I mean?"

"Who could forget?"

"Hideous thing, isn't it? Well, I'd taken that pipe and planted it in The Sweatshop earlier. Anyway, Jennifer and I went there and I let us in. Then I locked the door behind us and told her to follow me to the back. When we went through the curtain I picked up the pipe from where I'd hidden it and I bashed her. It was easy. Her head cracked like an egg."

I felt a shudder go through me. "Is that what you killed Fanner with?"

He nodded and went on. "Well, what to do now, huh? This is where my genius comes in. I put that pink wig on her head over the bloody mess I'd made and then I just switched her with the dummy in the middle, the one sitting down. I put a chain and padlock around Jennie's waist and fastened her to the chair with it. Then I wiped down anything I'd touched, locked up, went back to my gallery, washed off the pipe and put it back in the sculpture. That was my first creation in living-dead sculpture. Fanner was my second and you three will make it a nice five." This time he laughed loud, like a train bearing down on us.

I waited until the laughter subsided and then I asked, "What about Patrick Baker?"

Wayne said, "If I'd known anything, I would have told you, Fanelli. I believed this guy. I thought he was just nervous about the kid being under age."

"It's okay," I said. I believed Wayne. It was clear he hadn't known anything and that he'd told me he'd only seen Fanner's work once because it was the truth. But why had Fanner wanted a show for Morrison as well I asked George.

"I told him to ask for it. Two birds with one stone," he said. "Wayne is an even worse artist than Fanner was."

Wayne's head snapped up from his arms. "The hell I am," he yelled.

Joyce said, "You stink, Morrison."

"How would you know?"

I didn't want to get back on the lack of talent they all had. Not yet. "Mayer," I interrupted, "where's Patrick?"

"He's in a safe place. Safe from you and the police, that is."

"Making kiddie porn?"

"That's right."

As bad as that was, I felt relieved. The kid was alive. "Did he find out about your coke operation? Is that why you got rid of him?"

"You're such a smart man, Fanelli; it's a shame you were dumb enough to come here tonight. Yes, the little tyke ran away from wherever he lived and was sleeping in the gallery.

I didn't know about it but when my new show came in and I was unpacking with Doug we discovered him. Unfortunately, he'd also discovered us. I wasn't about to kill him with Fanner as a witness and besides, he was too pretty to kill and I knew a perfect use for him." He gestured with his hand and light glinted off the three silver rings on his middle fingers. "I have many businesses, you see. Many interests. Many creative endeavors."

"I can't believe this," Joyce said.

"You know nothing about me," he said acidly. "But I know everything about you, toots. I've known about you and Morrison from the beginning, for instance."

I decided the time was right. "And you've always known what a rotten artist she is," I said.

"I have, for sure." He turned to Joyce. "From the moment I pulled you out of that pig sty where you grew up, and took one look at your so-called talent, I knew you were tenth-rate. But you were young, nubile, as they say."

Joyce's rage had brought tears brimming over the rims of her eyes. "I sell," she cried. "I sell all over Europe."

"You sell nowhere," he said. "I sent my payments for the cocaine in your frames, my dear."

She screamed and jumped to her feet. Mayer slid down from the table, his eyes on Joyce. "Stay where you are, bitch," he commanded.

I braced my arms at my sides and pulled myself tight against the wall ready to spring. And then I asked a question I thought I knew the answer to: "What do they do with the paintings over there, George?"

"The frames they use over," he answered. "The paintings they burn."

It was the perfect answer, the one I'd wanted. Joyce Mayer leaped from her spot as if she could fly and George turned toward her just enough so that I could spring for his legs. I heard the gun go off as I tackled him, my chest thudding against his knees. We went down, he backwards against the table, which slid along the polished floor, I on top of him. The gun was still in his hand. I reached for it. With my other hand I chopped him in the Adam's apple. He choked and gagged but didn't let go of the gun.

He scrabbled away from me and then, shakily, he stood up. I got up, too, while he was nursing his throat. I knew he was going to be an easy mark as I hit him with a right to the head, a left cross to the chin and a right hook to the middle. He went down, doubling over. I flung myself on him and we rolled over, his chunky body crushing mine. I managed to get my leg up and knee him in the groin. There wasn't much force behind it but he groaned and doubled up again. I shoved him off me and got my arm around his throat. Then I grabbed his gun hand and pulled his arm into a half nelson. I bent his hand sideways until I heard the bone snap. He dropped the gun and Wayne grabbed it. At that moment a siren went off, drowning out George's shriek.

"What's that?" I asked, still holding Mayer under his throat.

"The front alarm," Wayne said, looking bewildered.

He was holding the gun pointed at George and me so I asked if he was with me or against me.

"Oh, with, sure."

I let go of George who was moaning and holding his broken wrist. Joyce was lying on her side, unconscious. There was a gaping hole in her leg but at least she wasn't dead. Nobody should be killed for being a bad artist.

We heard the sound of running feet and then Nick Scola and Father Paul appeared in the doorway.

"How'd you know I was here?" I asked.

"It was the broad," Nick said, sounding sober.

"What broad?"

"I come back to your place twenty minutes ago with the info and there's this broad sittin' in her doorway readin' a book. She asks if I'm lookin' for you and I tell her yes and then she says she's worried and tells me where you are. I went and got him," he said, pointing to Paul.

"You all right, Fortune?" Paul asked me.

"Yeah." Paul went over to Joyce and checked her pulse. My head was throbbing but I was okay. "You found Mat the Rat?" I asked Nick.

"Yeah. He got the pictures from some guy in the East Village. In Tompkins Square Park."

"That asshole," George whimpered, holding his broken wrist.

"What asshole, Mayer?"

He clamped his mouth shut, his lips disappearing.

I grabbed the gun from Wayne. "See this, Mayer? I'm going to blow a hole as big as a grapefruit right through your face if you don't tell me where Patrick Baker is."

"Will you get me a doctor?" he whined.

I nodded.

"Six-eleven East Sixth Street. Fifth floor. Now get me a doctor."

I gave the Magnum back to Wayne and got my .38 from the floor where it had fallen. "Call the police and an ambulance, Wayne. You think you can handle it?"

"Sure," he said. It was the first time I'd ever seen him looking confident.

I turned to Nick and Paul. "I'm going to get Patrick Baker. You want to come?"

They both said yes.

21

East Sixth Street is in the East Village. It is an area that resembles war-torn Europe. Back in the sixties there were hopes that it could be developed into what SoHo had now become. But the drug dealers got their hooks in before anything positive could happen.

At this time of night the streets looked quiet but I knew from experience that in almost every doorway, alley and burned-out building people were shooting up, getting raped, being rolled, maybe killed. The stores had solid metal grates in front of their windows and doors and some of the abandoned buildings were closed up with tin sheets over the windows. Empty lots, strewn with garbage, proliferated.

Number six-eleven East Sixth Street was between Avenues B and C. From the street we could see it was a five-story building. Four cracked cement steps led up to the front door; there were no lights anywhere. Paul parked my car near Avenue C and we walked back up the street. It was a short walk but my head was throbbing and something hurt in my chest. I hoped I'd make it through whatever we were going to find on that fifth floor. I should have asked George Mayer what to expect but I'd been too eager to get to Patrick.

Neither Nick or Paul had a gun so I took the lead as we went up the front steps and through double doors that had long ago lost their glass panes. We stood for a moment in a small foyer where, to our right, a yawning hole that had once held the mailboxes now housed broken bottles, used syringes and general garbage. A second set of doors, these tinned over, were closed but unlocked. As we entered the dark hall the smell of rot and decay assaulted us so hard we reeled backward for a moment as if we'd been slapped. We coughed and gasped for pure air but there was none. For a moment we stood still trying to adjust our eyes to the total blackness inside.

"You still with me?" I whispered.

Paul said, "Lead the way."

"Wit you," Nick said.

I could see what looked like the outline of a banister at the back of the hall and, like a blind person, I slowly shuffled my way toward it. When I got closer I saw that I'd been correct and took my first steps up. The building had the smell and feel of something abandoned, dead, and I wondered if Mayer had lied to me. At the top of the first flight, holding on to the banister, I stopped. I was feeling slightly dizzy and nauseated. As I was trying to regain my balance something crawled over my hand and I jumped, letting out a grunt of surprise.

"Jesus, Mary and Joseph," Nick said behind me.

Paul said, "What is it?"

"Nothing. A roach or something went over my hand, that's all. Let's go."

We crossed the landing to the next flight and started up. The building was cold but I was sweating, my shirt sticking to my chest and back. My hair felt soaked as if I'd just come out of a shower. By the time we hit the fourth floor my breath was coming in short stabs of pain. I wondered if I'd broken a rib or something in my fight with Mayer because I knew that I wasn't that much out of shape. And then I thought it was fear that was taking my breath away. Anything could be waiting for us on the fifth floor. These might be my last moments on earth. I had no desire to die in a scuzzy building in the East Village but I couldn't turn back now. If I let Patrick Baker spend one more minute of his life in this place my life would be worth zero to me anyway. I turned the landing and then I heard it.

We all froze. It was a sound I couldn't identify: squeaking and scraping like something that needed to be oiled.

"Rats," Nick whispered.

"What?"

"It's rats."

"Where?"

"Down there," he said, pointing past my shoulder down the hall into the blackness.

"How do you know?"

"I know," he said.

Paul said, "He's right. Listen."

I did. Now that I knew what it was I could untangle the sounds and I realized they were talking, squeaking to each other. The scraping sounds were their clawed feet scurrying along the corridor, scratching for food.

"Come on," Nick whispered. "Let's keep goin'."

I had no desire to stay with the rats and started up the last flight. It was clear that the building was empty and that no one was behind any of the doors we'd passed. I found it hard to believe that we were going to find anything different on the fifth floor but I had to go on. We reached the landing and stopped.

"Now what?" Nick said.

I didn't really know.

"How many apartments are on a floor?" Paul asked.

I'd tried to gage that as we passed each floor and I'd figured four, which I told them. Then I whispered, "We'll have to try each door."

We slowly made our way to the first door on the right. Listening carefully I heard nothing but the sound of our breathing in the hall. Holding my gun in front of me I reached for the doorknob and motioned to the others to step to either side of the door. The knob turned and the door opened. I was pretty sure if anyone was inside, the door would have been locked. The first thing I heard was the sound of rats scrambling across the empty room. I couldn't see much but I could feel the place was unoccupied. I stepped back and shook my head no. We tried the second door and found that apartment empty, too.

Then we crossed back to the other side of the stairway and stared at the last two doors. I felt like the guy in "The Lady or the Tiger," except that tigers were the only things that awaited me and my partners...if anything at all awaited us.

"What do you think?" I whispered.

"Who knows?" Nick said.

"I'd flip a coin but I couldn't see it," said Paul.

I flipped one in my head and it told me to go to the left. They followed and we proceeded in the same way as before. I tried the handle and it was locked. This was it. I looked down at the lock and saw it was a simple one. No police lock. But I didn't have my tools and I'd forgotten my wallet with my credit cards. I motioned the others back down the hall.

"Look," I whispered, "we're going to have to break it down and we're going to have to do it in one shot."

"No problem," Nick said.

I could see the outline of his huge shoulders and I thought he was probably right.

"If you do it, Nick, you'll be the first one through. Somebody could be waiting for you with a gun on the other side. I'll be right behind you but it might not help."

"Ah, what the fuck. Sorry, Father."

"You sure, Nick?"

"Yeah. Let's get the kid out."

I squeezed his arm and we started back down the hall. I stopped in front of the fourth door and tried the handle just to make sure. It opened into an empty space.

Back in front of the third door Nick was hunching his shoulders, getting ready. He scraped his feet as if he were a bull. I hoped he was. Paul stood to the left of the door and I to the right, my gun ready. Nick moved back against the opposite wall.

"Okay?" he whispered.

"Okay," I answered.

He launched himself from his spot and flew across the hall, his shoulder crashing against the wooden door, splintering it in a thousand pieces as it tore from the hinges, screaming in the silence. I was next through the door with Paul right behind me. I held my gun in front of me in both hands as I crouched, my legs spread.

"Everybody freeze," I yelled. "This is the police."

There wasn't a sound and then Nick, who had hit the opposite wall began moaning, or at least I thought it was Nick. Suddenly a flash of daylight washed over the room and I whirled to my left to see Paul standing by a window, a black cloth in his hands that he'd ripped down. Morning was breaking and we could see where we were. The room was empty except for a three-legged table and two folding chairs. I looked at Nick and saw that he was holding his shoulder but he wasn't making a sound. The moaning was coming from another room. As I moved closer I could tell it was the sound of someone crying. All three of us approached the second doorway, me first with the gun.

"Okay," I said, "come out with your hands up."

"Please, help," a voice came from the other room.

We all looked at one another and then I said again, "Come out with your hands over your head."

"We can't," another voice said. This one was male.

I stepped into the doorway, my gun leading. "Jesus," I said. I dropped my arm to my side and stared.

"Holy shit," Nick said.

Paul pushed past me.

Four narrow beds in iron frames jammed the room. In each bed were two children, five girls and three boys, a wrist of each fastened to the headpiece with handcuffs.

A girl said, "There's no one here but us."

I looked at all the faces then stopped at one. He was much thinner and his hair was shorter but I knew at once he was Patrick Baker. I said his name.

He looked at me quizzically. "Yes?"

Three of the children started to cry.

"Don't cry," Nick said. "We're gettin' you out of here."

"Are you really the police?" a boy asked.

"We're friends of the police," I said. "We're going to help you. Does somebody come to get you each morning?" I asked.

Patrick answered. "Yes. About seven o'clock."

I looked at my watch. It was five after six. I fumbled in my pocket for my well-worn address book. "Nick, take this number, go call Skelly at home. Tell him to get somebody over here with a hacksaw right away and that if he plays his cards right he can take a porno gang. Explain what's going on here."

"Okay, Fortune."

Nick left and Paul and I went to each kid and reassured them. Then I went over to where Patrick lay with a girl. I knelt on the floor next to him and told him my name.

"Where do they take you every day?" I asked.

"To an old warehouse. I could find it again," he said proudly.

I looked at his blue eyes. They weren't clear anymore and they looked like they belonged to someone middle-aged, maybe even old. His adolescence was over. But at least he was alive.

"How did you find us?" he asked.

"It's a long story," I said.

"But you knew my name."

"Yes."

He frowned. "Did my father send you?"

"No. Your uncle and Robert Sheedy."

"Oh." He turned his head to one side, away from me.

The girl next to him touched his chest with her free hand. "It's okay, Pat."

I couldn't believe the kid still had it in for Horton and Sheedy because they were gay. I said, "They love you, Patrick. They hired me to find you." I didn't say that his father didn't care.

He turned back to me, his eyes watery.

The girl said, "He feels guilty."

"Guilty?"

"I said some rotten things to Bob," he said. "Boy, was I stupid." He shook his head back and forth on the dirty mattress.

"Sheedy doesn't hold it against you," I said.

"Ah, you don't know," he said.

"But I do. He told me all about it. You can go back there if you want." I couldn't see handing him over to Carter Baker. He and Horton would have to work that out.

"You think so?" he asked, the dead eyes brightening.

"I know so."

He frowned again. "But what about my uncle?"

"What about him?"

"Won't he make me go back to New Jersey?"

"No. I'm sure he won't."

He smiled faintly. "Maybe my sister can come to New York, too," he said.

I swallowed hard. I'd forgotten he didn't know. This was no time to tell him so I just nodded.

Nick came back in the apartment out of breath. "Got Skelly. . . . He was bookin' Mayer. . . . Sending someone . . . to get the porno guys."

"Thanks, Nick." I stood up and motioned him into the other room. "Listen, could you make another call?"

"Why not?"

I wrote Sheedy's number on a piece of paper and gave it to him. I told him to tell Sheedy to get Horton down to his place and that I'd be bringing the Baker kid there soon. Nick left and I went back into the bedroom. Most of the kids were calmer now and Paul was finding out where they were from. One was from California and another from Texas. The rest were locals. I went back to Patrick and sat on the floor next to him.

"I have a son your age," I said.

"Yeah?"

"His name's Sam. I love him very much."

"He's lucky, then," he said. "My father hates me."

"I don't think that's true, Patrick."

"No, you're right. He just hates the world." His eyes clouded over and then he shut them.

I watched as tears squeezed out from beneath the closed lids and ran down the side of his face. I reached out and wiped them away with my handkerchief and then I took Patrick's free hand in mine while we waited.

22

As Nick and I left Sheedy's place I passed out. When I woke up in my bed the first thing I thought was that Meryl Streep was sitting next to me. And then I realized that it was Cassie.

"Hi," she said.

"Hi."

"Ready to eat something?"

I thought about it and consulted my stomach. "Yeah, I'm kind of hungry."

She left the room. I tried to sit up in a quick movement and I immediately felt a stab of pain in my side. I carefully slid back down and drew the covers up under my chin. I tried to remember how I'd gotten here but couldn't. I assumed Nick had brought me home. I had no idea what time it was because the shutters were closed but it felt like night. When Cassie came back with a tray I asked her.

"It's seven o'clock," she said.

"You mean I slept all day?"

"All two days. It's Thursday."

"Thursday?" I was supposed to be at my mother's. "My mother," I said.

"She's feeding your kids. And mine, for that matter."

"Really?"

"Yes. She's very nice. I like her."

"You met my mother?" Things seemed to be moving along very nicely without me.

"We spent part of last night here together and then she came by a few hours ago. She took the kids home with her."

"You mean we're here alone?"

Cassie laughed and I felt like I'd had a shot of adrenaline. I tried to sit up but the pain stabbed me again and I got dizzy.

"Let me help you," she said. "You're going to have to take it very easy. You have a broken rib and a bad concussion. You were clobbered twice in two days. Not good."

I discovered the tape around my chest. "You must think I'm a lousy detective. I mean, getting socked all the time. Come to think of it, maybe I am lousy."

"From what I heard you did all right."

I sat up against some pillows she fixed behind me and she brought the tray over.

"Soup," she said.

"You make it?"

"Your mother did. Chicken and rice. Your favorite, she told me."

"One of them," I said. I hadn't the heart to tell my mother that my tastes had developed beyond chicken and rice.

"Want me to feed you?" Cassie asked.

"I don't think it's a good idea," I said. There was something about having this woman feeding me that I didn't like. I wanted us to start on equal ground, if we ever got started.

She smiled. "Don't worry; I won't think of you as a baby," she said, reading my mind.

"You might. Let me try it myself."

I took the spoon from her and managed to get some soup in my mouth but most of it went on the sheet. What the hell! I gave her back the spoon.

It took us about half an hour for me to eat and then I went back to sleep. When I woke up the next time it was morning and Cassie was there again. The kids had gone to school. I had some tea and toast. I felt much better than I had the night before and I wanted to get up but she wouldn't let me.

"I have a message for you," she said.

"What?"

"Your ex-wife's secretary called. It seems Ms. McQuade has flown to the Coast, so she won't be able to see the children this weekend."

"Surprise," I said.

"The secretary couldn't resist telling me her boss had gone out there to see Paul Newman."

"What happened to Dustin Hoffman?"

"Beats me," she said. "I gathered I was supposed to gasp when she mentioned Newman's name, so I did."

I smiled. "That's nice. You must have made the kid's day."

We sat looking at each other for a minute. Then she said, "A Mr. Skelly called and said to tell you they got the guys when they came for the pickup on Sixth Street. He said those guys took them to the warehouse and they got the others. Nick told me the rest."

"How *is* Nick?"

"Well, he's been celebrating a little."

"You mean he's drunk?"

"Yes."

So what could I expect? After all, this wasn't some forties movie where everybody gets well in the end. Anyway, the guy had come through for me when I needed him and maybe I'd learned something about drunks. And myself. We could help each other if we tried...even if it was on a limited basis.

I wanted to know what else had happened. I said, "You know if any of the other kids got reunited with their families?"

"Father Paul was here and said that all but one has made contact. And she doesn't want to. Her home life must have been pretty awful not to want to go back after what she's been through."

"So what's going to happen to her?" I asked.

She shrugged. "I guess that'll be up to the state now."

"Poor kids," I said. "How about Joyce and Wayne?"

"Joyce is in the hospital but she'll be all right. Wayne is

okay, too. According to Nick he got drunk the other night and made a lot of speeches in Barney's bar about the state of the art world."

"Sounds right. What about George Mayer?"

"He's in jail. The judge set his bail at two hundred fifty thousand." She smiled knowingly.

"Good for the judge. Some justice for a change."

"Fortune, there's something else."

"What?"

"It's about Patrick Baker."

I felt scared and she saw it. She touched my hand.

"No, it's nothing to worry about. In fact, it's good. Charles Horton is really Pat's father. Jennifer's, too."

"What?" I said, astonished.

She nodded. "He apparently tried to be straight years ago and then his wife died when the kids were babies. He didn't feel he had the right to bring them up, since he knew by then that he was really homosexual, so he handed them over to the Bakers."

This was obviously what Sheedy wasn't able to tell me. Well, he was right: it wouldn't have made any difference if I had known but it sure was interesting. I said, "No wonder Carter Baker had such a thing about homosexuals."

"Yes. Apparently Baker told Pat that homosexuality runs in families and that Pat was a prime candidate for it because of his uncle. He taunted Pat for years, picking on the way he talked, walked, everything."

"Christ," I said. "No wonder the kid ran away."

"Pat practically believed that homosexuality was contagious so when he found out about Sheedy he was scared, even though things between them had been wonderful. He just got frightened and confused."

"Understandable."

"So he ran away and hid out in the gallery."

"And then he got caught by Fanner and Mayer while they were unpacking a coke shipment," I said.

"I know."

"So what now? What's going to happen to the boy?"

"According to Father Paul, there's no way Patrick is going to go home, although he'd like to see his mother again. And Horton's going to sue for custody."

"How does Patrick feel about that?"

"Father Paul said he seemed almost happy about it."

"I missed quite an ending," I said.

"At least it was a happy one . . . of sorts. Horton has already gotten in touch with a psychiatrist, which is great, because Pat will need a lot of help to deal with what he's been through."

"I'll say. I guess it could have been a lot worse."

"Thanks to you it wasn't," she said.

I waved away the compliment. "But while we're handing out thanks, I think I owe you one."

"What for?"

"For practically saving my life. Sending Nick after me."

"Did I really save your life?" she asked proudly.

"Well, almost."

She seemed disappointed.

Quickly I said, "You would have if I hadn't had a piece of luck a minute before. The point is, it was terrific of you to wait up for me like that."

"Couldn't sleep," she said in an offhand way.

"Whatever." I didn't want to push it. "Hey, how long do I have to lie low, as they say?"

"Oh, ten days or so."

"You're putting me on."

"God's truth," she said, making a crisscross with her finger over her heart.

"I'll never make it."

"You have to. It won't be so bad. I'll visit." She smiled and her eyes caressed me. "Say, can I come along on your next case?"

"No."

"Why not?"

"You want us both to end up in bed?"

The words hung in the air between us and then we started laughing. It hurt too much so I had to stop; then she did too. I took her hand in mind and felt the softness of her skin.

"Ten days, huh?"

She nodded.

"You won't get bored?" I asked.

"I won't get bored," she said.

She leaned over and kissed me, sweetly, lovingly. Everything in me stirred. When she moved away I took a good look at her and I saw that she no longer resembled Meryl Streep. Instead, she looked like Cassie Bloomfield and I was damn glad!